PAST PERFECT

Judith P. Stelboum

Alice Street Editions

Harrington Park Press
New York · London · Oxford

This is a work of fiction. No reference to actual persons, places, or incidents is implied or should be inferred.

Published by

Alice Street Editions, Harrington Park Press, an imprint of The Haworth Press, Inc., 10 Alice Street, Binghamton, NY 13904-1580 USA.

Cover design by Jessie Gilmer

Library of Congress Cataloging-in-Publication Data

Stelboum, Judith P.
    Past perfect / Judith P. Stelboum.
        p. cm.
      ISBN 1-56023-200-5 (alk. paper)–ISBN 1-56023-201-3 (alk. paper)
        1. Title.
PS3569.T3795 P37 2000
813'.54–dc21   00-025651

PAST PERFECT

Forthcoming Titles
Alice Street Editions

Inside Out, by Juliet Carrera

Facades, by Alex Marcoux

Weeding at Dawn: A Lesbian Country Life, by Hawk Madrone

Extraordinary Couples, Ordinary Lives, by Lynn Haley-Banez
and Joanne Garrett

*This book is dedicated to my much loved and loving partner
Martha Stephens, MD*

*And in memoriam for my mother
Jessie Lewis Stelboum
(1911-1998)*

Introduction to Alice Street Editions

To write, for a lesbian, is to learn to take down the patriarchal posters in her room. It means learning to live with bare walls for a while. It means learning how not to be afraid of the ghosts which assume the color of the bare wall.

–*Nicole Brossard*[1]

What are the implications, in the twenty-first century, of a new publishing imprint of fiction and non-fiction devoted solely to lesbian writing? What is the significance of isolating lesbian writing from heterosexual women's writing?

Alice Street Editions acclaims and affirms unique lesbian perspectives, offering in its pages the best cutting-edge fiction of the day. Defining "lesbian" may be ambiguous and sometimes contradictory, but lesbian writing is singular because it relates experiences and visions shared by a group of women who respond to the world in very different ways from women who are not lesbian.

At the start of the third millennium, we can respectably find ourselves in the Library of Congress catalog, and we can learn about ourselves in the newly formed academic field of Lesbian Studies, straddling the areas of Gay Studies and Women's Studies. We are, as Jill Johnston described us, the "lesbian nation," multiple, varied, composed of diverse entities, with particular customs and manners, but with our own distinct culture, history, and literature.

At the same time we are caught by those forces of our national culture that are ranged against us. Those who cannot accept our differences try to transform us into pop icons of lesbian chic, urge our assimilation, or call for our annihilation. We have been sexually neutered by queer theorists, and baby-boomed into a classification of same-sex "couples" by sociologists. We emulate heterosexual marriages with commitment ceremonies, and we join the patriarchal army. Lesbians are in danger of vanishing by being subsumed into the larger heterosexual culture if we do not consciously create our own worlds.

Lesbian visibility is disproportionate compared with lesbian accomplishments, as we remain an under-represented minority. Consequently, the categorical motivation for Alice Street Editions is an attempt to answer the question posed by one of the most famous political activists, Susan B. Anthony, who asked how we should ever make the world intelligent on our movement. Although Anthony was referring to the Suffragists, we, too, have to learn to brave the dangers of visibility in order to affirm our existence. We must encourage and develop all of the arts, as well as lesbian writing and continue to build strong lesbian identities. Though some of us are still individually invisible, we must never be culturally invisible.

Monique Wittig in *Les Guérillères* urges us to remember our pre-patriarchal past. "Make an effort to remember. Or, failing that, invent."[2] Inviting lesbians to re-member, or to invent our lives, beliefs, and desires, Alice Street Editions follows in the steps of those lesbian publishers who have courageously marked the path, allowing us the opportunity to hear a lesbian voice, or to be that lesbian voice. The joy and the thrill of recognizing our own desires and ideas in print is life sustaining, acknowledging the reality of who we are, our place in the world, individually and collectively.

To write about shared experiences transforms the love that has no name into the desire that demands to be realized, and articulates the ideas that can shape our lives into an exhilarating reality. Alice Street Editions will provide a voice for lesbian novels, memoirs, essays, and non-fiction writing, and will reflect the diversity of lesbian interests, ethnicities, ages and class. This imprint welcomes the opportunity to present controversial views, explore multicultural ideas, encourage debate, and inspire creativity within the lesbian sensibility. All genres of writing will be considered.

Lesbian fantasy, humor, and erotica will come to life in the pages of Alice Street Editions, in a publishing program that promises to be enlightening and entertaining. As Editor-in-Chief of Alice Street Editions, I'm looking forward to putting more lesbian writing into print and providing wider distribution for writers. The unique perspectives of the Alice Street Edition writers will become part of the articulated literature and lore of our lives at the start of the next one thousand years.

This novel, *Past Perfect,* examines the ways we remember events and people. With the aid of illusion and delusion, the past can seem perfect, especially if we can re-member it. *Past Perfect* begins with an Italian proverb declaring that fear is a bad counselor. The book focuses on the intimate lives of four women, following them through a period of time and locales from the East Coast to the West, while they sort out their feelings and move ahead with their lives. The graphic sex scenes are an integral part of this novel because sexuality is basic to the characters, and sex highlights moments of physical and emotional vulnerability that seem to be very pure. The structure of the novel mirrors the way we come to understand reality, through scenes and vignettes that illuminate individual moments of our lives, whose significance can sometimes be understood only in retrospect. Each scene is titled to reveal the intent of that particular moment to the reader.

Judith P. Stelboum
Editor-in-Chief
Alice Street Editions

NOTES

1. Nicole Brossard, *The Aerial Letter,* trans. Marlene Wildeman (Toronto: Woman's Press, 1988), p. 135.
2. Monique Wittig, *Les Guérillères,* trans. Peter Owen (New York: Viking Press, 1971), p. 89.

Acknowledgments

I would like to thank some of the people whose generous and loving support has encouraged my writing through the years. Lenore Hahn-DeSio, ideal teacher and mentor, challenging, creative, nurturing, and persevering. Arnie Kantrowitz, dear friend and colleague, untiringly and enthusiastically edited and reread many drafts. Martha Stephens spent many hours carefully editing and commenting on the final versions of this novel. Jessie A. Gilmer, whose life and family history was the inspiration for vital sections of this novel. Karla Jay provided opportunities for me to publish. Marny Hall's confidence in my writing made it possible for me to edit an anthology. Karen Kerner, always reassuring, liked the book even in the rough, early versions. Muriel Shine offered me her unqualified stamp of approval. I would also like to thank Helen Mallon, Bill Palmer and Nancy Deisroth of The Haworth Press. It has been a pleasure to work with creative publishers who care about writing. Appreciation to Melissa Etheridge for her passionate music.

PAST PERFECT

La paura e una cattiva consigliere.

Fear is a bad counselor.

–Italian proverb

Prologue

Carol walked slowly into the living room intent on rubbing the paint from her hands with an oil rag. She sighed and sank into a deep club chair in front of the portrait that hung over the fireplace. The painting covered the entire wall, affirming the passion that had been the painter's inspiration. The certitude of the artist astonished her. She studied it carefully, noting the details, the colors, the perspective, and the confident brush strokes. Carol had painted Elizabeth astride her horse in her favorite setting, a rolling meadow. Jewel, Elizabeth's German Shepherd, its mouth open, tongue hanging out, sat next to the horse. Elizabeth was wearing a brown and white herringbone riding jacket; tan jodhpurs that hugged her legs, and polished brown field boots. The braided reins attached to the shiny snaffle bit in the horse's mouth were held gently in her gloved hands, and the English saddle had a burnished gleam. Carol focused on Elizabeth, the sensuality in the thick, wavy brown hair falling to her shoulders, the warm hazel eyes that contradicted Elizabeth's expression of cold formality, bordering on arrogance. Looking straight out at the viewer, but through the viewer, the portrait revealed Elizabeth as enigmatic, contrary, and seductive. Carol turned away from Elizabeth's confronting stare, and walked to the French doors at the far end of the room. She focused on the elaborate perennial gardens they had designed and planted together.

In the beginning it was impossible to separate their love for this house from their love for each other. The house became the tangible evidence of their passion, an expression of mutual feelings of satisfaction, security, and comfort. Carol didn't want to admit that feelings of restlessness had been there almost since the beginning. She had long felt pinned down, tied to one place, one person. Growing dissatisfaction chafed her like physical bondage.

She had lost interest in the extensive gardens. She glanced around at the furnishings, stared down at the Persian rugs they had so carefully chosen, and she knew that they had become caretakers, tending all of the elements that were supposed to keep their private world healthy and alive.

She dropped her head and thought about the day she had shown Elizabeth the painting in progress, *"When I finish this, my darling, if I am able to do what I want, you will be quite naked to everyone who sees this."*

Elizabeth had held her from behind, admiring the painting. She breathed into her neck, "Yes, I will be naked for you, under that jacket, under those pants."

Now Carol knew she could no longer work here and was distraught thinking that she would never again paint anything as exciting as this portrait.

Elizabeth Sanderson

In spite of the warm spring sun flooding through the open French doors, Elizabeth shivered. Carol was gone and had taken everything with her. Sometimes she would find one of Carol's books, or an old shirt and these items became relics of a life she had lost. She was lonely. Every day, despite her depression, she went to her study, wrote, taught her classes at the university and sometimes went out for dinner with friends. She did what she was supposed to do. She wrote her class plans, delivered her lectures, but no matter how she occupied the waking hours of her day, at night in the cold bed and in the colder mornings she was alone.

Always so controlled, sure and confident, she now doubted almost everything she did and said. She considered and reconsidered uttering the blandest statement, afraid it would be misinterpreted. At department meetings and conferences, she spoke about her past projects, but when asked about her future plans, she was hesitant and vague. People thought she was reluctant to talk because of the project itself, but this was not the case. She couldn't understand why Carol had left, and although she didn't know what she had done, the fear of making more mistakes was paralyzing.

Pausing before the painting on her way out to the patio, Elizabeth thought of her horse, Red Cloud. He was buried on the property, and she liked to imagine his spirit still running through the fields and moving noisily through the woods. Sometimes when she walked in the woods abutting her house, she heard a loud rustling sound, and she would turn quickly, expecting to see her dog, Jewel, come running out of the brush. Then the memories of riding Red Cloud with Jewel running along beside them would be almost unbearable. Jewel was gone, too, buried two years ago in the "elephant graveyard," as they had called it, with all the assorted cats, and chickens. It was very quiet here, now. She looked at the painting she loved, and it tortured her with memories. They had shared a life together for more than twelve years.

She thought it might help if she took the painting down; instead she passively waited for some change. She acknowledged her pain, waiting for it to ebb, as if she were practicing some Zen exercise. But even after two years, it still felt like an exercise. It was not coming easily, not at all.

At first she had avoided her friends. What to say? How to explain? When she did see them again, she assumed a pleasant persona. Someone who was entertaining, could talk about ideas, about books. But her heart wasn't in it. Her heart had been dead for a long time, and maybe should be buried in the "elephant graveyard" with all the creatures she had loved.

Her friends tried to introduce her to new women. She could barely muster the most superficial questions asking what they did, where they lived, but beyond that, no one and nothing held any real interest for her. Some friends had even taken her to a women's bar one night. She had looked at the young women dancing, kissing, filled with the excitement of a life ahead of them, and felt even more alienated.

The final scene kept playing in her head. She was standing in the bedroom. The light wood floor and the beige rugs reflected the late afternoon sun. She smelled the roses through the open French doors and gazed across the lawn down to the river.

She was listening to herself pleading, crying, and screaming. Could she be angry with Carol-that beautiful open face, the fine blonde hair she had clutched in ecstatic moments? She heard her own voice. "How could you do this? Why do you want to do this? When did you decide this?"

"Don't yell at me," Carol shouted back. "I'm sorry. Things happen. People change."

"And me . . . us? We don't change? We can't change?" Elizabeth asked. "What are you talking about, Carol? Tell me what you want." Elizabeth tried to calm herself, but her heart was pounding, her head was buzzing, and her hands were shaking. She felt nauseated and dizzy, sure she was going to faint.

"I want to tell you, to try to make you understand about us," Carol said.

Carol was trying to speak to her reasonably, but Elizabeth heard each word as an assault. "... us ... never to be again. Talk ... this will never happen again."

Elizabeth sat down on the bed, and said, "Okay. What is it you want to explain?" She leaned back against the pine headboard for support. Outside the window she could see the strong flow of the river. Swallows were skimming the water, catching insects, and she heard the warblers and in the background distinguished the unique cry of a mockingbird. How beautiful, she thought, how peaceful, the real world. She tried to forget what was going on in her private world.

Carol paced back and forth in front of the bed and spoke with great agitation. The words came spurting out. "I can't explain why. I don't know. I want to leave. I'm not happy . . . I have to leave . . . I have to go someplace else . . . I'm dying here. I can't work anymore . . ." She paused. "I could drown in that river out there, just walk into it and drown myself. I will. I swear . . . I will if I stay here."

Elizabeth covered her face with her hands. "No, no." She could not stop shaking. Gasping once or twice, she gained enough control. "I don't understand."

Carol started pacing again. "Of course you don't understand. How could you? You never would. I've got to get out of here. It took me a long time, Elizabeth, to know what it was and it's this world we've created . . . so neat, so explainable, so safe. I don't want that. I want out. I want out of this house, this life, our life. It's killing me. I can't work here. I need chaos, disorder, more wildness. I can't explain it any more than that." She threw up her hands.

Elizabeth was angry. "What do you think I should say? Should I say you don't make sense? But now you don't want anything sensible in your life." Then she thought, "What's her name?" She brushed the air with her hand. "Susan or Phoebe or Cassandra . . . whoever . . . I hope she's wild enough for you."

Carol interrupted. "Her name is Jane." She paused and spoke gently. "I'm not talking about that part of our life. That part was wonderful for a long time."

"Yes, but not wonderful now."

"No. Not now." Elizabeth heard the finality in Carol's voice. "Elizabeth, it's not about sex. It's about passion, intensity . . . it's gone for me, and without it I can't paint and without that I can't continue to . . ."

Elizabeth choked back tears, and held up her hand. "I'm angry, and I'm sorry, and I'm sorry for you. If I weren't so much in love with you, I could hate you. You know I would be anything for you, say anything to have you love me still . . . but don't ask me to understand you . . . now." She paused for a longer time and shook her head. "Don't tell me any more . . . no more. . . . Not now. . . . Never. I don't know what to say because I don't know what you want. I'll just shut my eyes and then I'll wake up and one of two things will be real. This will be a dream-or you'll be gone."

She still had her eyes closed when she heard the front door open and close.

Veronica Santini

There had been three people who wanted the job, two young men and one woman. Elizabeth had their transcripts on her desk. She had known Joe O'Donnell and Tom Hallman for several years. They had been her students as undergraduates and were now going into graduate school. Either one would be acceptable. They were strong and both were quiet, so she knew that they wouldn't disturb her while she worked. The last applicant, Veronica Santini, from Newark, New Jersey, had transferred recently from Rutgers University.

"Why did you choose a graduate program in Connecticut?" Elizabeth asked.

Veronica smiled and took a deep breath. "That's not a simple question to answer. You might just as well ask how I happened to go to college at all. After high school I spent several years working in New York as a receptionist and secretary for a brokerage firm. Then I left and decided to get in touch with the roots of 'Amurica'." Veronica imitated a New England accent and grinned.

There were questions Elizabeth wanted to ask. Why did you become a secretary? Why did you leave? What happened to change the direction of your life? She posed only one safe question. "Were you always interested in horticulture?"

Veronica clapped her hands and laughed. "Yes, always. But you're right it does seem a strange career for a girl from Newark. A local Girl Scout troop I joined in Newark would take us on weekend trips to the Jersey Pine Barrens, Longwood Gardens or into New York to the Botanical Gardens. The Girl Scout leader, Mrs. Di Napoli, liked flowers and nature. She thought that the Girl Scouts was something like the Fresh Air Fund. You know, get a kid out into the country, give her a taste of another life before the corruption of the city snatches away the innocent child. Anyway, in my case it really worked. I liked walking in the Pine Barrens. I enjoyed getting lost in the paths through the Botanical Gardens. When I got older, in high school, I would pack a sandwich and just spend the day in the gardens, imagining that it was my estate. I started to learn the Latin names of the plants, trees and shrubs. First I read them on the little black markers in front of the plants. I copied them in a notebook and then asked someone who knew Latin, usually a priest, how to pronounce them."

She looked at Elizabeth expecting an interruption to her narrative, but Elizabeth seemed interested, so Veronica continued.

"Sometimes at home, when I'd lose my temper, I would curse, using these names. No one knew what I was saying. You *plicatum tomentosum,* you *hamamelis malus,* you *chamaecyparis.* Get out of here before I *larix* your *laricina.* It always seemed to work. My brother and sister would run to Mom saying, 'Veronica called me a . . . a . . . *plica* . . . and she said she would *lar . . . lar . . .* me.'"

Elizabeth laughed at Veronica's gestures and mimicry as she told the story.

"I knew that I wanted to be outdoors, work with plants and trees . . . and I wanted to leave New Jersey. So the decision to come here was easy. When I saw the announcement in the job placement office for the chance to work in your gardens, I filled out the application immediately."

Elizabeth quickly regained her professional distance. "I thought you were accepted in a special program in Colorado this summer to do some research on conifers. That's what Dean Smith told me."

"I was going to go, but I'm also interested in shrubs and perennials. I'm willing to postpone the Colorado program."

"You know, this is basically a summer job. My gardens are quite extensive, and there is some physical labor involved. For the really heavy-duty lifting and moving, I hire people, but we might have to do some transplanting and moving ourselves. Would that be okay with you?"

Veronica smiled and the corners of her mouth turned way up revealing her straight, white teeth. She flexed both of her arms at the elbow and proclaimed, "The bionic woman has nothing on me." Then she put both hands in front of her chest as if she were about to rip open an imaginary shirt. "This is a job for . . . Amazon woman." She laughed out loud.

Elizabeth looked at her intently. She liked her humor, exuberance and open manner, and was impressed by Veronica's pride in the strong body outlined by her tee shirt and jeans. "You're hired," she said.

Gardening

Veronica left the house very early for her first day at work. She wore her black aviator styled sunglasses to hide the excitement that would be reflected in her eyes. The very first week Veronica arrived on campus she had noticed Professor Sanderson. She watched Elizabeth walk across the campus, head back, shoulders squared, with a distinctive stride that might almost be a swagger. She was not totally surprised when Elizabeth and her friends walked into the local lesbian bar one night. This professor who rarely smiled or spoke that night intrigued her. When she saw the announcement for the summer job, Veronica realized that this was the opportunity to get to know Professor Sanderson. She impulsively gave up the summer fellowship in Colorado.

Following Elizabeth's directions, Veronica turned her motorcycle off the main road onto a narrow dirt road. The sign identified the road as part of a state forest, and Veronica thought she had made a wrong turn, but about a mile later, she spotted the identifying mailbox. She slowed down and shut off her engine. It was mid-May, and the leafy growth was already so dense that Veronica could not see very far into the woods, but she recognized some of the birdcalls coming from deep in the forest. She sat for a few minutes, enjoying the quiet isolation. When she started down the road again, she came to a single story, brown-shingled cottage, set in a large clearing. Veronica turned off the bike and removed her helmet. She walked towards the house on a footpath bordered by varieties of spruce, pine, hemlock set between maple, oak, birch and cherry trees. Veronica walked slowly, fascinated by the general design. It was more beautiful than anyone had described to her. Closer to the house, Veronica noted plantings of large leather leaf viburnum, oakleaf hydrangeas, varieties of rhododendron and mountain laurel. Color was subtly added to the textures by plantings of bleeding heart, pink, red and white astilbe, columbine, and the yellow variegated hostas. Bright green euonymous, and red-blossomed broom cascaded on to the sides of the path. Climbing pink roses were massed under one of the large bay windows. The entire garden was heavily mulched with shredded cedar chips, and Veronica inhaled the sweet scent of the cedar and roses. She wondered how one person could possibly maintain this, and nervously thought that what Professor Sanderson needed was not this lone student from New Jersey but a small army detachment to work here all day, every day.

Elizabeth, cup of coffee in hand, walked out the front door to meet her.

"Good morning, Professor Sanderson." Veronica smiled awkwardly. "Your gardens are magnificent . . . breathtaking! And the location is extraordinary. I know why the university sends interns and visitors down here all the time. If this isn't a remake of the Garden of Eden, it must be pretty close to it."

"Sometimes I feel that way myself." Elizabeth looked out at the dense woods. "We're in the middle of a state forest. The surveyor's office told me this was the only piece of land available, and so I built here, knowing it would always be private and protected. The perennial gardens are on the other side of the house, near the river."

Veronica looked back at the garden she had just come through. The careful, artistic planning, the diversity of the plantings, and the harmonious mixture of colors astounded her. "Did you do all of this yourself?"

"Yes, with some help from . . . friends." Elizabeth walked into the house. "Would you like some coffee? Have you had breakfast?"

"Yes, to the first. No, to the second."

"Well come on in, I'll get us both some breakfast. Oh, you can call me Elizabeth. That formality seems out of place now that we'll be working together so closely."

Veronica answered, "Yes, of course."

As she crossed into the entryway, Veronica noticed the brass doorknocker. The design in bronze was of a naked woman archer, arms tensed, muscles clearly delineated, poised with her bow pulled back. Veronica wanted to linger and study the sculpture, but was too self-conscious. She followed Elizabeth into a large living room where light shone through the floor-to-ceiling French doors allowing an unrestricted view of the back gardens.

"What a great house. I suppose you . . . and some friends just designed and built this, too."

"Designed, yes. Built, no."

Veronica stopped abruptly and stared at the painting covering the wall over the fireplace. If she wanted to spend more time examining the woman archer, the painting would take a few hours of observation.

"That's you, isn't it?" She looked at Elizabeth, then turned back to the painting. "It's . . ." She didn't know what she wanted to say. She swallowed and regained her cool tone. "It's equestrian of the year!" The colors of the painting and Elizabeth's gaze held her, but it was the expression on the rider's face that so flustered her. She saw what she had instinctively felt about Elizabeth. Beyond the formal, cold surface, was the passion, will, and sensuality she had imagined in her fantasy. She wondered who the painter was, to have been able to capture all of that. She tried to back off from her visceral reaction to the painting, telling herself that she really did not know Elizabeth at all and maybe she was just making it up. She kept looking back at the horse and rider as she followed Elizabeth into the kitchen.

Planting Time

It was unusually hot for early June. They had just finished moving a very large hydrangea. Veronica was kneeling to tamp down the dirt before adding peat moss and fertilizer to the soil. Elizabeth stepped back, took off her gloves, and noticed Veronica's muscled back and strong arms moving the plant into place. Elizabeth recognized a feeling she hadn't had for a long time. She fought it and turned it into an abstract, aesthetic observation, as she backed further away from Veronica.

"God," Veronica said, "It's so hot for June, I hope this isn't a forecast for the rest of the summer. Let's hope this plant will make it. It's a little late for transplant, but if it gets enough water it will be okay as long as it's not stressed."

". . . not stressed," Elizabeth repeated absently, still intent on the sweat dripping down Veronica's arms.

"It's too hot to work any more today," Elizabeth said quickly. "Why don't we stop?"

Veronica looked up squinting into the direct sun. "If you say so. No offense, but Colorado is looking better each day."

Elizabeth laughed to ease her tension. "How about something cold, a lemonade or maybe a beer?" She didn't want Veronica to leave just yet.

Veronica fumbled for a response, surprised by the invitation. After a few weeks, their working relationship had been friendly, polite and formal. This was the first instance of any social gesture and she was not prepared.

"I'm too dirty. I think I should just go home."

"Why don't you come in and take a shower?" Elizabeth pressed her. "Then we can sit and talk afterwards."

"Uh, oh, well I don't know. I have to get back. I, uh . . ." Although she wanted to get to know Elizabeth, and that had been

the reason for taking the job, during the past weeks Veronica felt
that working in Elizabeth's gardens had been the wrong approach
for a personal relationship.

Elizabeth was already walking towards the house assuming
Veronica was behind her.

"Okay." Veronica didn't want to make a fuss. She followed
Elizabeth. "I can get a clean shirt from my bag."

"Use anything you need," Elizabeth smiled, after showing her
into one of the bathrooms.

Veronica felt more relaxed when she emerged from the shower,
hair all clean, nails scrubbed, just like Girl Scout camp.

Elizabeth was in the kitchen. She, too, had showered and was
wearing a white shirt and green shorts. Her brown hair hung down
over the back of the shirt, and Veronica resisted the impulse to
move her hair aside and kiss her neck.

"Would you like a beer, iced tea, coffee?"

"A beer, thanks," Veronica said.

They walked to the patio, and sat under the shade of a maple
tree. Veronica looked across the gardens to the forest and then
back to the river. She thought that Elizabeth had succeeded in
creating reality out of a dream. The plantings were timed so that
there were brilliantly colored flowers or shrubs during the entire
year. The garden never looked desolate.

Elizabeth's question interrupted her reverie. "What's your family
like, Veronica?"

"There are five of us, Mom, Dad, Paul, Marie and me. I'm the
oldest. Dad's a retired fireman. Mom's active in the church. Paul is
in the local fire department. Marie's a physical therapist and about
to get married."

"And you? I'm sure that they look forward to your marriage?"

Veronica looked at her incredulously and laughed. She refused to
play the submissive, respectful student. "Hardly. I'm not the
marrying kind."

"Oh!"

"And you? Were you ever married?" Veronica calculated the

risk. She didn't want to reveal what she knew about Elizabeth. She wanted to see her reaction.

Elizabeth did not respond. Veronica interpreted her expression as puzzled and perplexed. "I hope that's not too personal a question? A southern friend of mine used to respond to personal questions by saying, 'Muh private life's muh ohwn.' That always made me laugh."

"Why? Don't you think privacy should be respected?" Elizabeth's voice became defensive.

"Sure, of course I do. But most of the time, 'private lives' are right out there in public anyway. Right on people's faces, what they say, and don't say. How they move. What they wear. How they look. Don't you think?" Veronica knew she was pushing her.

Elizabeth was moving her fingers around her glass. "Yes sometimes . . . maybe sometimes," she assented.

Why couldn't she just let Veronica go home? Instead here she was, asking inane questions, trying to recover lost skills of conversation. "Were you in the Girl Scouts a long time, Veronica?"

Veronica laughed. "I was in the Girl Scouts too long. I had every merit badge they ever gave and wore every last one of them on a large band that crossed my chest." Veronica paused. *Anymore and she would have to tell her about Leslie. Leslie and scouting; it was impossible to separate them.* She looked at her watch. "I guess I should be getting home now." It was about eight o'clock and the glow in the sky was beginning to signal sunset. The swallows had come out to skim the waters, and small birds were very busy at the various feeders scattered around the lawn. There was no human sound, only the river, the songbirds and the trills of the swallows. Veronica hesitated and then got up. She felt that there was much more to say, but she knew that it could not be said here and now.

"Maybe sometime you can stay for dinner?"

"Sure, I'd like to," Veronica said, picking up her knapsack on the way out. She mounted her motorcycle and waved goodbye.

Home Time

Veronica stopped her bike along Route 1 to watch the sun set over the calm waters of Long Island Sound. Elizabeth seemed interested in her, maybe the student-teacher formality was shifting.

One half hour later Veronica rode her motorcycle into a narrow driveway of a two-family house in the older section of New London and walked up the steep flight of stairs to an apartment she shared with her friend, Kathy.

She took the steps two at a time, anxious to give Kathy the latest progress report. The door was not double locked, so she knew Kathy would be home. Details of Elizabeth's portrait were fixed in her memory. The expression on Elizabeth's face clearly showed the remoteness, but also the vulnerability.

"Hi, Kath," Veronica greeted her.

Kathy was sitting at the kitchen table. "Hi. There's spaghetti, Ronnie. It's still warm."

"Thanks." Veronica squeezed Kathy's shoulder as she walked towards the refrigerator. "I think I'll have a beer first and relax."

"I have to leave for the hospital soon. This is one of those night shift weeks. How's it going out there in the Land of Oz? How are all the little plant munchkins, and the grand wizard herself? I'm eager for some nice gossip."

"I must be working the old Santini magic because the wizard seems to be transforming." Veronica twisted the cap and lifted the bottle to her lips.

"Really? Tell all and don't leave out the details."

Veronica teased her, assuming a detached tone. "I like my work. I like Elizabeth. The house is really beautiful and the gardens are wonderful. I'm learning a lot about perennial design."

Kathy was smirking. "Uh-huh. Well how come it's so hot and she's still so cold? I know why you took this job instead of going to Colorado. Just one look that night in the bar and you had to have her. Right? Am I right? I know you, Ronnie Santini."

Veronica ignored her comment. "Today was a real breakthrough. Nothing much, but she invited me to sit with her in the garden. A social event, I would say."

"The professor and her adoring, humble student take tea in the garden. I think I saw that movie."

Veronica sat down at the table. "No, Kathy, there's something there, and I don't think it's my imagination, or wishful thinking. I feel her looking at me, and when I try to look at her, she turns away and pretends it never happened. It's frustrating."

"Maybe the professor is trying to decide if you're worthy of the wizard?"

"Maybe . . . or maybe she's scared." Veronica was absently peeling off the beer label. "Try to help me out here, Kathy. What was her ex like?"

"I met Carol only once at a hospital Christmas party. They came with one of Kelly's friends and dropped in on their way to another party or a weekend trip. I forget."

"What did Carol look like?"

"She was attractive, tall, straight blonde hair like yours. I don't remember much. A few months earlier she'd had a big show of her paintings at the Hartford Atheneum and Kelly and I had gone to see it. I was impressed and curious to meet her."

"You never told me Carol was an artist!" *Of course, Veronica thought, she should have guessed. Only someone who knew Elizabeth so intimately could have painted that portrait.*

"Oh yes. She studied and lived in Europe for a while before coming back to the States. Kelly said that she's pretty well-known in the art world."

"What were her paintings like?"

"They were large landscapes of the southwest, desert landscape, mostly. I really liked her paintings, but I'm no art expert. The paintings were exciting, bright, vivid colors. There were also some portraits. One of Carol's father was very striking. He wore a western hat and suit and stood in front of a bookcase. All of her paintings had a mysterious quality. The subjects were real and recognizable, but they were also more than what they seemed." She stopped and laughed. "Maybe I should become an art critic. I can't believe I still remember that show."

"You're doing pretty well for a casual observer." Veronica was intrigued.

"You know, I still remember one small sculpture of a naked woman drawing back the string of a large bow. All of the muscles in her back, arms, and neck were strained. Her hair was pulled back from her neck and hung down to her shoulders. I whispered to Kelly that I'd really like to meet the model for this one."

Veronica realized that Elizabeth had been the model for the archer. "Did you see the large painting of a woman on horse-back?"

"Oh, yes. How could I forget that enormous canvas and that attractive rider. Of course, Kelly knew that the rider was Elizabeth Sanderson. How did you know about the painting?"

"It's covering an entire wall in her living room."

Veronica leaned forward, nervously peeling the wet label on the beer bottle. She shook her head, "I don't know, Kathy, I don't know. Maybe I'm out of my league here. I'm too unsure. I'm much younger, and I'm a student, and she doesn't seem to be interested. I don't know if I should have started this in the first place. Seems a little crazy now, giving up the project in Colorado for . . . I don't know . . . some ridiculous image of Elizabeth. You're probably the only one who would understand, and you probably think I'm over my head here, don't you?"

"Ronnie, I can only remember how you and I met at that sleazy bar. Two drinks–you propositioned me and off to bed we went." Kathy blinked her eyes and sighed dramatically. "Now . . . just friends as they say in the tabloids. No, Ronnie, my wonderful butch, you're definitely one to follow your feelings, and all these game plans with Sanderson, aren't like the Ronnie I know." She looked at her watch. "Oops, sorry I can't stay to talk about this."

She walked over to Veronica, lifted her chin up so that they looked at each other, and kissed her gently on the mouth. "Got to run. Take it easy. You'll be asleep by the time I come home, but if you're still lonely, leave a note on my pillow, and I'll take your mind off school work." She laughed. "See you tomorrow."

Veronica went into the living room and turned on the TV. At 9:30 the telephone rang.

"Hello, Veronica, it's Elizabeth Sanderson. I hope I haven't disturbed you, but I forgot to tell you that I'm going to the Arnold Arboretum tomorrow. My old friend Jim Pike has arranged for me to see a new variety of peony from China. I know it's short notice, but I wonder if you would like to go with me."

Veronica didn't want to appear too excited. She hesitated before answering in a tentative voice. "Sure, sure, sounds interesting."

"Wonderful, I was hoping you'd want to come. I'll pick you up at seven-thirty."

Veronica gave instructions to help Elizabeth find her house, and said she would wait for her outside.

Veronica took more time than usual, the next morning, deciding on the right outfit, jeans, work boots and a faded blue, short-sleeved denim shirt. She was ready at seven o'clock. She went downstairs, sat on the steps, and remembered how excited she and her brother Paul used to get before the yearly family picnics. They would wake up early, dress quickly and check their baseball gloves for the big game with their cousins. *I should have offered to pack a lunch for today. No, that would have been too forward. Maybe Elizabeth only wants me along to help carry some of the plants back and that's all.*

The beep of a car interrupted her musings and she waved to Elizabeth. When Veronica stepped into the car she saw that Elizabeth was not dressed in work clothes. She wore tan pants, a cotton shirt and a tan linen blazer. All Veronica's hopes for the day were gone. She was destined to remain the college student to Elizabeth, and nothing more. Elizabeth smiled at her, but the dark

sunglasses made it impossible for Veronica to interpret any meaning more than a simple welcome.

"You know, Veronica, I would like to introduce you to some
people who might be helpful to you in the future. People in our
profession don't make a great deal of money, but that's not really
what attracts people to horticulture anyway. There are always a
few famous landscape designers who get huge commissions for
government projects or large corporate developments, but those
people are the exceptions. There are still many opportunities to
work with small landowners and arboretums or botanic gardens, or
to go into forestry, if you'd still like to do that."

"What you mean is that the days of the great gardens,
Sissinghurst, Longleat, are finished."

Elizabeth laughed. "Yes, sorry your vision of managing the great
estate belongs to an era long gone. Can't live in the past now!"
*That advice would be something to remember myself, Elizabeth
thought. Veronica was an interesting distraction . . . nothing
more. She wondered if Veronica had any feelings about her.
This thought made her nervous, or was it excited, or was it just
jumpy? She couldn't tell, and she couldn't assume anything
about Veronica's feelings either, and there was always the issue
of Veronica's being a student. True, she was a graduate student
and older than the usual grads. She couldn't decide if her
attraction to Veronica was something that she was pleased about
or not. It had been so long. She was grateful to be recovering
from the hold that Carol had on her. But the actual act of
moving on, finding someone else was frightening.*

She explained to Veronica, "In graduate school, Jim and I worked
together on several landscape design projects, but Jim's interests have
evolved more and more into species preservation. He travels all over
the world, collecting rare and endangered plant species that he brings
home to the arboretum and tries to propagate."

"Important work," Veronica replied in an attempt to remain the
amiable student.

*   *   *

During lunch, Jim talked about the latest developments in peony varieties and mentioned his trips to China and England. They discussed the recent debates on soil amenities on plant growth rates, and when Elizabeth told him how Veronica was so very interested in garden design, Jim turned his attention to Veronica.

Elizabeth knew she wasn't really concentrating on the discussion. She was conscious of Veronica's physical presence. Everything about Veronica was sensuously appealing to her, Veronica's large, tanned hands and long fingers, the muscled forearms and the broad shoulders. Her blonde straight hair, so much like Carol's, clung to the sides of her neck in the humidity. Elizabeth watched Veronica's mouth as she spoke to Jim. She wondered if Veronica knew about Carol, and was just being polite last week when she asked if Elizabeth had been married. Surely campus gossip still exists. Even so, Elizabeth wanted to tell her the truth, but she had always found it difficult to get to know someone, even if she wanted to, and she was not sure she wanted to allow anyone into her private life. She didn't want to begin again. Yet, in spite of her memories of Carol, and the age difference between herself and Veronica, she couldn't deny her feelings for Veronica. She sensed that Veronica liked her, but she was worried that she was assuming too much about Veronica's intentions. Any rejection would be too much for her and worsen her depression. She concentrated on the conversation about peony species and put her feelings in the back of her mind. They spent the next few hours walking around the arboretum, with Jim explaining all of the projects for the next few years.

On the way back to New London, Elizabeth felt the strain of the day beginning to get the better of her. When she and Veronica were working together there was a purpose in being together, there were specific topics of conversation relating to the work. She was not used to spending so much of her time socializing with a person she hardly knew. Earlier, she had felt energized at the thought of spending the day with Veronica, but now she realized that this was not going to be the beginning of a romance. She resolved that there would be no more emotional involvements or attachments. After all, she hadn't even gotten another dog after Jewel died. No, she was determined to remain a friendly, supportive mentor to Veronica.

She turned to look at Veronica, and their eyes met. Veronica smiled and Elizabeth wondered if she could really maintain the distanced role of professor to this woman.

"I really want to thank you for today," Veronica said. "Meeting people as intensely involved in species preservation as Dr. Pike makes me feel a part of an important, worthwhile community. Even though everyone speaks about ecology and environment, you never seem to meet people who have dedicated themselves so clearly."

"I'm glad that you enjoyed the day and the arboretum. If you decide to stay in this area, Jim knows everyone in New England and could be a big help."

"That's very nice, thanks."

They chatted politely about the various plant specimens in the arboretum and soon were back in New London. It was evening when Elizabeth dropped Veronica at her house, saying a quick good night which she knew would prevent Veronica from extending an invitation to come up to her apartment.

The River

A week later, Veronica was just leaving the house when the telephone rang.

"Veronica, I'm glad I caught you before you left. Jim called last night and he's sending down several varieties of hemlocks. He wants to test them for resistance to woolly adelgid in the coastal area. He thinks the arboretum may have developed a technique for hemlock resistance. The trees are coming today."

"How many are there, Elizabeth? Can we handle them?"

"No, no, don't even think of it. They're too big for us to deal with. He's sending a crew from the arboretum to put them in. They're bringing everything with them. I only called to say that if you wanted to take the day off, you could as I'll be busy supervising the planting."

"I'd like to watch and observe the procedure, see Dr. Pike's techniques put into practice. I'm sure that there'll be something I can do to help."

"Great . . . Veronica, why don't you bring your bathing suit? It's going to be a hot day today. There's a place on the river where . . . I . . . swim."

"Sure. Okay. I'd love to swim." Veronica put the phone down, poured herself a cup of cold coffee, and wondered what caused Elizabeth's sudden familiarity. She was nervous but excited.

Veronica parked her motorcycle in the driveway and, with her helmet under her arm, walked up the path to the house. She noted that the new plantings they had put in last week would need water before the sun got too strong. Elizabeth was right. It was going to be a real hot day. Her fingers traced the sensuous curves of the archer's body, and she felt the smooth contours press into her hand as she knocked on the door. She reluctantly released the archer from her grip and called out, "Hello."

"Good morning. I'm in the back here. Be right out. Coffee's made. Help yourself."

Veronica looked around the kitchen. She admired Elizabeth's taste–the white-tiled floor, the simple maple cabinets and the black-granite counter tops. She compared this house to her family's small home in New Jersey–a tiny front yard surrounded by two-foot hedges with pink azaleas and the usual foundation plantings. All the houses had the same living room furniture, bedroom sets, and even the same paintings on the wall. Elizabeth's unique presence was everywhere in this house. How could it not be with that huge painting staring down anyone who approached it? Walking into the living room, Veronica looked at the painting. How well Carol had captured that distant look in her eyes, the stiffness in Elizabeth's back and shoulders. Yes, there was definitely a real coldness in Elizabeth, that was true, but there was something else, something beyond the superficial impression that Carol had been able to recreate. Carol understood the depths of this woman that Veronica could only sense.

She heard Elizabeth call from the hallway. "I'll be right there. Could you get me a cup, please?"

Veronica walked back into the kitchen and started to pour the coffee. Elizabeth appeared in jeans, work boots and a dark green short-sleeved shirt. She was drying the ends of her hair with a small towel.

"I don't know why I'm bothering with my hair. It's so warm already, if I just walk outside, it'll dry in about two minutes." She smiled at Veronica. "I should have put on shorts, it's going to be so hot, but I somehow feel very exposed when strangers are here."

Veronica nodded. "I know what you mean."

The house vibrated as the large truck pulled onto the dirt road. Both put down their coffee cups and went out. Elizabeth had already chosen the spot where the trees were to be planted. It was quite a way from the house and near the border of the state forest. There were no other hemlocks nearby, so if the experiment didn't work, nothing else would get infected from these particular trees.

They worked all morning and into the early afternoon, Veronica and Elizabeth getting the men cool drinks and making sandwiches for the lunch break. They directed the spacing and location of each tree, and the crew used heavy digging equipment to prepare the holes. Veronica relayed the water through a series of hoses she had connected. They didn't have quite enough hose, so the last few hundred feet had to be carried by hand.

"We'll get some more hose tomorrow," Elizabeth grunted, lifting up a water bucket.

"Absolutely," nodded Veronica. "We'll be doing this watering for . . . the rest of the summer." She wanted to say for the next three years, but stopped herself from such a presumption.

When the men left in the afternoon, both women were relieved and exhausted. Now that the work was finished, there was a tension about being alone together. It was late afternoon, still very hot, when they sat and leaned back against a rock, surveying the planted and watered grove of hemlocks.

"It's hard, physical work but that's what I like about it." Veronica was animated. "You feel all of the working muscles of your body straining. It's sometimes better than sex." Elizabeth frowned, and Veronica knew that she had crossed the line that was the unspoken boundary between them. She was annoyed that Elizabeth had the power to stop her spontaneity. A furrow appeared between Veronica's brows, and she ran her fingers, slowly, through her hair.

Elizabeth tried to relieve the awkward moment. "Veronica, how about a swim to cool off? I'm going to show you a really special place. Come on."

She stood up and held out her ungloved hand to Veronica, who looked up at her. The sun was just behind Elizabeth, and Veronica saw only the outline of her shape. The expression on her face was indecipherable because of the angle of light, but Veronica responded to the enthusiasm and playfulness in her voice. Elizabeth pulled her up, almost jerking her off the ground.

"Follow me." Elizabeth walked quickly into the woods. Veronica followed, curious to see yet another wonderful aspect of this marvelous property. She couldn't imagine what or who had tempted Carol away.

Elizabeth stopped and turned. "Hope you have a bathing suit. It's private here, but sometimes people do come hiking through the woods."

"I'm wearing my suit," said Veronica.

"Good. Mine's in my pack here." Elizabeth pointed to the small fanny pack around her waist.

Elizabeth held up her hand and motioned for Veronica to stop. "There, hear it?" She turned excitedly towards Veronica.

Veronica stopped. This was Elizabeth's territory, her world. Veronica was the student again. She tried to put that thought out of her mind as she concentrated on listening to the sound of rushing water. "Waterfall." Veronica grinned.

Elizabeth nodded and they continued to walk deeper into the woods.

"Through here. It's shorter." Elizabeth ducked under a pine.

They walked into a dimly lit grove. The fresh smell of the pines was invigorating. The air was about ten degrees cooler and the soft forest floor was covered with pine cones and brown pine needles. Saplings of birch and poplar grew between the pines, and the afternoon sun was filtered into a pale golden haze. Veronica wanted to sink down on the floor and just stay there.

"You should have told me to bring my sleeping bag. This is marvelous."

Elizabeth looked out at the dappled light. "Yes, this is one of my favorite places. I once had a birthday picnic here." She turned from Veronica. *It hurt to remember. A private affair, Carol had said. She carried a picnic basket with cold salmon, champagne and strawberries. She spread the blanket on top of the soft pine*

needles, uncorked the champagne, and poured it into the
glasses.

"To you." Carol kissed her. "I love you so much."

"To us . . . always," Elizabeth replied, and they sipped the
champagne. Carol lowered Elizabeth onto the blanket, opened
up her shirt and unzipped her shorts. The champagne bottle
rested against a tree, and by the time they resumed their
toasting it was warm.

Elizabeth felt the old paralyzing sadness creep over her. She had
violated some private space by bringing Veronica here. *Stop it!*
This is not the sacred Indian burial ground, and I shouldn't
continue to cast myself as the suffering victim.

"Let's walk down to the pool." Elizabeth pointed to a small
footpath between two pines. The sound of the water almost
drowned out her voice. "It's steep, so grab the tree branches as
you climb down," she cautioned.

Veronica shook her head, then scrambled down the slope. She
reached the bottom, almost sliding down the trail, out of breath.
Elizabeth guided her along the pool to a grassy area downstream
where they could speak without shouting.

Veronica took off her shirt and jeans, made a little blanket out
of her clothes, and sat looking into the water.

Elizabeth went into the woods to change into her bathing suit.
When she returned, she felt exposed and self-conscious as she
stood in front of Veronica.

Assuming a formal, professional tone in her voice helped her get
through the moment. "Thanks for all of your help, Veronica. I
really appreciate it."

"Aw shucks, ma'am, it weren't nothing, just doin' muh job."
She looked up with a subtle smirk on her face.

"Well, I don't want to feel that I was depriving you of your
summer in the Rocky Mountains, but you have to admit that New
England has its own charm. You should see these woods in the fall

with all of the colors of the leaves. Everywhere you walk is golden and red. It's quite magical."

"I look forward to the fall and experiencing all of the mysteries of New England." Veronica leaned back on her elbows and smiled up at Elizabeth.

Elizabeth spread her shirt out on the moss-covered bank. She cleared her throat, but her heart was still beating faster and she knew it was not from the climb down the trail. "I really don't know very much about you, Veronica. I've wanted to ask you some things, but I felt that I would be getting too personal."

"What did you want to ask me?" Veronica felt herself tense up, apprehensive and cautious.

"Well, maybe it is too personal," Elizabeth continued. "If it is, I know that you'll tell me to mind my own business, right?" Now she looked directly into Veronica's dark brown eyes, expecting to find the answer without having to ask. She tried to sound detached and impersonal. "I'm really interested to know how you changed the direction of your life and why."

Veronica looked at her. She picked up a twig from the grass and started to chew on it. She exhaled and said thoughtfully, "That's a complicated question to answer. There are so many reasons I could give you." She got up and walked towards the water, turned back and sat down again near Elizabeth. She so much wanted to be honest with her, to tell her the truth, if she could find the right words. She couldn't explain everything all at once. Elizabeth was still a stranger. She struggled with her response. "I could tell you about being in a dead-end job. I could talk about my dislike of the city, my dislike of certain styles of dress that I was required to wear. I could mention my alienation from the other women in the office. My life was slipping away from me. I was disappearing. I was losing control. I forced myself to leave. I wrenched myself out of my job, away from my home and family in order to survive." She paused abruptly. "It's all I can say, now, that you would understand." Veronica turned towards the river.

"Veronica . . ." Elizabeth held up her hand. "Please, I'm sorry

if I was prying. I would usually never ask anything so personal."
She had to find some answers. Carol had felt this urgency to
change her life, to tear herself away from her home and from
Elizabeth.

Veronica looked at Elizabeth and saw, for the first time the
vulnerability that Carol had captured in the portrait. "Let's forget
the past, Elizabeth. It's such a beautiful day. Do we get to actually
go in the water or just sit here? Any snapping turtles, black
snakes, bottomless holes, whirlpools? Now you have to be truthful.
Tell all. C'mon, I really have to know before I go in. You wouldn't
want to endanger your best worker would you?"

They both laughed.

"No, no dangers in these waters, just the risk of death by
frostbite. It's pretty cold."

"I'll chance it. Today's a day that could melt icebergs." Veronica
walked into the water and swam towards the falls and the deep
pool.

Elizabeth focused on the sound of the falling water and the
strong strokes of the swimmer making headway against the current.

Why We Dream

Elizabeth was frightened and trembling, holding onto Veronica, knowing that the real motivation for this impulsive ride was an attempt to understand Carol. What had Carol meant when she said she wanted more wildness? She tried to imagine the requisites of Carol's world as she unsuccessfully struggled with her immediate panic. She was afraid of falling off the bike as she was pulled backwards and pushed forward. She was afraid of the speed. Most of all, she was afraid of the confused feelings she had for Veronica whose hard back she pressed tight against her chest. Her arms circled Veronica's waist. She wanted to rest her head on Veronica's neck, on the back of her shoulder. "Just a ride," Veronica said. "I'll show you what it's like." Elizabeth was instantly sorry, but it was too late. She was not dressed warmly enough. The breeze raised goose bumps on her bare arms. Her stomach turned as if she were on a roller coaster ride. Every few feet street lamps flashed light through her closed eyelids.

She felt the motorcycle dip and knew they had turned a corner and then the bike shifted to a lower gear and slowed down. She opened her eyes as they pulled into a dark parking lot. She was shaking, her legs still pulsating from the vibration of the engine as she stepped off the bike. She blinked a few times, and recognized where she was.

Veronica removed her helmet and moved closer to help Elizabeth unbuckle. She lifted up Elizabeth's chin, held it for a moment, and smiled. She wanted Elizabeth to know that Veronica was now in control. Elizabeth had given up the role of professor when she joined Veronica on the motorcycle. Veronica took her arm and they walked into the bar.

They sat opposite each other, silently sipping their glasses of white wine.

Veronica took the moment to be bold. She would risk it all now! In a carefully measured voice, she said, "Did you guess I would take you here, Elizabeth?" She bent over the table, leaned closer. "I want to tell you something." She took Elizabeth's wine glass, placed it on the table and held both of her hands in a firm grip. "I've wanted to tell you this for some time. I know you better than you think. I've seen you here before, but you didn't see me. You didn't even know me then, but I'd been watching you at the college since I arrived. I wanted to bring you here so you would know that."

Elizabeth looked around the bar and spoke in a controlled whisper. "Let me go. I want to go." Elizabeth attempted to pull her hands away, but Veronica was too strong.

"No. I can't do that now. It's too late. You'll never want to see me again. That would be a big mistake for both of us. I've just revealed how I feel about you. I know you think I'm strange." She let go of Elizabeth's hands. "I don't want to frighten you, but we had to move off of square one." Elizabeth tried to get up from the chair, but Veronica pulled her arm, forcing her to back down.

"You can pretend that you don't understand, but I think you do. I know when you look at me. I know I make you nervous. Maybe you confuse nervous with excited. Could that be, Elizabeth? Why did you want to ride with me?"

She let go of Elizabeth's hand, leaned back in the straight chair, and held Elizabeth with her eyes waiting for an answer. "You're not speaking, huh? You don't know what to do?" She leaned forward again. "What do you want to do, besides run?"

Veronica took her hand again, turned it over and stroked inside her palm. Veronica's smirk curled her upper lip, creating a small dimple in her right cheek. She said, "Let's dance while you think it over."

They moved around one small spot on the dance floor. Elizabeth felt Veronica's warm breath on her neck below her ear. Veronica insinuated a leg between Elizabeth's thighs, and pressed on Elizabeth's back, forcing her closer.

"Are you crazy, Veronica?"

Veronica whispered, "How do you want me to answer that? Have I ever been committed to an institution? Am I crazy about you? Is what we're doing tonight, crazy? Are you crazy for going along with it? What answer would you like? Pick one. Don't tell me what it is. Put it back in the deck and let me guess. Just like I'm going to guess what you like, how I'm going to make love to you. Would you like me to tell you that? Would you like to know what's going to happen, or should I let you guess? Maybe we'll let the tension build up for a while, let your nerves get real ragged and jagged. Then, when you're not expecting it . . . then . . . pow. I'm there."

Elizabeth recoiled. "Veronica, let me go. Don't do this! I'm frightened of you. I don't know who you are anymore."

"But, Elizabeth, you're the one. You're the one I've picked. Picked up. Don't you see? It has to be you."

Elizabeth dropped her head on Veronica's shoulder. She had stopped squirming to get loose.

"Yes, yes, just relax. It's going to be great. You'll see. Relax. That's it. You can't escape anyway, so you might as well enjoy it." The tone in Veronica's voice changed. Elizabeth recognized the student she had known for the past few weeks. "Elizabeth, I'm doing this so that we can know each other in a different way. I'm risking everything for you tonight. Just for you."

Veronica caressed her back and stroked the back of her neck.

Veronica switched her persona again to create the bravado she needed to pull this off. "You're a great dancer, Elizabeth. Last time I saw you here you didn't dance, but I could tell by the way you walked that you'd be a good dancer, the way you move your hips, so natural, no effort at all. Your body has a will of its own. Am I right? Isn't that true?"

Elizabeth didn't answer and Veronica felt her body stiffen, she pushed Elizabeth back and stared into Elizabeth's eyes.

"I want you to tell me when you're ready to go. You will tell me that, won't you, Elizabeth? You will! When you're ready?"

"You're really scaring me. Do you mean to do this? Do you mean to scare me?"

"Why are you scared? Of me? Of yourself? Of what we're doing? Of what I'm saying to you? You know it will happen. We will make love. We may even become lovers. Maybe you'll like it. Maybe you'll even like me."

"I . . . I . . . You're wild, no restraint, impulsive. You're Carol." Elizabeth said.

Veronica tightened her grip. "No, Elizabeth. Don't lie to yourself. You know it's me you want. I can feel how you are."

"I can't believe what I'm doing . . . with you," she stammered. She wanted to speak to Carol, to say . . . "I'm ready. Just keep holding my hand, so I don't run away."

"You mean away from me, Elizabeth, away from yourself? Say what you mean." Veronica was impatient and pulled Elizabeth closer. "Tell me. You can tell me. I want to hear it . . . all of it. Always . . . whatever it is."

Elizabeth finally understood that Veronica wouldn't let up or let her off. In some ways she was relieved not to have to continue to fight. She welcomed Veronica's forceful coercion. They sat down and watched the other women dance for a bit, and then Elizabeth reached up and placed a trembling hand on Veronica's cheek. "Yes."

"Wait here." Veronica paid the bill and came back to get her. They walked out together.

Veronica fastened Elizabeth's helmet and then her own. She swung her long leg over the seat of the motorcycle and patted the space behind her. Elizabeth obediently got on. They sped off with a roar, kicking up some of the gravel. Elizabeth cried out and reached down to touch her ankle. Veronica put her hand on Elizabeth's knee, gunned the engine and roared off through the dark streets.

* * *

Veronica locked the bike and led Elizabeth into the house.

"When you dropped me off here a few weeks ago, you didn't

give me a chance to invite you in. Weren't you curious? Now you can see where I live."

She opened the door to her apartment and took Elizabeth's hand as they walked in together. Kathy was asleep, but the door to her bedroom was open signaling an invitation to Veronica. She walked to Kathy's bedroom shut the door, and led Elizabeth to the adjoining bedroom.

Elizabeth turned, "I can't. I want to . . . but I . . ." She started for the door, but Veronica was too fast. She bolted the door and held Elizabeth by the shoulders.

Her voice was low and sounded strangely seductive to Elizabeth. "Didn't I say you couldn't get away? You know that. Don't try it again." She paused, and added, "Maybe later, you won't want to leave. Ever think of that?"

"No! No! I have to leave. Veronica, I can't do this. Let me go. Please, Veronica, I'm not joking." She pleaded. "I feel trapped. This is a mistake."

Veronica leaned back against the closed door. Her voice was calm and she spoke slowly. "Get undressed, Elizabeth. I want to watch you. I don't know what turns me on more, undressing a woman or watching her get undressed in front of me. I wonder which you prefer? Start with the pants. Shoes first, of course. Then work your way up. When you get to the shirt, leave it on. Then I'll come to you. And then you'll come to me. Won't you? You'll have to. You have no choice, no decision about that."

She sat down in a chair and placed Elizabeth directly in front of her.

"You can begin now. Lift up your foot and put it on my lap. I'll do the shoes."

Obediently, Elizabeth stood with her hands resting on Veronica's shoulders, allowing Veronica to remove first one shoe and sock, then the other. The bruise from the gravel had cut Elizabeth's shin-bone and there was some blood. Veronica licked the ankle and gently released it.

"Now the belt. Undo it. Now the zipper. Let the pants fall down to the floor and step out of them. Good. Stand still for a minute and let me look at your legs. I want to look at you for a long time before I touch you. I want to see the color of your skin before I feel it. Now do the shirt. Begin with the top button and stop before you take it off. Have you ever watched a woman remove a shirt, Elizabeth? It's one of the most beautiful moments. When the arm begins to move out of one sleeve and the shoulder rises and the whole torso turns and the breasts become visible one at a time, then the shirt slips off the arm and falls off the other one and . . . voila! There you are. And here you are . . . so beautiful. A body any artist would want to sculpt, just to touch it, to pose it, just so. Stand like this. Yes!''

Elizabeth stood in the dimly lit room, cold and naked, while Veronica sat looking at her. The temptation to run was strong, but she knew that Veronica would not let her go. *Do I want to get away? I have never felt like this. Veronica said not to think. Better not to analyze what I'm feeling now. Just stand here and let her look at me. Look at her looking at me. Her fingers moving over my mouth. Studying. Examining.*

"The bathroom is that way." Veronica indicated pointing her thumb over her shoulder.

Elizabeth washed, then looked at her face in the mirror. She was scared and excited. *I wanted this to happen. Veronica was right. It would never have happened if it were left to me. I want to leave because I'm scared. I've never done this before, I'm scared and I want to leave, but I want to stay, too. Veronica knows this too.* She walked out of the bathroom with a large towel wrapped tightly around her body.

Veronica smiled coldly. "And what is this, some more false modesty, some more denial? Drop the towel."

"I can't," Elizabeth replied. "I feel too vulnerable."

"Drop the towel," Veronica demanded. Elizabeth undid the towel and let it slide to the floor.

Veronica walked over to her. She ran her fingers through

Elizabeth's thick brown hair, pulling her into a tight embrace, pressing Elizabeth's mouth to her own.

"I've wanted you here, like this, for a long time. Enough time to fantasize making love to you. I want to do everything to you, everything all at once."

Veronica lifted off her own tee shirt and lowered Elizabeth on to the bed. Elizabeth reached up and covered Veronica's exposed breast with one hand.

"Yes," Veronica murmured and closed her eyes. Veronica leaned over Elizabeth roughly taking a nipple in her mouth. She slid her hands under Elizabeth's hips and caressed her. Elizabeth stiffened. "No, don't. No one . . . I never . . . "

Veronica grabbed her roughly by the shoulders. Elizabeth's head fell back on the pillow.

"Don't tell me what to do. Not now." Veronica continued to stroke her. "Yes," she whispered as Elizabeth surrendered to her touch. "Yes, that's better."

Veronica spoke softly. "Elizabeth, you must know that this is a difficult game to play." Her hands stopped moving and she took a deep breath. "You came with me tonight. Let me take you where you really want to go. Trust me!"

Her voice sounded gentler than Elizabeth had heard it all evening. "Yes. Yes. Show me what I want."

"I will. I want to," Veronica said, and she bent down to kiss her. "You're so wet." Elizabeth opened her eyes and put up her hands. Then she let them drop to her side. Veronica put two and then three fingers inside her. Elizabeth spread her legs wider, moaned and Veronica thrust deeper. She slid a thumb into her ass pushing and pulling slowly and then increasing the tempo responding to Elizabeth's excitement.

"Yes . . . yes. . . ." Elizabeth was hard to hold down. Her whisper became louder. "Oh, yes . . . don't . . . don't stop . . . don't!"

"You feel so good. Now! Now! Come! Come now! Come to me! To me! Come now!" Veronica urged her on.

"Yes . . . now . . . for you . . . yes," Elizabeth yelled out. Her hips jerked up from the bed and then she fell back. Her head moved from side to side as she moaned and wet her lips. She gasped. Her hands clenching and unclenching, matching the spasms inside her body that she couldn't control.

The knock on the bedroom door startled both of them.

"Ronnie, are you okay?"

She looked down at Elizabeth and spoke with difficulty, "Yes, yes . . . Kathy . . . fine . . . don't come in."

They lay still for a few minutes, and then Elizabeth stirred and moved her arm around Veronica's waist. She pulled her down onto her and held her close.

"You really are crazy. I don't have to ask that anymore." She spoke into the darkness. "I mean, crazy, wild . . . like . . . not like me. Veronica, or Ronnie, whatever you want to be!"

Elizabeth began to cry softly, nestling her wet cheek in the hollow of Veronica's neck. Veronica held the yielding body and stroked her hair. She felt Elizabeth's tears running down her neck and shoulders, and then they both slipped into an exhausted sleep.

It was still dark when Elizabeth woke up. She was disoriented for a second, but remembered when she looked down at Veronica, asleep on her stomach. Her even, deep breathing reminded her of a child. *She's so young, and I'm too old for these games. No one forced me to do anything. Veronica sensed what I wanted, and I acquiesced. Last night was not real, and yet it was.* It had been so long since she felt anything except numb, that even fear was a welcome emotion. She brushed some hair away from Veronica's face and looked at her closely. She bent down and kissed her cheek and the corner of her mouth.

Veronica opened her eyes and turned over on her back. She reached up for Elizabeth and pulled her down on top of her.

They could not stop the kiss because it was too fragile, too delicate. They could not look into each other's eyes for that would require an acknowledgment of what had happened.

Veronica kissed her breasts, began to suck her nipples, and

Elizabeth shook her head, closed her eyes and ran her tongue over her lips.

Veronica's hands traced Elizabeth's body. She turned Elizabeth on to her back and moved both her hands under Elizabeth's buttocks, lifting her slightly. She took her very gently, moving her tongue up and down, just touching the opening to Elizabeth's vagina.

"Oh, oh." Her hands twisted in Veronica's hair. Veronica pushed harder. Elizabeth gasped and bucked against Veronica's mouth. Veronica put her fingers inside, and held back a little, letting Elizabeth set her own pace and intensity.

Elizabeth groaned guttural sounds from deep in her throat. The sounds suddenly became a scream and she stopped moving. Her body shook convulsively and Veronica could feel the contractions inside as the fluid seeped on to her hands. Veronica moved her fingers once more, and Elizabeth shuddered.

They lay still not speaking, then Elizabeth slid her hands down Veronica's shoulders to her breasts and rubbed her nipples. Veronica closed her eyes. Elizabeth moved further down on the bed. She savored the clear liquid, salty and sweet.

Veronica clutched at the bed sheets, her fingers opening and closing to the internal throbbing of her body. The rhythm set by Elizabeth's tongue. Elizabeth moved her fingers inside, demanding entrance.

"Oh God!" Elizabeth breathed out loud. "I had almost forgotten how it feels."

Veronica came with a deep moan and pushed down on Elizabeth's hand, almost forcing Elizabeth's fist inside of her.

Afterwards, Elizabeth rested her head on Veronica's thighs. Neither one knew what to do or say next. Elizabeth opened her eyes and stared at the design tattooed on Veronica's belly. She ran her hand over the tattoo that looked like a medallion pinned to the soft skin.

Elizabeth lifted herself on one elbow and smiled at Veronica.

"You're just full of all kinds of surprises," she quipped. "What's that?"

Veronica pulled her close so that their lips touched. "That's my sign," she smiled.

"What month is that?" Elizabeth smiled back.

"Must be the month of Lesbos." Veronica's grin was wide.

"According to the Sapphic calendar, right?" Elizabeth responded in a musing voice, her fingers gently tracing the outline of the tattoo. The labyris was about six inches over all. The double headed blades were deep lavender and the ornate handles holding the crossed blades were black with a small orange line running down the length of the handle. Flowing ribbons of green were wrapped around the handles of the axes. The blades were decorated with curlicues in red and blue, giving the whole tattoo a Celtic design.

"I guess you weren't joking when you referred to yourself as Amazon. You had it tattooed right on your body."

They both laughed. Veronica moved the hair back from Elizabeth's face. This was a gesture she could see herself making for a long time.

"When did you do it? Why there? Did it hurt?"

"Well, as I've told you, muh private life's muh owhn, and I guess muh private parts are, too, but since you ask in such a nice way . . . yes it hurt to have it done. I did it when I was sixteen. It was my private sweet sixteen celebration."

She sat up and pulled a pillow behind her head. "I don't mean to sound flip. It means much more than that to me. It's personal and has to do with my family. I don't know if I can explain this to you, because you don't know them."

"Please," Elizabeth ran her hand down Veronica's breast. "Tell me. I want to know. I want to know more about you."

Veronica kissed the top of her head. "It was my answer to the pearl necklace that my parents gave me on my sixteenth birthday, my answer to the sugar cube corsage that I had to wear to school that embarrassed me so. I saw the expression on my parents' faces when they gave them to me. They wanted to surprise me. It had cost them so much to do this that I had to pretend that I really wanted that necklace, that I was really sweet like the corsage. I knew what they expected of me. I was sixteen, and soon I would have a boyfriend, get married, have children and move into a house near Mom so we could spend all day together and watch the kids, etc. etc. I felt as if I were drowning in that sweet, cloying, candy make-believe world. I did it so I would never, for a minute, forget who I really am, no matter what. It's my badge, my identity."

Elizabeth studied her. "Yes, I understand." Elizabeth leaned forward and kissed the tattoo.

They stroked each other's body, learning the feel of each other's skin, memorizing the special places that they each hoped would become familiar landmarks in their future lovemaking. Although they were still strangers, this was what each of them desired.

Sleeping/Dreaming

"Mnnnn . . . No! No! Please . . . no!" Veronica was forced awake by the recurring dream. She never knew when it would happen, and months could go by before the same images would rise up from her unconscious. Always in the dreams, as in real life, she was too late. She woke in a sweat, opened her eyes, breathed deeply and leaned back against the headboard. She moved closer to Elizabeth. "Hold me. Please. I need you to hold me."

"Veronica, what's the matter?" Elizabeth took Veronica in her arms, and smoothed the damp hair back from her forehead. "What is it?"

"It's my dream about Leslie." She bit down on her lower lip. "It wasn't my fault. We were so young. How could anyone know?"

Elizabeth held Veronica tightly. "It's all right."

Veronica whispered fragments. "I got her the job in the brokerage house. That's where she met Mike. I told her it wouldn't work. I begged her not to do it. She wouldn't listen. She thought it would be the easiest way out. Marry Mike and no one would ever know. She never even considered how I would feel."

She lifted her head to look at Elizabeth.

"You know what she wrote in the stupid high school yearbook? She wanted to make her parents proud of her. Lots of kids write things like that. I laughed when I read it. I thought it was a joke, but it wasn't. We couldn't be lovers and make her family happy. She got a job to make her parents proud. I got a job to be with her, to make her happy. Then she married Mike to make him happy. Everyone was supposed to be happy, but no one really was. She thought she could control her life and her feelings." Veronica beat her hands on the bed cover in frustration. "We should have stopped after Mike. I knew that. We tried, but it was too hard. All those years in camp, church, high school, we had each other. I miss her so much, Elizabeth."

Elizabeth stroked her back. "What happened?"

"Her car went off the road into a ditch and turned over. She was going too fast. They said it was an accident. She wasn't wearing a seat belt and her neck was broken. She had a little boy, three years old, and even her love for him couldn't stop her, and, of course, she left Mike. He was . . . he is a nice guy. I wanted to believe it was an accident, but I knew better. And when her letter came, I wasn't really surprised. She had mailed it the same day she killed herself. It was only one line, 'I still want you'."

Veronica began to cry and Elizabeth held her gently, protectively in her arms.

Genealogy

Veronica's mother stood at the open door welcoming them. She grabbed Veronica in a bear hug and kissed her on both cheeks.

"Veronica, my beautiful baby, I'm so happy you came, so we can spend some time before the wedding . . . just the family. Paul and Marie will be here soon. Marie's so excited, Veronica. She bought you the most beautiful dress for the maid of honor and she has it hanging upstairs waiting for you to try on."

"Mom, this is Elizabeth Sanderson. She's a professor at the university."

Here we go again. How do I introduce someone to the outside world? The differences which you were just beginning to convince yourself were philosophical always became real in the outside world. What did that make Veronica's world? The inside world? That's what inmates called a prison, "the inside." The rest of the world was the "outside." Sometimes–no, all times– that was how she felt. What should she say? Mom, this is my–friend, lover, companion, woman-I'm-in-love-with-and-hoping- for-a-longer-more-meaningful-relationship-with-person? She imagined the rest of the conversation.

What does that mean, Veronica?

Well you know, Mom, she's the one who gets me off, sucks my cunt, sticks her fingers up all of my orifices, holds me at night, wraps her legs around me and kisses my breasts and plays with my nipples till I want to scream and then she lowers herself and slides down the length of my body making me shiver and have tiny jerky fits till she gets to my pussy and starts to lick me and take me in her mouth. She's the one who gets me so wet I should really walk around all the time with a sanitary napkin to protect myself from all of the unclean, unsafe things that we do. You know Mom. I don't have to tell you. You know who she is!

"Oh it's always nice to meet one of Veronica's teachers. When she was in Sacred Heart we knew all of the sisters who were her teachers. They always said such wonderful things about her. Joe and I loved going to parents' nights. We always felt so proud."

*   *   *

Veronica fidgeted with her napkin. Her brother Paul kept one arm around her and laughed at her stories about "WASP heaven" in Connecticut. Marie and Frank were wrapped up in each other, holding hands and basking in the family's approval. She looked over at Elizabeth trying to imagine what she might be thinking. *We can't sit here and hold hands. I shouldn't let it bother me, but it does. There's that line, the barbed wire fence between the inside and the outside.*

She suspected they knew about her anyway. But, they would be shocked if she took Elizabeth's hand, and kissed her the way Frank turned to kiss Marie. Everyone was being so nice, but if she moved out of line, just once, gave them the opening to condemn, question, reject her, it would be finished. They would never accept her.

She glanced over at Elizabeth who was saying something to Marie. Elizabeth looked back at her and smiled. She decided that the promise in that secret smile would have to do. It would have to be enough to get her through the day.

Her father, his arm around her shoulder, walked around the small backyard garden, asking questions about his tomatoes, asking her advice about the mildew on the roses and lilac leaves. She followed him to the garage to look at his supply of garden chemicals.

"You know, Veronica, it's too bad we didn't live in a nice house when you were growing up. We probably would have spent a lot of time together in the garden."

Translation: How did this happen to us, to you? It's my fault, I didn't have money. Didn't give you a real house, so you had to go away summers to that Girl Scout Camp with Leslie and who knows who else. All because we didn't have a garden for you.

She wanted to say, *Dad, my life is fine. In fact it's wonderful. Even though you see that, you still look at me as if I were some kind of misfit. I hate that patronizing–she can't help it, she's just a victim look.* She wanted to show him the tattoo. *I'm an Amazon, strong and tough, because that's how you have to be if you want to survive your family, your friends, the kids at school, Father Mancuso and Sister Irene and all the others. I have to be tough to stop you. You love me and you would destroy me. You think it's for my own good, but it's for you. It's a war that I will win. I will win. If I keep saying that to myself and touch my belly, just here . . .*

Veronica rejoined the others who were sitting in the backyard talking about the wedding. She had gone upstairs to try on the pink satin dress that her sister wanted her to wear. It needed some alteration, but basically it fit so well, her mother cried anticipating the actual wedding day, and her father rushed to get the camera and take a picture. The tension inside her was becoming unbearable. She mouthed the right words, smiled the right way, kept her eye on Elizabeth, conscious of not looking too often, so no one would notice or feel uncomfortable. She let them believe the lie that Elizabeth was her professor, a friend from Connecticut, but the cost was too great.

"Mom, Dad, I'm afraid that we have to get back. I have to work tomorrow, and it'll be a long ride with lots of traffic. Anyway, I'll be down in a few weeks for the wedding." Veronica got up and started to gather her things together. "Sure," said Rose, "let me pack some of the leftover food in an ice bag for you."

At the door, Elizabeth held out her hand to Veronica's mother. "Thank you for a lovely afternoon, Rose." *The WASP way,* thought Veronica. Rose Santini laughed, pulled Elizabeth close to her and gave her a big kiss on the cheek. Then each Santini, including Frank, gave Elizabeth a big hug. Veronica sensed Elizabeth's discomfort with this overt display of affection and wondered if Elizabeth would comment on her family. How did the New Jersey Santini's compare with the Connecticut Sanderson clan? Veronica was certain that she would soon find out.

Seeing Elizabeth's discomfort was a minor distraction for Veronica, but by the time she got to the car the tension of the day had caught up with her. Her head was thumping, and her fists were clenched. She asked Elizabeth to drive and took deep breaths hoping that Elizabeth would not notice how upset she was.

Elizabeth pulled the car around the block and shut off the engine. "What's wrong?"

"Nothing. I don't want to talk about it." Veronica slumped in her seat moving her fingers back and forth through her hair. Elizabeth recognized the characteristic nervous gesture.

"I think I know what's bothering you, too much of a good thing, a case of familyitis . . . a pretty bad one, too." She took Veronica's chin in her hands and looked at her blank face. "We may have to quarantine you to permanent Dyke quarters if you don't show signs of improvement soon."

Veronica brightened. "I guess that wouldn't be so bad."

"So, let's go, Veronica. Let's go to Dyke heaven. Sapphic paradise on the river. What do you say? Are you up for it?" She paused and looked out the windshield. "There's one problem . . . how do we get out of here?"

Veronica smiled. "That's what I'd like to know. How do I extricate myself from this place?"

"Well, my dear, that is a personal problem. Right now, I'm just talking about the fastest way onto the highway."

Veronica gave directions and Elizabeth quickly found the entrance to the highway.

"How do you feel when you visit your family?" Veronica was rubbing the furrow between her brows.

"I don't have a close family like you do, Veronica, just have some cousins in Massachusetts and I rarely see them." Elizabeth looked over at Veronica. "I guess you want more of the details right? Yes, knowing you it's only the intimate details that will do. Revealing more of me than I ever wanted to put into language. You demand a lot, Veronica."

Veronica smiled again. "Yes, but I'm worth the sacrifice of your privacy. Right?"

"Let me tell you now, and later I can regret I revealed so much of myself to . . ."

Veronica retorted, ". . . to a stranger. Is that what you were going to say? Revealing too much to a stranger. Me?"

Elizabeth reached over and patted Veronica's hand. "I was never really close to my parents. I was an only child. My mother died when I was in my twenties and my father a few years later." She squeezed Veronica's hand. "Now comes the part you really want to know. They had suspicions about me that I never confirmed or denied. Then, it no longer mattered." She paused and shook her head. "There's nothing you're going to learn from my experiences. My family was so different from yours. It's clear, to me, your mother and father and Marie and Paul love you very much, but I think that you already know that. Your family just don't know yet how you're going to fit in. Let's assess the situation objectively. Your mother has one daughter to give her the grandchildren and to maintain her community status, so you're in a pretty good position there. Your brother obviously adores you, and he wouldn't care if you brought home the creature from the black lagoon." She ran her fingers along Veronica's cheek. "He looks just like you . . . gorgeous." She moved Veronica's hair away from her face. "The same blonde hair falling over his eyes, the same intense expression. . . . I was jealous. They're all so proud of you Veronica. If I were you, I would try not to concentrate too much on the other part."

"You mean focus on the parts of my life they can accept and not think so much about who I am?"

"Yes, and don't be sarcastic."

Veronica moved her hands through Elizabeth's hair on the back of her neck. "I guess one of the reasons I'm so crazy about you has to be your great survival skills."

"You're being sarcastic again, aren't you?" She stroked Veronica's knee and insinuated a hand between her legs. Veronica leaned back and sighed.

Love Shouldn't Be So Hard

It was a chilly night in late August. Arms and legs entwined, they tasted themselves on each other's lips as they lay under the warm quilt that Elizabeth had taken down from the closet. As Veronica and Elizabeth became closer, contrary to what either of them expected, there was an increasing strain.

"You never say my name when we're making love. You've never said Veronica, since that first night. Elizabeth, I need to know you want me, Veronica, here with you, now, in this house. Why won't you say my name?"

Elizabeth evaded answering the question, pretending she didn't understand what Veronica needed from her. "I do want you, Veronica. When I'm alone here, I miss you, but I'm not the replacement for Leslie, which is what I think you're aiming for."

"No, and I'm not Carol. I never wanted to be a replacement. Why are you doing this? Is this all you want from me, a few nights, some hours here and there? Is that all I am to you? Maybe it's the age difference, or don't you really like me? I know I'm not like Carol. Is that still it?"

Elizabeth smiled. "Actually, you remind me very much of Carol, maybe that's why I keep you at a distance. This affair is all too real for me." *As real as the closing of a door,* she thought.

"You mean being loved, loving is too frightening to you now? You want to think of this as something superficial. You won't take a chance."

Elizabeth got up out of the bed and stood in front of the French doors staring into the night and listening to the river.

Veronica watched her for a few minutes, and then took the comforter off the bed and draped it over Elizabeth. She stood in back of her, holding the comforter tightly around Elizabeth. She placed the palms of her hands against the sides of Elizabeth's head and applied some pressure.

"Wouldn't it be easy if we could squeeze out all of the painful memories of our lives? Then the harder I pressed, the happier your life would become."

"That's called a lobotomy," said Elizabeth sharply, "and it's only done as a last resort."

"Yes, so we have to remember and we have to live with the memory, but the operative word is . . . now."

Elizabeth was impatient. "Why are you pushing me like this? You want more from me than I can give you."

"I want to believe that I'm more than an interlude in your life, more than a sex machine or a comforter like this blanket thrown over you. You should want more. That's why I have to be a real person, someone instead of something. I'm not asking for us to begin to monogram the sheets, buy the china, write up the living wills. I'm just asking for the possibility to exist."

"Veronica, I know what you want. I'm sorry, but I think this is as far as I can go. This is as much as I can give to anyone." Elizabeth walked away from the window and got back into bed.

"Veronica, I want to tell you something about an accident I had when I was a child."

Veronica walked back to the bed and placed her arm around Elizabeth, rhythmically stroking her soft arm, enjoying the feel of the strong muscles underneath.

"What was it? What happened to you?"

"I don't know why I'm thinking about that moment now so much."

"You've never told me very much about your childhood."

"I must have been about ten years old, and I was riding my favorite horse in a local show, not very far from this house, as a matter of fact. We were a class of young girls, about seven of us, and we would compete against each other in English equitation."

"What's that?"

"Oh, that's when you walk, trot and canter your horse round the ring. Your horse has to be on the right lead, and the transitions between the gaits have to be very smooth. The rider has to direct the horse with her legs and her hands, just slight pressures, very subtle. It's pretty standard fare, especially for the kids."

"What's a lead?"

"Veronica, you don't have to learn everything about horses and riding in a few minutes. I'll try not to be so technical. Just listen and don't interrupt."

"Do I get quizzed afterwards?"

Elizabeth pushed her away.

"Relax. Just a joke," Veronica laughed. "My, you have lost your sense of humor. Okay, I promise not to interrupt anymore. I'll save my questions for the end as they say in all the lectures. Except I can't write them down now, can I?"

She ignored Veronica's attempts to make light of their conflict. "My mother and father always came to the shows. They were sitting around the ring. They knew I would win the blue. Our house was filled with all sorts of trophies and ribbons, photos of each of them winning various events, jumping, dressage . . ." Elizabeth lifted her head slightly, "and don't ask me what that is either." She stroked Veronica. "Horse shows are not low key and no one is really having a fun time, because there is a tremendous pressure to compete and to win. I was an excellent rider and loved riding. I would go for rides through the woods on my favorite horse, Sunny. He was a large Morgan, very gentle and willing. Sometimes we would hitch him up to a cart and he was beautiful at driving, too. My parents wanted me to enter into more and more shows. Often they would have friends out to the house for weekends and bring them to the shows to see me ride. They bought a horse trailer and would take me to shows in towns farther away. Maybe they saw a career for me in riding, I don't really know. On that particular weekend, my father invited some business friends up. They had come a few times earlier, and I didn't like them very much. They stayed up late and made lots of noise so that I couldn't get very much sleep. The morning of this particular show, I braided Sunny's mane and tail. He seemed so relaxed, it really helped to calm me down, too. I was doing fairly well in the ring. The instructor was calling out the gaits, and I was concentrating on my hands and legs as I had been taught. I must have lost my concentration for a moment because when she called out 'canter,' we started out on the wrong lead. I tried to get him to switch over to the correct lead, but it was already too late and we were heading for the turn in the ring. Sunny slid out from under me and fell over on his side. He was off balance, and it was my fault, not his. He was just following my signals."

Veronica could feel Elizabeth tense. She held her closer "Were you hurt? What happened?"

"When Sunny fell over, I panicked and didn't take my foot out of the stirrups. My leg was caught under him, and I couldn't free it. I knew that Sunny would never hurt me. He tried to get up, and he pulled me up with him. I heard a cracking sound, and then I must have fainted."

Veronica sat up stiffly.

"I didn't pass out for too long because I remember people running towards me. Sunny must have thought the crack came from something in him because he started to lose control and run around the ring. Finally someone stopped him, and they took my leg out of the stirrup. My right leg was so badly broken that the doctors didn't know if I would ever walk without a limp or a cane.

"But you're fine now, aren't you?" Veronica felt queasy and anxious.

"The break was a clean one, I was strong and I mended well. I was laid up for the remainder of the summer, but that's not the point of the story. The physical pain was nothing compared to the way my mother and father looked at me afterwards in the hospital. I knew what they wanted to say. They wanted to yell and scream at me and call me a stupid girl who forgot everything and almost got herself killed. But they were quite calm and matter of fact about everything. My mother didn't blame me at all. My father never told me that I had done anything wrong. When I asked how Sunny was, they told me not to worry about the horse. He would be just fine. About a week later they confessed to me that they had sold him that very day. I never knew where he had gone, who he was with. I never saw him again, and I longed to know that wherever he had been sent, he was loved and well treated. I tried to explain to them that it was my fault and not Sunny's, but they wouldn't listen. I couldn't have been careless, not their little girl, not the daughter of all the trophy winners. I cried all the time in the hospital, realizing that Sunny had been punished because of me. It was so unfair. I also knew that my parents never wanted to know the truth about anything, especially when it concerned their daughter. That was the summer I detached myself from them. My bones knitted together, but the rift between us was never healed. I learned to hide my feelings, to pretend that things didn't matter to me. Most of all I learned to protect myself from being hurt again. Carol, somehow, got past all those psychic sentries who had kept me aloof and protected. When she left and the door slammed shut, it was not the door I heard, it was the sound of that crack.''

Maid of Honor

"Now, Veronica, when you hear the music, start to walk . . . slowly." Father Thomas demonstrated the correct walk. "Right foot, left foot. That's it. Slowly, in time with the music. Make sure you smile." He took Veronica's arm and led her to the altar. "Wonderful, Veronica, now move to the side and wait for the bride." He watched apprehensively as Veronica followed his instructions. "Good," he sighed.

"Now Mrs. Santini and Paul. Slowly, slowly. There's no hurry here. At least we hope not."

Everyone laughed.

"Mr. Santini and Marie . . . right foot, left foot." Father Thomas shook his head and stopped them. "Slowly! Slowly! Everyone always wants to go too fast. Let's all take our time. It's so beautiful, and we want to savor every second. Let the guests get to enjoy the scene, too. Try not to be nervous."

Mrs. Santini gave a tight laugh and placed her two hands on the sides of her head. "Oh, that's easy for you to say, Father, but it's not your daughter and this is the first wedding in the family."

Mr. Santini put his arm around her. "Rose, you know you're going to look beautiful tomorrow. Don't worry, Father Thomas, we'll all do fine. We'll do exactly what you said and make sure that we walk slowly. After all, we do want everyone to ooh and ahh over the beautiful bride." He walked over to Marie, smiled and kissed her on the cheek.

Veronica felt the stress of the moment. She looked at the ushers and the bridesmaids, cousins and friends of Frank and Marie. *You can't tell from looking. One in ten, maybe more. Occasions like this always emphasize the difference between us and them, but I'll really try to fit in.*

She smiled warmly at her father, who walked towards her. "You especially, Veronica, will be the most beautiful." He whispered in her ear, "Just make sure you don't outshine the bride, or I'll never hear the end of it from both of them, much as they love you." He hugged her and they laughed.

* * *

Later that night, lying in her bed, Veronica wanted Elizabeth to be there with her. She could have asked her parents to invite Elizabeth to the wedding, but it would have involved too much explaining.

Veronica felt like a soldier the night before the battle. She picked up the phone and dialed Elizabeth.

"Did I wake you? Yes. I'm sorry, and it is pretty late, about twelve-thirty. I was anxious. I'm nervous about tomorrow . . . the night before the big show jitters. I wish you were here with me, next to me now. I need a little Dyke support.

"Of course, I'll be very good tomorrow. I won't display my tattoo . . . especially not to Father Thomas." She laughed.

"It's so hard to explain why I feel this way . . . you don't have the family ties that I do. You don't know what it's like . . . the expectations. I want to be part of the family wedding. Tomorrow scares me because I know I can lose control."

She listened as Elizabeth tried to joke about the control Veronica used the first night they were together. Veronica responded angrily, "Forget about that night! Forget it. . . . I sound agitated because I am." She forced herself to speak quietly. "It was a game, Elizabeth. A game you'd never played before. A game of seduction. You seemed to like it. Lucky for you and . . . lucky for me . . . Elizabeth . . . It's difficult to continue this scene now. I keep getting jammed on Marie's wedding, tomorrow."

She responded again to Elizabeth's attempt to make light of her anxiety. "Of course, why didn't I think of that? I could go to church early tomorrow and go to confession. Confess it all. Reveal all of the intimacies, intricacies of my hidden life. Give Father, what's-his-name, a real thrill.

". . . No, no that was just a joke . . . it's going to be a long day, complicated and conflicting, and I can't share my feelings about it with anyone. Here in body and not in spirit? It's all very sad. It's happening already. It must be in the air, fomenting all those little guilt and sin germs that creep back into you like a virus, the herpes virus that goes away temporarily and then re-appears just when you don't want it to.

"I know you understand, Elizabeth. Of course, you don't have to be Italian or Catholic to experience isolation and family pressure, but you don't have the church along with it. You don't have the school . . . I don't know why I'm rambling on so. Thanks for listening to a monologue." She bit her lower lip. "I miss you Elizabeth. I could lose myself making love to you, watching you become excited. Sex is the best tranquilizer," she said laughing.

Veronica ended the phone call and sat propped against the pillow for a few moments, picturing Elizabeth. Her thick brown hair spread against the pillows. *Even I could paint a portrait of her if I keep at it.* She snuggled down into the warm sheets and fell asleep.

Loud talking awakened her, opening and closing of closet doors just outside her bedroom door. She looked at the clock on the bed table. It was only six-thirty, but everyone was up and getting ready. She smiled and shook her head. Nothing had changed. Soon they would be knocking on her door, assuming that she would still be asleep through all this noise. When she was young, Veronica used to put the pillows over her head to muffle the noise. Later on she put a hook latch on the door to keep them out. She remembered how grumpy she used to be, how she complained about the early rising to go to church.

No, she told herself, only positive thoughts for this day. *I'm going to have to do better. It's only six-thirty in the morning, and if I start like this now, I'll never even make it to the church, let alone the reception. Okay, take lots of deep breaths, smile, look demure.* She winked at herself in the mirror. *Don't show your tattoo . . . and for god's sake . . . don't grab any of the bridesmaids in the ladies' room.*

She slipped on her bathrobe and went downstairs. Paul was sitting at the kitchen table in his undershirt and jeans, a cup of coffee in his hand. He, too, had just been awakened, and his eyes were not fully opened. His blonde hair was freshly cut, shorter than he usually wore it.

Everyone makes sacrifices, she realized. *You're not the only one. Don't be so selfish. After all it's Marie's day, and everyone wants it to be as perfect as it can be for her.* She kissed Paul on the top of his head and poured herself a cup of coffee.

"What do you think the rush is?" he asked. "We don't have to be there till noon." He rested the cup against his forehead.

"I guess they want us at the church before anyone else gets there. You know, to greet the guests, make sure everything is okay."

"Yeah, yeah. I know. I'm not really complaining. I'm just tired, that's all."

"We've got a long day in front of us, Paul, so we'd better take it slow. Begin slow and go slow. That's the word."

He looked at her, and a playful grin spread across his face. "So that's the word, huh? I wondered what it was. All night I'm saying to myself, so Paul what's the word? So now I know. Slow. The word is slow. Tell me, Ronnie, does anyone else know this word, or is it just a secret between the two of us? Can we write away for the magic decoding ring with this word?"

He was really waking up now, and the little boy she used to play cops and robbers and cowboys and Indians with was sitting in front of her.

Veronica shook her head, laughed as she sat down across from him. "Who you gonna write, huh? Huh? Think you're tough, huh? Well let's go a couple of arm wrestles and we'll see."

"Are you kidding, Ronnie? You must be joking? I'm a big boy now. There's no contest."

Veronica held her hands in front of her face. "Okay," she

laughed. "It was just a joke, Paul. I can see what a big guy you've become. Man, no messing with you now. No sir. Why, a tough like you could probably wrestle my arm right out of its little girl socket, couldn't you?"

"Veronica, I didn't mean anything. I . . . I'm not a . . . Oh crap, Ronnie, I'm not like that. You know. I'm no macho Italian stud. I don't have to prove myself to you. Why do you have to twist things so that they come out all wrong?" He shook his head. "I don't understand you anymore."

"I'm sorry, Paul. I know you didn't mean anything. I'm too sensitive. I'm sorry. Really. It's . . . it's a hard day for me, too."

She walked over and put her arms around his neck.

He patted her shoulder. "Yeah, I'm sorry, too. Just got carried away. I know it must be difficult for you. I never wanted to ask you anything, Ronnie . . . about your life, I mean, but I think about you a lot. You seem so different since you moved away. I'm still living at home, followed Dad into the fire department. Marie's getting married and moving into an apartment not far from here, probably have a couple of kids soon and Mom will be over there all day. But you . . . you left. Is it so hard for you to be with us? Why?"

"Paul, you make it sound as if I'm an international drug dealer leading some secret life."

"No. That's not what I meant at all." He raised his hands over his head in exasperation.

"Sure it is." She was losing control. She tried to stop, to calm down. *This is unexpected. I'm not ready for this now, not today.* "Paul, you're my brother, and I love you, but I don't want to talk about my life today. I want to . . . enjoy Marie's wedding."

"I know, I do too, but we never seem to get the chance to talk anymore, the way we used to. I miss my sister who I could count on for advice."

She wanted to talk to him about her life. She really wanted to be honest and tell him what she was feeling. He was important to her.

He pulled on her arm and forced her to sit in a chair next to him.

"Maybe this isn't the right time, Ronnie, or even the right place, but I want you to know, as if you didn't know, that I love you. I always have and always will, no matter what."

She assumed a flippant, sarcastic tone. "You mean when the FBI catches me with a boatload of drugs off the Miami coast and sends me up for life? Even then, huh?" She popped him on the back of the head and he got up from the table. They chased each other around the living room a few times, laughing hysterically and then each plunked down into a soft armchair.

"What's all this noise here? Veronica, Paul, why aren't you getting ready?"

Paul's eyes rolled in his head. "Mom, there's plenty of time. Ronnie and I were just trading decoding rings." He looked over at Veronica and winked.

"You two, just like when you were kids, always making up stories and secrets together." Veronica was warmed by her mother's loving look.

"Come on now, let's get ready. I'm so nervous. Your father and I hardly slept."

Paul got up from his chair, grabbed his mother around the waist and danced her around the living room.

"Isn't it romantic," he began to sing.

Rose pushed herself away from him after a few steps and he let her go, extending his hand and bowing from the waist. "Okay, honey, catch you later."

He dropped into the sofa and sprawled out, his legs dangling over the side of the sofa. "And as for you," he said, looking at Veronica, "I'll just have to catch you later on, too."

"I hope so, Paul. I really do." She blinked back the tears.

Her Sister's Wedding

The organ music was peaceful. Veronica closed her eyes and pretended she was at a concert, shutting out the excitement in the church, the shuffling relatives, their nervous murmuring above the music. Actors, she thought, must feel this way while waiting for their cue, before stepping out on-stage.

She was an actor, waiting with the rest of the cast, rehearsing and planning their moves for the big march down the aisle. She watched the others and was again aware how easily they blended together, made small talk. *Damn it! Why am I always on the outside looking in? Why do I make myself an outsider? Could I once-just once-be a part of this world? On the happiest day of my sister's life, please let me fit in. Let me feel her happiness and let it be real to me.* She hated herself for being different.

During high school, she couldn't talk about her love for Leslie. She developed the habit of biting her lower lip, swallowing her feelings, no longer sharing them with her family. She realized she had lost her spontaneity. Her confidence and self-esteem were being compromised. Everything about her relationship with her family was an act, as she fought to kept the real Veronica hidden away.

And it was so easy, because they assumed certain things: that I wanted to go to the prom with Tommy, that all those nights at Leslie's house were spent studying. And now, too, I'm an impostor at my sister's wedding. In drag-wearing the pink satin dress Marie chose. I never have been that little girl they thought they knew.

Father Thomas came in and announced excitedly, "It's time, everyone! Get in order! Mr. Santini just before you start walking you'll have to check Marie's gown and make sure the train is straight. I'll try to come back to help before you go, but just in case I can't . . ."

Her father looked stiff in his tuxedo, and he sounded stiff, too. "Sure, I'll check it. Don't worry."

"Remember, everyone, listen to the music, and just follow the tempo. Don't walk too fast. Just relax and smile, and you'll all do fine." He beamed a patronizing smile. "You all look lovely."

Veronica walked over to her sister. "Marie, I have to tell you again, how absolutely beautiful you look."

Marie hugged her. "You're the one who is truly beautiful, Ronnie, my big sister. I know that someday you'll be as happy as I am right now."

Veronica pulled away from her. "I . . . I'm . . ."

Marie squeezed her hand and looked into Veronica's eyes. "Veronica, we all love you so much! Frank, too!"

The music started, and the wedding procession made its way into the church. Veronica walked down the aisle alone. Everyone was looking at her. She couldn't remember ever feeling so nervous and shaky.

She imagined that everyone could see through her act. She thought she heard:

"That's Marie's sister, she'll never get married."

"That's Marie's sister. She's a lesbian."

"That's Marie's sister. She's a pervert."

But no one could see her secret. *Let the performance begin.*

With a simpering smile, Veronica walked toward the altar. She turned to watch her father and Marie walk down the aisle to Mendelssohn's Wedding March. She watched the smiles and heard the murmurs of approval from the wedding guests. Veronica tried to look interested as the priest spoke, but she was barely listening to the ceremony. She had dismissed her religious upbringing as primitive drivel.

Leslie had been shocked by her vehement attacks on the Catholic church. She had fond memories of some of the nuns at their high school, but Veronica was angry at the ways they'd tried to shape her mind. She mournfully remembered how upset she would get with Leslie for not being strong enough to resist this religion that proclaimed them sinful.

Marie has always believed in the church. She, Frank, and their children will be part of it, preserving it, and perpetuating it.

And how did I escape, she thought. I don't know. Did I?

"I do."

The ceremony was going by so quickly. The priest blessed them. They exchanged rings. Frank kissed Marie, and soon they were walking back up the aisle.

She was relieved that the ceremony in church was over-now she just had to get through the social agony of the celebration. The matinee performance was over, now for the evening crowd. She took a deep breath, knowing that her performance was only beginning. She had the second female lead in this piece, and she would really play it up.

*　*　*

She shook hands with someone from Frank's side of the family, and then leaned forward to kiss her cousin, Connie, and Connie's husband, John.

"Oh, you look so beautiful, Veronica. Doesn't she, Johnny?"

"Thanks, Connie, you look good, too. I love your dress."

Veronica watched Marie and Frank laughing and talking with their guests. *Marie looks particularly beautiful today. There will never be a day like this in my life. No! I don't want a wedding. I don't want to imitate them. I just want to exist in their minds. To exist in a world of my own . . . of our own. There will be no ceremonies like this to make me feel good about myself. No one will stand around praising my love. They'd throw bottles, not rice. There'd be insults instead of toasts.*

Sweat trickled down her armpits, and beaded up on her forehead. She had to get out, but she felt trapped, her smile frozen on her face. She took deep breaths to try to stop the panic. She told herself she wouldn't think about these things now. She tried to focus on Marie and Frank, but they started to blur together. She bolted from the line and ran to the ladies' room. She was nauseated. Her forehead was wet with sweat as she bent over the toilet. She retched a few times and then leaned back against the cool stall door. Her breathing was shallow, and she felt faint.

At the sink, she wet her face with a paper towel. She looked at herself in the mirror, rouged, lipsticked, eyelinered, hair moussed; completely artificial and unnatural.

Everyone had been telling her how beautiful she looked, but Veronica thought she looked awful, like a wax figure, a mannequin. *But that's the point–be what they want, not what you are. Just think of this as a costume party. I'm dressed as a femme. Actually I've always resisted being so femme; let's see how I like it.*

She patted her face dry and returned to the celebration, just as her brother, Paul, was toasting the bride and groom. Everyone applauded.

Veronica was cornered by her Aunt Sally.

"Veronica, I saw Sister Irene the other day. She asked about you. I told her what you were doing with school and all. She seemed pleased. You were one of her favorites." Aunt Sally gazed toward the head table. "Oh, Marie is so wonderful, and Frank is so nice. They should have a wonderful life. You'll find the right boy, too, Veronica. Don't settle! Take your time. You have all the time in the world. All that school–high school, then college, now a special school for learning agriculture–it makes it harder to find the right guy." Aunt Mary stroked Veronica's cheek. "We're all so proud of you, Veronica . . . the first one in the family to go to college, the brains of the family."

"Actually, I'm studying horticulture, not agriculture." She stared blankly at her aunt. "I guess I should walk around and talk to the guests."

"Yeah, sure, Veronica, that's good. You look gorgeous!"

The band started to play and some couples got up to dance. Veronica leaned back against the wall and watched.

"Hi, aren't you Veronica Santini?"

"Yes."

"Don't you remember me? I'm Buddy, Buddy Riggio, Frank's cousin. We met a few months ago at Frank's mother's house."

She had no idea who he was. "Sure. I remember. Hi. It's nice to see you again. Great wedding, isn't it? Are you having a good time?"

"Yes. You really look terrific tonight. I like that dress. Your hair looks different, though. You know, after we met, I asked Frank for your phone number, but he told me you lived out of town."

"Yes, I live in Connecticut. I'm in graduate school."

"Oh, what are you studying?"

She tried to make it simple for him. "Forest ecology."

"Now that sounds interesting and different from the usual stuff people study."

She questioned him. "You mean subjects that women study?"

Buddy laughed. "Okay. Yeah I picture all those hard hats and heavy boots. Guys tramping through the forest cutting down trees, you know, lumberjack types."

"I'm studying how to save trees, not cut them down."

Buddy's expression became very serious. "Oh. I know. I know that."

Veronica started to walk away. Buddy followed her.

"Veronica, would you like to dance? Would you dance with me?" He opened his arms, ready for her to walk into them.

She couldn't believe this was happening. Buddy was not in the script she had studied for this evening. She smiled awkwardly. "It's been a while since I danced with . . ." She decided not to fill in the blanks.

He held her around the waist and they joined the other dancers on the floor. He was an old-fashioned boy, this Buddy. She could tell the way he held her that she was in the "Madonna" category, not "whore." But she knew that if she married him, she'd quickly become the ball and chain. He was so predictable. She had grown up with guys like him and all the others–Frank, her father, her brother. She knew how they thought. She knew all their stereotypes of women.

The band was playing a Dean Martin song . . . "When the moon hits your eye, like a big pizza pie . . ." Everyone was singing and dancing with the band. Buddy looked at her, smiled, and sang, ". . . that's amore." She returned his big, broad, happy grin, with a weak smile.

Veronica noted that Buddy's palms were moist with perspiration. There was small line of sweat on his forehead and on his upper lip. She wondered if he were nervous. She wondered what he was thinking. Veronica noticed the stubble of his beard beginning to show and shyly looked away.

She saw her mother and Paul looking at her. They were saying something to each other, and then Paul gave her the thumbs-up signal. She was in good hands, she was doing the right thing.

Veronica was pleased to have her family's approval. She didn't want anyone to think that she wasn't enjoying this dance. She tried to forget how awkward and uncomfortable she was in Buddy's arms, with his hand on her back, guiding her across the dance floor. His direction, his desire, his strong arm pushing and pulling her . . . just like married life.

Panic began to creep over her again. How could she continue this? Her throat clenched up and she knew she wouldn't be able to talk. When the dance ended, and he offered to get her a glass of champagne, she could only smile and nod.

He took her arm and led her to the bar, where he continued talking about being a fireman and getting to know her brother Paul.

He didn't seem to notice her discomfort. He was probably used to women who let him ramble on, listening passively to his thoughts, dreams, ambitions, feelings. That was what a girlfriend was supposed to do.

But Veronica was panicking, clenching her teeth and trying to maintain some outward composure. *If I drink more, I'll relax and be able to continue with all this.* Buddy handed her the glass of wine.

Veronica felt Buddy taking control of her. He ushered her to some chairs and continued talking. She knew that Buddy was oblivious of her state, probably assuming she hadn't said a word because she was shy. She would never see him again after tonight. She breathed slowly and deeply. The breathing worked. She smiled, but quickly worried that Buddy would interpret the smile as flirting. He took her hand and asked if he could visit her in Connecticut.

"Uh . . . Um . . ." She didn't want to encourage him, but she didn't want to be rude. He was Frank's cousin, and he worked with her brother, Paul. She hoped that he would forget about her after tonight, so she mumbled, "sure." It was a safe bet. She didn't think he would really travel all that way to see her; they had just met, after all, and she hadn't done much to encourage him . . . except for the smile . . . and the dancing.

"Veronica! Veronica, hurry! Marie's going to throw her bouquet." Her mother called to her.

Marie and Frank were kissing everyone good-bye, leaving on their honeymoon. Veronica's mother stood next to her.

"You stand here, Veronica, and Marie will make sure you catch it. It's good luck, and I just know that you'll be the next Santini bride."

"But Mom, Mom, I . . . I don't want . . ." Her throat tightened again.

Her mother held her around the waist and waited for the toss. Veronica had seldom seen such concentration on her mother's face. She had to have that bouquet. Perhaps seeing her dancing with Buddy. . . . She knew what her mother was thinking. Veronica just had to meet the right man, and her adolescent feelings for women would vanish and she would become one of them, a married woman with children who went to church. It was what her mother lived for. How could she protest against it?

Marie located her sister and her mother in the crowd, blew a kiss, and tossed the bouquet over her shoulder. Mrs. Santini pushed Veronica, and Veronica saw all the other girls step away. It was her athletic instinct that made her raise her arm to catch the projectile that was aimed for her face.

She inhaled the scent of flowers as the other women congratulated her. Her mother embraced her with tears in her eyes. Marie and Frank smiled as they walked to her. They kissed her, and Frank said, "You know, Veronica, Buddy never forgot you from the last time he met you. He was excited about coming here today and seeing you. He's such a great guy."

So this had all been planned, she thought. Buddy, the bouquet, next her wedding, then a few kids. The sweat trickled down her armpits.

"Sure, sure, he's very nice," she blurted out to pacify Frank and the others.

This was all happening so fast. She was losing control. Her true self was being swept away. She had to think realistically. *This is not my wedding. They are only hoping for my wedding. They want to plan my wedding, but I don't have to go through with any of it.*

Her mother dabbed at her eyes with a handkerchief and clasped Veronica's hand. Veronica saw her father and brother talking to Buddy.

The three men walked towards her. Each one kissed her on the cheek and congratulated her on the catch. Paul kept patting her hand and he looked so proud.

"Paul," she said, holding out the bouquet to him, "I think these should be for you. You should be the next one."

But he turned away and continued talking to Buddy. The band started up again, and the crowd applauded as her father led her mother onto the dance floor. Paul pulled Veronica onto the floor, and everyone applauded again.

Buddy insisted that Veronica dance with him for the rest of the evening. She felt everyone's eyes on her. She knew she was encouraging her family to believe that she was interested in Buddy, and she hated herself for the pretense.

Buddy led her outside. Veronica had had several glasses of champagne, and events were becoming hazy, but at least she wasn't panicked.

"Veronica, this night has been real special for me." He was holding both her hands turning them in his. "I like you so much, Veronica. I hope we can see more of each other. I know it's hard for people to date long distance, but I'd like to try to make it work. What do you think?"

She was frozen. "Buddy, you're a nice guy and all, but . . ."

He put his hand up to stop her from finishing the sentence and shyly looked down at the ground.

"Yeah, well . . . we really don't know each other. But I want to get know you. I want to see more of you. I'm serious. I want you to think of me as a serious contender here. I know someone with your looks probably has lots of guys hanging around. I'm just a fireman. You should be used to that with your father and brother. Maybe that's in my favor, although you probably know lots of smart college guys."

He stared into her eyes with an intimacy that amazed her. It seemed that Buddy already owned her.

Her eyes must have betrayed her shock.

"Have I come on too strong?" He was pleading with her.

She felt sorry for Buddy, sorry that he had chosen her, sorry that he probably wouldn't understand when she told him the truth. She didn't want to hurt him. She didn't want to encourage him. She would have to choose her words carefully. It was Elizabeth who was home waiting for her. Elizabeth to whom she would tell this incredible story as they lay in each other's arms after making love. Elizabeth's body naked and warm was the presence between them.

"Buddy, no. No, you've been fine. It's just that I am not interested in . . ."

Buddy stopped her again. "I know you want to finish college. Even if we dated, I would never interfere with that. I'm not one of those old fashioned guys who thinks a woman should sit at home with the kids. Please don't think that."

"Buddy, you make it so hard." She wanted to scream it so he wouldn't doubt her, and she wouldn't doubt her own feelings.

Buddy, I'm a Dyke, a lesbian. I don't want you. I want her, and she would point to any woman in the room.

Instead she said, "Buddy, listen to me. I . . . I don't want to get married. I'm not the marrying kind."

He laughed. "Oh is that all? I thought you were going to tell me you had some special guy in Connecticut. Listen, . . ." He squeezed her hand, and shook his head as if relieved. "We can take it slow. I used to feel the same way. I thought I'd never want to settle down. I guess I just needed to meet the right girl. You know what they say . . . you gotta grow up sometime."

She took her hands away. "Don't say anything now, Veronica. Let's see what happens. Don't stop this before it even begins."

"But that's just it. It can never begin. I don't want it to happen." She walked away.

He quickly followed after her. "Some bozo must have really hurt you, right? Well things like that happen. I've been hurt lots of times, too, but I think it's worth it to keep looking. We're not all so terrible you know. Veronica? Veronica?"

He turned her around to face him and he saw the tears running down her cheeks. He took out his handkerchief and gently wiped them away.

"This must be a hard day for you, your younger sister getting married, catching the bouquet, all those people looking at you. I should have known."

He lifted her chin and kissed her on the mouth. His lips felt soft. He pressed his cheek against her and she could feel the roughness of his shaved face.

"I'm sorry, Buddy. I'm sorry."

He pulled her close to his chest and stroked the back of her head.

"It's okay. It'll be okay."

Exhausted, Veronica let her head rest on his chest.

The band started playing Italian favorites again. After a few minutes they walked back inside. She hoped that no one would notice that she'd been crying. Buddy looked longingly and protectively at her for the rest of the evening. She did not object when he pressed her closer to him.

People were finally leaving, and Buddy had to take his parents home. He squeezed her hand. "I'll call you soon."

She nodded weakly.

Night Life: Some Kind of Submission

On the drive back to the house, Veronica listened as her family talked about the wedding. "My baby, my little girl." Her mother kept wiping at her eyes, clutching Veronica's hand. Aunts, uncles, cousins, friends were dissected; what she wore, what he said, who looked happy, who had put on weight. Her father was smiling as he reminisced about his favorite relatives, repeating stories she had heard all her life. Paul was drunk, waving his arms and humming one of the pop songs the band played earlier. Veronica slouched deeper into her seat.

It was past two o'clock in the morning before the Santini family calmed down enough to sleep and the bedroom doors were all shut. Veronica sat on the edge of her bed trying to move her fingers through the sticky spray that plasticized her soft, fine hair. Mechanically, she stepped out of the pink satin dress, showered, washed her hair free from the spray, and scrubbed off the make-up. She put on her black leather jeans, black sweater and leather jacket. Quietly she walked down the stairs and out the back door, locking it behind her. She pushed her motorcycle into the darkened street and down the middle of the block before starting it up.

There was little traffic in the streets so early in the morning, and Veronica could really let the bike out. With the wind blowing against her body, Veronica felt she was riding farther and farther away from that girl who had so passively and politely endured hours of family wishes for her future wedding. The only thing I have in common with her, she thought, is my name. She wanted to shout out loud in time with the pumping pistons of the motorcycle. "I am the real Veronica Santini." She smiled broadly, letting the wind pummel her shoulder and sting her lips when she opened her mouth to yell. She roared through the Holland Tunnel with the zeal of a convert and the excitement of the born-again.

When she got to the bar, she circled her bike a few times. She turned off the ignition, and heard the loud, pulsating blast of the music. She unzipped her leather jacket, removed her black helmet, and swung her blonde hair free. Excited with anticipation, she paid the cover charge, checked her helmet, and quickly walked through the smoke-filled, noisy room to the bar. It had been some time since she had been a regular here. Beer in hand, she turned, leaned both elbows back on the bar and surveyed the scene. The place was packed. She had known it would be on a Saturday night. Where else would they all go? She breathed deeply. The smoke made her eyes blink and burn, and the insistent beat of the music made her heart imitate the bass sounds of the speakers; yet she felt comfortable and began to relax. After a few minutes she noticed individual women, and she cruised the ones she found attractive, her eyes moving quickly along bodies, scanning breasts, asses, legs, arms, hair and faces. They were all ages, but she wasn't that particular. She quickly glanced away from couples clinging together, and turned her attention to women alone or with friends.

She approached a young woman wearing a tee shirt and jeans and a studded black leather band on her upper arm. She seemed younger than Veronica, probably in her early twenties, with thick black, curly hair that reached to her shoulders. Her pale skin was almost ghostlike in the flashing lights of the bar. She was standing with two women, both dressed in black leather jackets similar to Veronica's.

"Hi, do you want another drink?"

"Sure. Thanks." The woman smiled as she looked Veronica up and down. She put out her hand. "My name's Lindsay."

"Veronica." She held Lindsay's hand and squeezed it.

"Are you from the city?"

"No, no. You?"

"No, I came with some friends from Staten Island."

"Oh."

They could hardly hear each other talk over the music. Veronica suggested they go downstairs. Lindsay spoke to her friends and followed Veronica. The downstairs area was quieter and dimly lit. A few women, smoking cigarettes and holding cue sticks, were huddled over the pool table in the main room. The old carpeting kept in all of the musty, mildew smells, and Veronica remembered her first time here when she had been so turned off by the grunginess of the place that she had almost left. Now it didn't seem to matter at all. There were a few chairs around, and Veronica motioned Lindsay to two that faced each other in a corner.

"Why did you come to this particular bar, Lindsay?"

She had to make sure that Lindsay knew what she was getting into.

Lindsay looked at her, shook her head and laughed quietly. "I know what I'm doing here. Do you?"

Veronica let out a whistling sound from between her teeth, smiled, and held Lindsay firmly by the chin. They laughed together. She took Lindsay's beer and put it down on one of the tables. Then they got up and walked down the narrow corridor towards the smaller rooms underneath the main dance floor. Veronica felt the vibration of the music from the walls and floor. She stopped and turned to face Lindsay, taking her hand and patting it with her own. Lindsay's eyes were wide, and Veronica thought she seemed scared. Veronica pushed her gently against the wall and moved her hands up and down the sides of Lindsay's body, touching her nipples with her thumbs and squeezing her breasts gently. She kissed Lindsay's neck and inhaled the scent of lavender.

"I love the way you smell, Lindsay, but my taste is for something more natural."

She reached down, spread Lindsay's legs and rubbed her fingers along the seams of the jeans. She smiled to find that Lindsay was already giving off heat and was more than a little bit wet.

Lindsay raised Veronica's face to hers. They kissed, and Veronica opened Lindsay's mouth tonguing her lips and pushing against her teeth. Lifting Lindsay's black hair, she put her hand on the back of

Lindsay's neck. They turned, looked at each other, and silently entered one of the rooms.

The room was dark, but they knew that they were not alone. They heard sounds coming from every corner. For Veronica this was part of the excitement of the place. When her eyes adjusted to the dim light, she could discern other bodies. Veronica turned to Lindsay and began to lift off her tee shirt. When Lindsay's head was through, she stopped pulling on the shirt and it held her arms pinned together over her head.

"Did you know that this was what I wanted?" Veronica whispered.

"Yes," Lindsay answered.

"Good."

Veronica pulled Lindsay to her, caressed her face and kissed her. Lindsay moved her body closer to Veronica's and rubbed herself up and down the leather jacket, her arms still stuck up above her head. Veronica ran her hands over Lindsay's exposed breasts. She loved the feel of the smooth, thin skin covering her rib cage and waist. She pushed her thumb into Lindsay's navel and pressed down. Lindsay raised her fettered arms and encircled Veronica's neck, the cotton fabric of the tee shirt handcuffing her wrists. Veronica's arms tightened in a viselike grip, and her mouth hardened as she pulled Lindsay's naked torso tightly against her, knowing that the zippers and buckles of her jacket would mark and cut Lindsay's delicate skin.

Veronica placed one leg behind the pinioned Lindsay, causing her knees to fold, then lowered her, backward, to the floor mat. She opened Lindsay's jeans and pulled them down over her legs. Lindsay was still caught up in the tee shirt, which stretched her arms over her head. Veronica knew that she must be uncomfortable. That's the way she wanted her to be. Lindsay said nothing. Veronica removed all of her own clothes and lay down on top of Lindsay.

"Do you need some help here?" A large dark-haired woman

came over and kneeled down above Lindsay's head, looking straight at Veronica.

Veronica looked down at Lindsay. Her lips turned up at the corners into what was almost a smile. "Do I need help with you?"

"Yes, maybe you should have someone. I . . . I would like . . ." Lindsay looked up at both of them with half-closed eyes and moved her tongue over her open lips.

Veronica turned to the bigger woman, "Okay. Just hold her arms there like that. Make sure that she doesn't move."

Veronica fondled Lindsay's ass as she pulled herself up, resting between Lindsay's legs.

The large woman held Lindsay's slender arms out straight in one hand and with the other began to stroke her exposed breasts. Lindsay moaned, and Veronica slid her hands up her thighs. Veronica felt the heat between Lindsay's legs. She stroked Lindsay's clit, and wetness covered her fingers. She took the rubber glove from her back pocket and slipped it over her hand, letting the latex slap against her wrist. Lindsay opened her eyes briefly and smiled at Veronica. She rocked her hips slowly from side to side and closed her eyes.

"Lindsay," Veronica breathed in a low, husky voice, "I'm going to fuck you very slowly and for a very long time and there's nothing you can do to stop me. I don't care what you want or how you want it. You'll do what I want now!" She bit Lindsay's neck and pinched the skin. She moved her tongue over Lindsay's lips. Lindsay tried to move her head up from the floor to meet Veronica's mouth, but she was being held firmly by her arms and was helpless.

Veronica spread Lindsay's legs as far as they would go, forcing Lindsay to raise her knees off the floor. Even though Lindsay was so wet that she didn't need much lube, Veronica slowly rubbed a generous amount on her glove. First her overlapping fingers entered Lindsay, then her thumb, folded inside her palm. Moving slowly, in and out, deeper with each thrust, she pressed further and further inside, past the widest part of her hand. Her hand curled to fit and fill the shape of Lindsay.

Lindsay was shaking her head and starting to gasp, but the woman over her removed her hand from Lindsay's breast and clamped it over her mouth so that Lindsay could not scream. Veronica gave her the nod when she stopped moving her arm, and the woman released Lindsay's mouth and went back to her breasts. She rubbed Lindsay's nipples. Then she bent down and took Lindsay's small tit in her mouth to bite on. Veronica knew Lindsay would have some bruises, but hoped that she would have good memories to go with them. She concentrated now on the feeling of being inside this woman, of stretching her wide and pushing into her so deep. Lindsay was breathing hard and fast.

"Lindsay. Lindsay," Veronica whispered.

Veronica opened her hand just a little bit and felt Lindsay contract and try to move away. Veronica would not let her escape. She pulled Lindsay's hips forward towards the arm that was planted inside of her and sat looking at Lindsay's face.

"What do you think?" asked the woman at Lindsay's head. "Want something for this little one's butt?" She called to another woman who was leaning against the wall watching, her hands between her naked legs.

"Hey, Sue, can you get us some of that equipment from the closet over there? She motioned with her head, not wanting to remove her hands from Lindsay's breasts.

The woman nodded and returned with a large dildo, a butt plug, and a condom. "You can use this harness when you want." She placed all of the items next to Veronica.

Veronica glanced down at the pink dildo and black leather harness. She was deep inside Lindsay and didn't want to think about other possibilities. *I don't even know her,* she thought. *Probably Lindsay is not even her real name. But, at this moment I know her better than anyone in the world, and she knows me. She trusts me not to hurt her.* Slowly, she began to move her arm and spread her fingers inside Lindsay. The woman at Lindsay's head held her, squeezed her breasts and pulled hard, twisting her nipples.

Veronica was very excited. She tried to control herself. Each thrust and opening of her fist brought her closer to orgasm. She was waiting for Lindsay, so her own orgasm would be intensified. She leaned her head and shoulder on Lindsay's belly and began to talk to her, urging her on. She whispered how good Lindsay felt, and how open she was. She told her she wanted them to come together.

Lindsay came while the woman above her had her tongue inside Lindsay's mouth. Veronica felt the contractions deep inside Lindsay, and felt her own body respond in unison. Everything seemed to stop; the movement, the noise, the throb of the music, the moans from Lindsay. The room was removed from the world. They were floating, swimming, flying together, no longer tied here to this earth by their bodies. They were flying high, looking down, joined together in their most intimate parts, never to separate, never to let this feeling go, infinite and finite together. Veronica kept still inside Lindsay for a long time, then slowly and carefully removed her hand.

Sweat covered Lindsay's body and Veronica motioned for the woman above Lindsay's head to release her. Veronica gently pulled the tee shirt off, lowered Lindsay's arms to her sides and wiped the sweat off Lindsay's face, neck, and breasts. She moved up to Lindsay's side. "Lie still. Don't tense the muscles in your stomach. Just relax. You'll be fine."

"Yeah, I know. I feel just fine already." She smiled. "More than fine. Great." Lindsay reached for Veronica's hand and pressed it to her lips.

"Yes," Veronica said, smiling back. "I know what you mean."

Veronica leaned back against the wall, held Lindsay in her lap, and let out a long sigh. At last her body slumped and she closed her eyes.

*   *   *

The sun was already up when Veronica turned her motorcycle into the driveway of her parents' home. She was surprised to find her mother sitting at the kitchen table so early the morning after the wedding. She had planned to slip quietly back into her room and into bed before anyone saw her.

Her mother stared at her. "Veronica, I thought you were still sleeping."

She tried to act nonchalant and tucked her helmet under her arm, but she knew that the boots, black leather jacket and dark mirrored aviator glasses were too much of a contrast to the Veronica who had so pleased her mother just a few hours ago. Tough, she thought. This is the real me.

"Mom, I . . . I just couldn't sleep . . . all the excitement of the wedding. I thought I would go for a little ride."

"I hate that motorcycle. You and Paul fooling around with those . . . bikes, you call them. It's dangerous. Every time you come down from Connecticut on your motorcycle, I worry."

Veronica knew they were avoiding the real issue. Playing another game, she thought. What must she think of me now?

"I'm always careful. You shouldn't worry so much. You know I don't ride in the winter, or when it's wet outside. It's okay, really."

She walked over to her mother and kissed her on the cheek. "I'm really tired, Mom. Think I'll just sleep for a little bit this morning."

Lying on her bed, Veronica was conscious again of the extremes that she took to reinforce her identity. It didn't matter and she didn't care. She was in new territory, and she wasn't afraid. She was excited about the possibilities. She would create her own world if she had to. She would do anything to keep who she wanted to be alive and intact. But most of the time it took all of her energies to invent herself in so many different ways. Everyone and everything was trying to force her into those selves already known. She knew what she didn't want. It wasn't as clear what she did want.

She wondered what she would tell Elizabeth about tonight, or if she would say anything at all to her. She wondered if she would ever be in a place where she felt secure, where she wouldn't have to push or test herself again and again. Who would she be then? What could she be like? She didn't know and was too tired to think anymore. With her right hand lightly covering her face, each inhalation of Lindsay softened her hard, tense body into sleep.

The Visitation: Fantasie

One day, in late October, the letter for Elizabeth finally arrived, as Veronica had known it would. She placed it on the small pine chest in the entryway underneath the bills and announcements, but there was no hiding it, no hiding from it. This letter demanded to be read. *Found at last. Eureka. Eureka. The final act. The end. Curtain down. Eureka.* But it was only the postmark–Eureka, California.

"Carol is coming to New York for a show. She would like to see me and spend a few days in Connecticut." Elizabeth tried to sound calm, but Veronica knew Elizabeth's hopes.

In November, Carol arrived. The sun was behind her as she walked up to the front door and touched the archer's body. *How many times has she done this? Will she do it again? This visitation is full of mystery, like the other one they taught me about in Catholic school, the outcome unknown, except to a few. How long will we have to wait until its significance can be understood, written and spoken about by friends, explained by critics, physicians, and prison wardens?*

Her hands are on the archer's body–breast, legs, face, fingers, everywhere. Carol's hands are larger than mine, with much longer fingers. "The better to . . . you with, my dear." *The brass figure on the door moved. Did it move? It seemed to move to the touch of those mysterious, familiar fingers. Certainly Elizabeth will want them, the known, loved fingers. She will want them and will know the feel of them on her, inside her.* Then Carol entered and took possession of the house. Possessed it by her presence–prescience.

Everything seemed to hold still while Veronica waited for the inevitable pronouncement. She spied on Carol and Elizabeth, looking out of Elizabeth's bedroom window, feeling like an intruder.

". . . and who's been sleeping in my bed?" asked the big bear.

"Only me. Little me, and it's much too big for me. It doesn't fit. I have to go home to some small place."

"And who's been loving my woman?" asked the big bear.

"Only me, but don't be angry. It doesn't matter. She's still yours. I just kept her warm for you. Warm and wet. It's for you, though, for you. It's not mine."

They walked across the green lawn, Carol in tan pants, black turtleneck and tweed jacket, Elizabeth in her jeans, dark blue sweater and sweatshirt. Everything was golden, orange, red, flaming around them. It was a cold day and they were burning. She watched them walk, gesture, draw closer to the river, their backs toward her. She couldn't see their faces. She couldn't interpret their physical gestures.

Veronica stood, hands in her pockets, her front teeth gnawing on her lower lip, studying, memorizing, feeling that if she turned away from the window she would miss some clue to the puzzle. Each time Carol and Elizabeth started to physically drift apart something pulled them back together. Releasing and pulling, Veronica thought, till the tension must relax or snap. Now they faced each other. Carol brushed some hair from Elizabeth's face. *Did Elizabeth move her head towards that hand, press into that palm? Did she? Did she move so that Carol's fingers could caress her face, her hair?*

Veronica watched as Carol took both of Elizabeth's hands into hers. *How long will they stand like this, gazing at each other? Are their lips moving? Are their eyes speaking? Are their hearts beating as fast as mine? Should I imagine a dialogue? Make it up. Something to go with the action. Superimpose stage directions? Okay, now you move down right, cross over, take her in your arms. Kiss her–now–hard.*

No! No! Yes–they are. They heard me. Their bodies moving together, arms enclosing. Is that Elizabeth's hand on the back of Carol's head? On her neck? I can feel it. It tingles. It burns. I feel that body pressed against me, that mouth breathing on my neck, the hair tickling my face, the soft lips glazing my skin, the body moving and the lips and the tongue and the fingers and the legs.

Carol and Elizabeth parted, still holding hands, looking at each other. As they walked, and Carol put her arm over Elizabeth's shoulder, pulling her close to her side. Elizabeth put her arms around Carol's waist and they walked towards the river. Carol had threatened to drown herself in this river. *No! Don't! No need to. I'll leave.*

Veronica turned away, leaned her back against the window and slumped down to the floor. She sat there for a long time rubbing her hands through her hair. *This is what it must be like to be in an asylum, repetition of physical acts. Just like this–comforting, mindless gestures.*

The Real World

Veronica felt she was no more than a buffer between them.
Carol had made the first move, but who would make the last?
Veronica knew the answer. It was just a matter of time. She was
jealous of this talented, determined woman, so sure of herself and
outwardly relaxed. The strain of being the outsider grew more
intense, and Veronica sensed that a buffer between Elizabeth and
Carol was no longer needed. When the distance between two sides
of the bed seemed greater than the distance between California
and Connecticut, Veronica retreated to her own apartment.

* * *

Elizabeth sounded very formal on the phone, and Veronica heard
the hesitancy in Elizabeth's voice. "Carol's gone down to New York
to prepare for the show. Do you want to come over?"
"Oh, is the coast clear?"
"What do you mean?"
"Nothing. Nothing! I guess I don't know what to say."
"Veronica, I'm sorry if you left because you felt uncomfortable.
Carol and I are just friends. She invited us both down to New York
for the opening of her show. I said I would speak with you."
"You're going, whether I go or not. Right?"
"Of course, I'll go. It would be an insult not to, and I want to
see her latest work. Veronica, please come over so we can talk?"
Veronica felt like a trespasser entering Elizabeth's home. Carol's
presence was everywhere. "Why don't we call ghost busters?" she
joked.
Elizabeth responded with a bewildered look, and Veronica
realized that soon she would have to accept the inevitable.
Elizabeth would reveal her feelings for Carol. These feelings were
not dead, had only been dormant. She had only been protecting

herself. Of course, Elizabeth would go back with Carol. She would go anywhere with her. Veronica knew that before Elizabeth did. Only one question remained, did Carol want Elizabeth? Why had she come here if not for her?

In spite of Veronica's doubts, Elizabeth convinced her to drive down to New York for Carol's gallery opening. She said that they would spend a few days in New York at a hotel near the Metropolitan Museum of Art, take a break from the garden, walk around the city, go to some museums, and have some wonderful dinners. Veronica wondered why Elizabeth would plan such a romantic weekend with her now? Veronica would go with her, but she couldn't trust her. Veronica wanted to hide in her apartment and lick her wounds, but she also wanted to see this drama out to its final moments.

Although the opening wasn't until later in the evening, they left early in the morning to spend the day in the city. When they reached the exit for Hammonasset State Park, Elizabeth pulled the car off I-95 and headed towards the beach. She turned to Veronica and smiled. The smile was so warm and so intimate, so full of feeling, Veronica knew that it was meant to reassure her. Veronica would have to accept whatever happened.

They walked along the beach in the sun. "Take off your shoes and socks," Elizabeth said. Although it was cold, they rolled up their pants and walked barefoot in the shallow water.

Veronica took Elizabeth's hand and asked tentatively, "What did Carol have to say after all this time?"

"She told me about her life in California, about the paintings she's doing now." Veronica knew she wouldn't get the answers she wanted, but she allowed Elizabeth to go on with this superficial talk, because she couldn't figure a way to turn the conversation.

"She said it was very different from her work in the East and that location had a big influence on how one saw the world. Her perspective is different in California."

"Was she referring to her painting or to her life?"

"Both, I think."

"So what is her new perspective? Did she go into detail? I'm interested." She took a deep breath. "Oh crap," Veronica said, "I don't know what to ask you. I don't know what to say to you. I've lost my courage. Carol is very intimidating. She's a hard one to compete with."

Elizabeth was calm. "Why do you talk of competition? Carol and I are just friends now."

Veronica shook her head. "That's not true, Elizabeth, not totally true. Remember, I'm a careful observer."

They continued to walk along the beach. Elizabeth ignored Veronica's comment. She moved closer and pressed her head against Veronica's shoulder.

"You remember that first night when you took me on your motorcycle to the bar? I was so scared and so excited, and the more frightened I became, the more excited I got. You broke through to me that night. I would never have allowed myself to feel anything for you. There were too many barriers, too many fears. I didn't know anything about you, but you had the courage and strength to take me there . . . to take me, to make me want you. You made me something else that night. I understood, for the first time, the idea of surrendering myself to the moment, forgetting my fears and allowing things to just happen. You really could have been crazy, could have hurt me. I didn't care."

Veronica faced Elizabeth and took her wrists. She said in a matter-of-fact tone, "It was a strategy of seduction, Elizabeth. It would work or it would backfire. I had to take the chance. I couldn't continue seeing you every day, having the same dead conversation. I hoped it would be a way to involve you." She paused. "I wanted you, Elizabeth. I usually don't wait so long when I want someone."

Elizabeth looked at her and laughed. "So, you've changed, too."

"You made me nervous and uncomfortable. I gave up a job in Colorado for a fantasy of you. I wanted to test the truth of my illusions. Nothing would have stopped me." Veronica's hands tightened around Elizabeth's wrists.

"What are you saying?" Elizabeth's tone changed, and she attempted to free herself from Veronica's grasp. "You mean you really wouldn't have let me go out that door?"

"I could never let you go, not then, especially not now."

Elizabeth spoke with some bravado. "How would you have kept me? How would you stop someone who wants to leave? How do you hold someone against her will?"

"You don't really want to know that, do you?"

There was a sinister quality in Veronica's voice. Elizabeth was frightened realizing they were alone on the beach, yet she goaded Veronica on. "Yes, tell me how you would have stopped me. Show me."

"Why now?"

"Tell me!"

Veronica pulled Elizabeth close against her chest. "I would not have let you go, Elizabeth, not under any circumstance, not if you had begged me, not if you had begun to cry. Nothing would have worked. I was determined to get what I wanted . . . to get you, to have you, and you were not going to stop me."

"Even if I didn't want you?"

"Yes, yes." Veronica's voice was low, detached, and cold. Her grasp on Elizabeth's wrists was tighter, harder. "Don't you understand? There was nothing you could do . . . nothing. I would have done anything, gagged you, tied you up, locked you in a closet, starved you for a few days, drugged you."

"Is that true? Is that really true? Would you have done those things just to have me?" Veronica started to speak, but Elizabeth put her hand over Veronica's mouth. "No, stop. That's enough. I don't really want to know. It doesn't matter. What you do, and what I do and say is what's real. It happened. We both wanted it to happen. You didn't do anything to me that I didn't want. That's the truth."

"You know, this is a hard scene to keep playing, Elizabeth." Veronica looked away, and her voice was soft. "It's difficult to sustain the performance."

Elizabeth pulled away from her and walked on. The wind was picking up now and she zipped up her blue woolen jacket. Her shoulders were hunched against the chill and her hands thrust into her pockets. She walked up into the dunes and lay down in a protected hollow. Veronica followed and stood over her.

"Now!" Elizabeth looked up, shielding her eyes from the sun. She demanded. "Here, now."

This was not what Veronica expected. This was not what she wanted . . . now. She wanted to talk. She wanted Elizabeth to tell her the truth about what she was feeling for Carol, for her. Maybe she even wanted Elizabeth to lie to her. But here was Elizabeth, wanting to make love. Veronica wanted that, too, but she wanted too much. She had created the scenario for this. From the beginning she had the feeling that the approach was all wrong, and now they were caught in the roles they had created. In spite of her reluctance, her body was telling a different story, and she couldn't deny the rush and pounding beat of the pulse in her temples.

Veronica lay down on the sand next to Elizabeth. Leaning on one elbow, she put her other arm around Elizabeth's waist.

"Don't you think it's a little cold? Will you be cold?" she asked solicitously.

"Yes, of course, but parts of me will be warm . . . are . . . hot."

They grinned and Veronica unzipped Elizabeth's woolen jacket and moved her hands over Elizabeth's breasts.

"This is what you want, Elizabeth." Veronica looked into her eyes and saw the desire and the confusion, "But it will not be how you want it. I know you now. I know what you need. Take it from me, because I won't give it to you."

She was very slow, very gentle. Elizabeth could hardly feel her at all. She forced Elizabeth to come to her, forced her to move up towards her, and as Elizabeth moved up, forward, pressing and pushing, Veronica continued to move away. Veronica watched the desperate expression on Elizabeth's face as she slapped her hands on the sand at her sides and beat Veronica on the back with her fists.

"No, no. More! Harder! Deeper!"

Veronica paid no attention to Elizabeth's entreaty, but kept to the same slow pace, kissed her neck, covered her mouth with gentle kisses, in spite of Elizabeth's thrusting attempt to pull Veronica into her frustrated passion.

Elizabeth came finally. She lay there, exasperated, panting. "Why did you do that? Why didn't you do what I wanted? You knew what I wanted."

"Because I knew. That's why."

Elizabeth raised her hand. She was shaking with rage. The superficiality of her orgasm had left her even more upset than before. She moved her open hand to Veronica's face, but Veronica caught her hand and held it. She brought the open palm to her mouth and began to kiss it, all the time looking straight at Elizabeth.

Then she pressed her body over Elizabeth's and held her against the sand.

"You're so impatient, my darling. We have a whole weekend coming up. This was just something to whet your appetite. Yes, I know what you want, but only you know who you want. Now you'll think of me all day and into this evening, too, when we're at Carol's show. When Carol is looking at you, talking to you, you'll be wiggling in your pants. You'll be wet, and you'll be thinking of later, thinking of me back in our hotel, later."

"You always know how to get what you want, don't you?" Elizabeth's voice was resentful.

"It's some sort of protection, like life insurance." Veronica laughed quietly and nuzzled Elizabeth's neck. She could feel Elizabeth's body soften and relax. Elizabeth moved her arm around Veronica's neck and pulled her head down, forced Veronica's mouth open and kissed her hard. "Will you make love to me? I want to make love with you so much."

"Yes, of course. You know it's what I want."

Tell Me, Does She Love You?

The gallery was on the first floor of a large loft building in Soho, the chic area in New York for artists from all over the world. Although Elizabeth had told her the show would be reviewed in several newspapers and magazines, Veronica had no idea that Carol was so well-known, and she was surprised to see people overflowing out onto the sidewalks of Greene Street, drinks and canapés in hand. When they managed to push their way inside, Veronica quickly spotted Carol talking with some men and women. She was wearing a white silk shirt, black pants, and a brocaded vest. Silver Indian bracelets, turquoise earrings, and a large turquoise necklace highlighted her pale skin and light blonde hair.

"Do you know anyone here?" Veronica asked Elizabeth.

"No, I don't think so. It's been a long time, and I was never really that involved with Carol's friends."

"You sound sorry you weren't more involved, but when you get back together you can change all that. Right?"

She waited for Elizabeth's reply. "Caught you off guard, haven't I?" Elizabeth didn't look at her. "I think you've just answered my question. I already knew the answer anyway. It was almost rhetorical. I think I really should go now and leave you and Carol." She walked towards the door.

"Veronica, let me show you around." It was Carol. She took Veronica's arm and led her back to Elizabeth. "I want you both to see some of my favorites."

Walking around looking at the paintings, Elizabeth took Veronica's hand, squeezed it and whispered, "Don't leave me. You're wrong. Wait . . . please! We'll go together."

In spite of her anger, she acquiesced to Elizabeth's entreaty. *But what am I waiting for, more rationalizations, more lies which she expects me to sanction or ignore, like some perjuring witness? The tuth is there for anyone to see. Why can't Elizabeth just do it, just say it? Why do I have to be a party to this self-deception? No, it's too much to agree to again, the lies, the denial of her true feelings.*

Veronica watched as Elizabeth followed Carol with her eyes. Elizabeth's face appeared indifferent, almost blank, but Veronica saw beneath the facade, beneath the set mouth, and the aloof look in her eyes. Carol had understood the subtleties in that reserved expression which hid and revealed so much. It was there in the painting, and yes . . . Carol knew, too, how seductive those contradictions were.

The three stood in front of Carol's latest canvas of a mountain landscape in northern California. The vitality, sensuality, and overwhelming strength of the natural world that Carol created in her paintings made Veronica feel insignificant. Her own strong feelings for designing landscape had led her to choose a life outside the narrow world planned by her parents. As Carol spoke of the spectacular redwoods and forests of her new home, Veronica planned her letter to the Forest Service in Colorado, or Montana. She could work with the conservation projects in Alaska, or maybe Nebraska. Soon she would be as far away from Elizabeth as Carol had gone. It was a small comfort to know that the world of nature still held the possibility of escape for Carol and for her.

*   *   *

"I'm glad you didn't leave the gallery." They were walking along the hotel corridor. "I want to talk to you about Carol. You're wrong about her. She's not interested in me anymore. She has a girlfriend in California. If I know Carol, she has more than one."

Veronica did not respond. She realized that the resemblance between herself and Carol was more than physical. Elizabeth must have felt that. That unconscious recognition is what attracted Elizabeth to her in the first place. Now, Veronica understood it all.

Elizabeth continued her appeal to Veronica, "You surprised me with your assumption that Carol and I would get back together. I couldn't give you a direct answer because I was so shocked that you would think such a thing." She unlocked the door to their room.

Elizabeth locked the door then leaned against it. "Do I dare put out the 'Do not Disturb' sign?" She smiled coyly at Veronica.

She ignored Elizabeth's question. "Your non-verbal answer seemed clear to me. Your longing for her is obvious. Your sexual excitement today . . . it's triggered by Carol. It's not me you see and feel when we make love." Her voice was hard-edged and sarcastic. "You know I love fantasy, but I want to be included in it, at least, sometimes."

Elizabeth was exasperated trying to explain what she herself couldn't or didn't want to understand. "You push too hard, Veronica. You always push too hard."

Veronica started to take off her jacket and shirt. She paused and smiled sardonically. "That's not what you said this morning on the beach. In fact you were disappointed that it wasn't hard enough."

Elizabeth looked at her, shook her head, and laughed.

"You know, Veronica, one of the other qualities I admired first about you before I knew of your . . . physical skills . . . was your sense of humor. It adds a realistic perspective to situations . . . like this one."

"So what do we do now?"

"You're still pushing." Elizabeth would not admit to anything. "What answer do you want me to give you? There are no written guarantees here. You should know that. You started off by telling me that. What do you want me to do? I'm here, and I'm with you. It's all in the moment. Isn't that your credo? We have this moment, in New York together in this hotel . . . now." She looked away out the window. "It may be all I ever have to give. It has to do."

"You're wrong, Elizabeth." Veronica lay down on the bed, her arm draped over her eyes. "It's not enough for me. It won't do. Never make do! *You* should know that."

"I know what I want now, but Carol seems to loom like a third person in this room with us."

"Well," Veronica moved her arm away from her face. "Let's not forget Leslie. She's always here, too. We all bring our pasts, I guess . . . except that you can get yours back."

"So that's it. Leslie is dead, no real competition there, except the happy myth of what might have been. But Carol is still with us, and the possibility is always there for renewal."

"What do you want me to do now? Help you pack up your belongings for the move out west?" Veronica asked.

Elizabeth sat down next to her on the bed. "I'm not going to let you go on with this ridiculous scene, when we have another one which is much more enjoyable. We have other unfinished business before you pack me up and ship me out." She started to laugh as Veronica pulled her down on top of her and began to unbutton her blouse.

"If only I could maintain some perspective about you," murmured Veronica.

"As someone told me this morning, 'don't be so impatient'."

The warmth in Elizabeth's voice was reassuring, even soothing. Veronica laughed with her. "The moment, yes . . . of course . . . my philosophy."

"Veronica." Elizabeth was repeating her name, pulling Veronica's shirt out of the pants, undoing her belt.

There was so much that Veronica wanted to say. There were so many unanswered questions, but their bodies were responding to each other in spite of the conflicting emotions.

"I promised you something more for this morning, didn't I?"

"Go inside me . . . now . . . please. . . ." Elizabeth gasped, pushing herself against Veronica, and forcing Veronica's hand inside. Veronica could feel Elizabeth's openness, her vulnerability. She was giving herself over, opening herself to Veronica in ways she had never risked before, but it was too late; Veronica sensed Elizabeth's emotional desperation.

Veronica's fingers were wet and sticky, slipping in and out so easily. She wished she could give more of herself to Elizabeth. She wished it would be enough. She wished it would be everything Elizabeth needed. She wanted to hold her down. She knelt between Elizabeth's legs.

"Oh, God, I love how you taste." Licking, at first slowly, moving her hand in and out, her fingers hitting the walls inside Elizabeth. For the first time, Veronica felt that she was in possession of this woman. Licking along the sides of Elizabeth's clitoris and inside her cunt, her tongue glided over her own fingers with each stroke.

Elizabeth seemed to be gasping for breath. "Uhh, uhh, ohh, ahhhh."

The moans spurred Veronica on. Elizabeth was writhing. She was screaming and turning her head from side to side. Her arms lay rigid on the sheets. Her hands opening and closing with each contraction.

"Veronica, stop. Don't . . . stop . . . stop. No!"

Elizabeth's ecstatic movements were triggering Veronica's excitement. She didn't care anymore whether Elizabeth knew whose fingers, tongue, mouth, or body was on top of her. Veronica wanted more. She wanted to go deeper, harder and faster. More! It was moving so fast.

Veronica could feel her contractions. She wanted Elizabeth to cross the line. She lifted her head. "No, just a little bit more, just some more. Stay with it. Stay with me."

Elizabeth screamed out. Her body lifting, she almost pushed Veronica off her, but dropped back exhausted her face and body clammy with sweat. Elizabeth crossed her arms over her breasts, her hands clenching and unclenching. Her brow was furrowed, and her eyes squeezed shut.

After one last lick directly over the clitoris, Veronica took her mouth away. She felt Elizabeth shudder. She left her hand inside and slid on top of Elizabeth.

Elizabeth moved one of her arms off her breast, held Veronica, and murmured, "Don't leave me yet. Stay in me." She moaned and nestled her head against Veronica.

"Yes, oh yes. You know I will. I want to. I want to fuck you all night like this."

Veronica moved her tongue inside of Elizabeth's mouth as she had moved it in her cunt, and Elizabeth shuddered again as she tasted herself in Veronica's long kiss.

"You like us like this?" Veronica whispered.

Elizabeth's eyes were still closed. "Umm, yes, I like it. I like what you do, how you do it, what you do to me."

She held her tightly in her arms. "Veronica, please, don't let me go. Don't."

Veronica took her hand out of Elizabeth. She brought it up to Elizabeth's mouth. "Close your mouth." She smeared the warm wetness over Elizabeth's lips. Then she bent and kissed her. "I love the essential you. I love the essence that is you. I don't want to come out of you. I don't want to leave you, not like this, not when we're like this . . . so close." Elizabeth opened her eyes to look into Veronica's.

There was no sleep until early morning. Just at eight the telephone rang. Veronica moved Elizabeth aside to get to the phone.

"Hello, Elizabeth. It's Carol."

She came awake suddenly. "Carol, no, this is Veronica. I'll put Elizabeth on."

She turned towards Elizabeth whose eyes were opened wide with what Veronica read as a look of alarm.

Veronica went into the bathroom. When she returned, Elizabeth was sitting up in bed twirling her hair around one finger and staring blankly ahead.

"Heavy thoughts, huh?" Veronica held Elizabeth's hand and smoothed the hair off her face.

"Yes." She pulled Veronica close to her. "She wants to have breakfast with me before she goes back to California."

"Oh?" Veronica looked at Elizabeth. "Guess you'd better get up and get dressed. Rule number 12 in the *Dyke Manual,* never keep an ex-lover waiting, especially one who no longer wants to be an ex."

"You make it sound as if I've already shipped the steamer trunk."

Veronica assumed a thoughtful expression. "Actually, Carol may want to come back to the old homestead. After all, it was her home, too. So you may be right on that score. Maybe the two of you will just stay here in the East."

"Veronica, I can never tell if you're joking. Your sense of humor is sometimes so borderline. I don't know how to react." She was annoyed. "This is a breakfast with an old friend who is returning to her home on the other side of the continent. Why are you being so sarcastic?" Elizabeth got up out of the bed and walked over to Veronica. They were both naked, and Elizabeth put her arms around her. Veronica did not respond. Elizabeth picked up Veronica's arms and placed them around her waist. "I want to feel you. It's never enough."

"Then call her back; tell her that you want to stay here with me. Tell her you want me to suck you and fuck you all morning, afternoon, night. Tell her. Pick up the phone."

Elizabeth moved away from Veronica. "I can't do that."

"You mean you won't do it. Damn it, Elizabeth, say what is true. Say what you're feeling. If you don't want to say it to me, at least, for God's sake admit the truth to yourself. I can't stand being involved with another life filled with lies. It's enough I have to put up with the lies for my family, but I have to draw the line. I don't want to listen to your denials. I won't."

"Veronica, you don't understand. We're friends now. You must know that. True, she is an ex-lover, but so what? We want to be friends now. I have no expectations for getting back together. I'm here, now, in the present. Don't you know that? What was last night all about? What are all the nights and days about if that isn't truth between us?"

"You don't know what the truth is, Elizabeth. I see it in you. She is not your old friend. She is your ex-lover. She is a woman you lived with for a long time. You built a house together. You almost had a nervous breakdown when she left. You love her. Don't lie to yourself. I won't listen to it."

Elizabeth looked at her and walked silently into the bathroom.

Veronica got back into bed and flipped on the TV to a talk show about cheating wives and their grieving spouses. Veronica thought she had something in common with straight women.

She watched Elizabeth dress, and the silence between them was finality enough for Veronica. She would leave as soon as Elizabeth left. She would make her way back to Connecticut on the train. This affair would end now. She was already objectifying it in her mind, calling it an affair that was circumscribed by a beginning and an end. Now it was over. Sex had been the most important aspect of their relationship, and why not, at least it was honest, she thought. The body doesn't lie, the excitement of the body . . . what she really wanted. Watching Elizabeth dress, with the pure taste of her still in her mouth and on her lips, the scent of her on her fingers made her very sad.

"Will you be here when I come back? I want you to be. Please, Veronica, be here for me, for us."

"I wish I could come back with a snappy retort, but I can't. I'm underwhelmed by all of this. Undermined. You understand. I can't answer you. That would give you too much power over me . . . and us. Have a nice breakfast."

Reunion Breakfast

What Elizabeth couldn't deny was her accelerated heartbeat when she saw Carol wave from a corner table of the restaurant. Perhaps Veronica was right and she had been lying about her feelings. She did want Carol to see her as attractive, did want Carol to desire her again. But that didn't mean that she wanted to go back to what had been. She had made a new life and developed new perspectives. Then she remembered that Carol had said that to her just a few days ago.

She walked over to the table and sat down. Carol leaned over and kissed her on the cheek.

"I'm glad that we could have this time together before I left. Being in Connecticut brought back so many memories. It made me very sentimental, but I'm glad I went. I hope my visit didn't create any problems between you and Veronica. I sensed a tension at the gallery last night." Elizabeth thought Carol was warm and especially friendly.

She spoke directly, without expression. "I left her alone in bed, so I could come to breakfast with you. She will probably be gone when I return, and I don't know what our future will be or if we even have any at this point."

Carol looked at her intently. "I . . . I'm sorry. Is there anything I can do?"

"Well, what should we order here?" Elizabeth picked up the menu in front of her, trying to keep her hands from shaking. She wondered if Carol could still tell what she was feeling by the tone of her voice.

Carol put her hand on Elizabeth's and pulled the menu down so she could look at her directly. "I'm always subjecting you to these roller coaster rides, aren't I? Even during this short visit, I've managed to upset you. I'm sorry. I wanted time with you. I really wanted to see you, to know how you've been getting on. I've missed you."

Elizabeth cut her off. "Veronica thinks that you want to get back together. Is that true, Carol? You never even hinted at that in Connecticut."

"Why do you think it's true?"

"I don't think so, but Veronica does. She's better at understanding people, or reading between the lines. I'm pretty good with plants."

"Yes, I remember." Carol smiled. "We all have to cultivate our gardens in this best of all possible worlds. Isn't that right, Liz?"

"No one calls me Liz anymore," she said matter-of-factly.

"Probably scared to death to call you that." Carol smiled again.

"Why? Tell me. Why should someone be scared to call me Liz? You weren't."

"You're so smart, but so dense sometimes. It just slipped out of my mouth one day, and I was petrified that you would take offense, not tell me and just hold some resentment towards me. You never said what you were feeling or thinking so I had to guess. I did that based on reading your behavior and your reactions."

"Our life together was one thing for you, Carol, and another for me. Is that what you're saying?"

"I think that's an oversimplification, Liz."

Elizabeth was exasperated. "Oh, I wish I had your perceptions and the ability to express them as well as you do in your paintings. I wish I had a better understanding of you, me, our lives. I wish knowing people were as simple as knowing plants and shrubs. You know when to prune, fertilize, transplant, how much water, shade or sun. Some answers are not so difficult."

Carol said, "Liz, maybe seeing each other was a mistake."

Elizabeth attempted to protest, but Carol stopped her.

"No. No. Let me finish. I don't want to upset your life. I thought that after these few years, we could become friends." Elizabeth raised her eyebrows. "Yes, I've met lots of women out in

California, but they're new friends. You're special to me. The part of my life with you will always be important to me. I know you understand, and I was hoping you would feel the same way."

"Yes, of course I feel that way, too. I told you when you were at the house, I want you in my life again. I know we can be friends," she took Carol's hand, "best friends."

Carol visibly relaxed. "Anyway it's in the Dyke tradition, right? Ex-lovers become best friends."

Elizabeth smiled faintly. "Now who's oversimplifying?" She was thinking of Veronica and how she could make amends to her.

"I guess that's one of the pluses of lesbian life, never losing contact with the ex's."

"Well, just *one* of the pluses."

They both laughed.

"You know, Liz, I have something to confess to you."

Elizabeth looked up sharply. "What is it?"

"This is not my first trip back east. I've been in New York a few times before this and never gotten in touch with you. It's always bothered me to be so close and never call you."

"Oh." How was she supposed to respond to that? How did she feel about that?

"At first, I was so involved in my new world, I wanted to forget the past and begin again . . . and it was still too painful for me to see you. I had started on a new adventure and I didn't want anything tying me down, bringing me down. It's hard to work when you're carrying around a negative emotional weight. I try to be on the edge all the time. I have to concentrate, let myself believe I can do it and that my work is good, good enough for me to devote myself to it."

She listened. "I understand."

Carol went on. "Painting is an act of faith, and I waver between belief and doubt. The doubting could kill me because if I let myself doubt, then everything I am becomes meaningless. It means that I have selfishly focused my life on creating something that is not worth anyone's time to look at, contemplate, be excited or moved by. I have to believe in myself, and anything that will help me believe is taken in. Anything or anyone that adds to the doubt has to be dismissed. The dismissal is not so easy, especially when it's someone you love very much." Carol studied her face. "Do I make any sense to you, Liz?"

She was puzzled. "Are you saying that I wasn't supportive and encouraging about your work? Do we have to talk about this now?"

"No, no, of course we don't. It's just something that I've wanted to tell you for a long time. It's difficult to articulate."

Elizabeth said thoughtfully. "You know, Carol, it took me a long time to get over you. Today is difficult for me because of Veronica and . . . because of being with you. I don't know if I can deal with all of this. I'm sorry."

Carol spoke quickly. Elizabeth could hear how embarrassed she was. "Sure, sure. Liz, I'm the one who should be sorry. Maybe we should have just let it go by. I should never have called you. But it's been almost two years, and . . . ."

Elizabeth interrupted. "I'm glad you called. Really, I'm glad we're going to be friends again, but I don't think I can bear to hear about Jane and all the rest of them. I can't begin again on that note."

Carol looked away from her. Elizabeth reached across the table.

"I loved your new paintings, Carol. The intensity of the color, the scale, and the magnificent landscapes are breathtaking. I am, as always, in awe of your passion and your vision."

"Liz, I wish you could come out there and see the redwoods and the Cascade Mountains. You would really love it." She played with one of Elizabeth's fingers. "I would really like to show you that part of the country."

"I wasn't fishing for an invitation." Elizabeth felt the old anger coming back. *Carol left, and now she has returned. Everything is still the way Carol wants it. I can't tell her how dead I felt without her. I don't want to appear that helpless and vulnerable. How can we be friends? How can we be friends and* not share these feelings? It's too complicated. I can't describe my confused feelings to Carol. Why was I so eager to meet her for breakfast? Did I expect Carol to supply some clue that would explain everything?

Carol was talking about camping in the mountains. In some ways Carol seemed like a stranger to her, yet she couldn't forget what they had meant to each other then. She remembered when they had first moved into the house. It was a cold day in January, and because of the heavy snow, they had decided to stay in and cook the only thing they had in the house, spaghetti. Suddenly the electricity went out.

"Well, it's a good thing we have the fireplace," Carol said.

They got out their bedrolls and lay down in front of the fire. Elizabeth went to get more wood, and Carol opened a bottle of wine.

"To keep you warm." She came up behind Elizabeth, who was stoking the fire.

Carol kissed the back of Elizabeth's neck, then turned her around. They kneeled on the floor facing one another.

"Elizabeth?"

Carol was asking her something. She concentrated on her reply and let the romantic memory go. "Yes, I would like to see the redwoods and northern California." She hoped Carol wouldn't pin her down to a specific time. There was too much conflict, too many memories. *Can we be just friends? Is it possible? And Veronica? She's so young, so different from me, but she makes me feel. Is that what Carol wanted then, too? Was that what she meant about being wild?*

She forced herself to pay attention to what Carol was saying, but it was difficult to erase the images of their life together. Carol's visit had reinforced her loneliness. *Maybe Carol had been put off by Veronica's presence? Veronica had only been a distraction for her. But that was it. It was just sex. Hadn't Veronica said that even from the beginning? That was what she wanted, and that was what she had gotten. No one had lost anything. She* stopped, shocked at how easily she could betray her feelings for Veronica and exile Veronica to the fringes of her life. Whatever had been between them was finished. That was certain. Carol was her real life. It was Carol she really wanted. She promised herself that she would pay more attention to what Carol considered important, be more sensitive to her moods and feelings, listen more carefully to what she was saying and try to be more social with Carol's friends. If necessary, she would give up her work in the East to be with Carol. She was excited thinking about the possibility of their being together again. This time, she promised herself, it would be different. She would make it different. Carol could be happy with her and would be satisfied. Now she believed Carol had come east to renew their relationship. She convinced herself that Carol wanted their life back as much as she did.

Retreat

Kathy picked her up at the railroad station, but Veronica didn't say much. She had never seen Veronica so upset. Her eyes were red, but her defenses had already put up an impenetrable wall that stopped any communication between them. For weeks, Veronica sulked around the house. Kathy tried to interest her in some social activities, but Veronica refused to go out of the house, except to go to classes and then come straight home. Elizabeth called several times, and left messages on the answering machine, but Kathy knew that Veronica never returned the calls. Nor had Veronica answered the doorbell when Elizabeth showed up in person.

Kathy began to worry and took a day off from work to be with her friend. They listened to music, and she got Veronica to go to a movie with her.

They were home eating dinner, and Veronica blurted out, "You know, Kathy, as soon as I walked into her house and saw the portrait, I had my doubts that it would ever begin, but I knew this was the way it would end. The woman who painted that picture really understood Elizabeth. To know someone like that, the way Carol knows Elizabeth, meant there would be no real competition from anyone else. Even with Carol gone, the portrait was always there. She was always there and *her* presence was the reality, not mine. I didn't understand the hold Carol had at the beginning."

"Ronnie, give yourself a break. You'll get over it. You didn't even know her that long. It only started out as a one-night scene anyway. Wasn't that all you wanted from her?"

"Oh, Kathy, yes!" Veronica was impatient. She ran her hands back and forth through her hair. "But it became more, much more. I was falling in love with her. Finally, allowing myself to love, after my failure to help Leslie."

"I know, Ronnie." Kathy sympathized with her.

"I thought I could get whatever I wanted, create whatever I wanted. Like the night I brought her here. You remember you almost walked in on us. She believed all I wanted from her was sex."

"But that was true, Ronnie!" Kathy wanted Veronica to acknowledge the basis of her interest in Elizabeth.

Veronica slammed her fist down on the tabletop. "Yes, damn it. At first, sure it was. It's what I know best. It's all I ever want from anyone. It's all I need."

Kathy jumped. "God, Ronnie you put up so many defenses. How was Elizabeth supposed to see through the poses and the bravado? Did you ever say anything to her? Did you ever ask her to be anything more for you? Sometimes, Ronnie, you give the impression of being so hard."

"I am tough. I want to be tough. It's how I learned to survive. But I still can't believe she left her house, the college. She left everything for Carol." Veronica shook her head.

"The only thing to do at this point is to forget it. Concentrate on your studies, Ronnie. Make new friends. Get involved again. There are other women in this town. You'll meet them if you want to."

Veronica got up from the chair. "Not now, Kathy, not now. I have to think about this, about Elizabeth and Leslie."

"So, I take it you won't come to the bar tonight?"

"How can I go with you? I'm not interested. Anyway, I would just be a downer for you."

"I'm sorry you won't come. I'm only trying to help, Ronnie. It's important to get out, even if you don't want to. You don't have to talk to anyone, just sit there and listen to the music. Maybe have a nice slow dance with me?" Kathy smiled.

"Sure, and we know where that one would get us? You're a good friend, Kath. You're one person I can say I fucked but didn't fuck up or fuck over." They both laughed.

"At least your sense of humor is intact."

"Elizabeth always liked my sense of humor. She said it was one of my survival skills."

"She was right. You need a sense of humor. It gives a third dimension to your tough butch image."

Veronica smiled again. "I'm going to sleep, Kath. Don't wake me when you come in, no matter who she is." She walked to her room and shut the door.

She lay down on the bed and wanted to cry. Maybe this weekend she would go home, see how Marie and Frank were doing. She hadn't seen them since the wedding. She had spoken to her parents a few times. She couldn't talk with them either. She never told them about Elizabeth. *First, I lived through Leslie, trying to believe that her marriage wouldn't change our lives, now Elizabeth lying to herself about Carol. How could I have gone along with their self-deception? What a jerk I am. How stupid!*

She couldn't be still anymore. She was restless, angry, and frustrated. *I failed with Leslie and I failed with Elizabeth. My approach was all wrong. I should never have worked for Elizabeth. That had made our positions unequal. I tried to fix that with sex. Power for power, I thought. That backfired. We never became closer emotionally, only sexually.*

She knew she couldn't ride her motorcycle all the way down to New Jersey. She was too distracted and upset. She would call her parents and tell them that she would take the train Saturday morning.

She sat down at her desk and began to go over some notes for her class in forest management. She imagined redwoods and pines, hemlocks and spruce. She suddenly caught herself thinking of Elizabeth again, thinking about where Elizabeth was now, at this very minute. "Very sneaky, Santini," she said out loud.

After preparing for the test which was coming up, Veronica got back into bed and fell into a deep sleep. She was awakened a few hours later by laughter from the other bedroom. First she was startled. Then she realized Kathy was home and was not alone. Good for you, Kath, she thought. She turned over and went back to sleep.

Dear Veronica

"I thought about calling you, but you would probably hang up the phone or screen the calls through your answering machine. You never answered my telephone messages before I left Connecticut, and refused to see me when I showed up at your apartment. That says it all, I told myself. Let it go. But it's not so easy to let you go, not as easy as I thought it would be. What I did was so unexpected and impulsive, I'm still in shock. When I look in a mirror, I wonder who this person is. Displaced, transported 3,000 miles. The department gave me a leave of absence on very short notice. I wanted to resign my position, burn all my bridges, so that I would have nothing to come back to. The Dean told me to take the leave and to think about an official resignation after a year. I am determined to stay here with Carol, so I will send in the letter of resignation soon. I know you will understand how difficult it was for me to leave my home and my gardens. The college arranged for a visiting professor, his wife and family to stay there for the year. She likes to garden, but seemed intimidated by the amount of work it would entail to maintain all the property. The university agreed to send over some students and keep the gardens as an internship project, so I don't quite feel that I have abandoned that, too. But it's you, Veronica, I feel worse about than anything else."

Veronica put the letter down and blinked a few times. She wanted to crumple the rest of the pages and throw them, unread, into the wastebasket. She viewed this latest attempt from Elizabeth to get in touch with her as a provocation, but she was also curious to find out what lies and denials Elizabeth would write now about her situation. Elizabeth's letter, complete with return address, had arrived five days ago, and Veronica's first angry impulse was to tear it up and throw it out, but she couldn't do that, so she tossed it into a night table drawer. This afternoon, she was alone in the apartment, and Kathy was at work. Sitting with a cup of coffee, forcing herself to remain unemotional and detached, she took the letter from the drawer.

It was true; she would have hung up the phone if Elizabeth had called. There was nothing more to say. Now Elizabeth was trying to feel less guilty, trying to believe that she had made a mature decision going off with Carol.

". . . I tried to explain this to you when I came back from New York. You wouldn't see me."

She got up and walked into another room as if she were walking away from Elizabeth, leaving her talking to an empty room, talking to herself.

For a while she stood in front of the window in the bedroom, looking out on the street, moving her fingers through her hair. Then she closed her eyes and saw Elizabeth's face, heard her voice reading the letter. She slowly opened her eyes and took a deep breath.

Screw it. It was just an affair. Nothing to get so upset about. Kathy was right. It just never got off the ground. There was no chance. Leslie and Carol made sure of that. What did Elizabeth want her to do now, manage a polite good-bye? Give her a chance to say what she never got to say in person?

She went back into the living room, sat down, and picked up the letter.

"I do care what happens to you, Veronica. Being with you I learned so much about myself, about what I needed and how to get what I wanted. You taught me that."

Veronica laughed. "Oh baby, you really did learn something." She shook her head, tore the letter in half, and threw it into the wastebasket. Staring down at it, she felt drained of all energy and emotion.

When the telephone rang for the fourth time, she picked up the receiver.

"Hello."

"Is this Veronica Santini?"

"Who is this?"

"Veronica, it's me, Buddy. Don't you remember me from the wedding?"

She held the telephone away from her ear, wondering whether to lie and say she was someone else.

"Veronica? Veronica? Is that you?"

"Oh, Buddy." How did he manage to catch her at the most difficult times?

"Did I interrupt something? Is this a bad time for you? I can call back."

"Well . . . uh . . . I . . . I've been pretty busy studying and working now. Exams are coming up and I have to keep up my grades. I . . ."

"Well the thing is that I'm here . . . here in New London. And I was wondering if I could see you."

"What are you doing here?"

"I came up with some friends to visit the Coast Guard Academy, but I thought I'd give you a call to see if you were free. Just for a little while. I . . . I know you must have school work to do, though, so . . ."

She rubbed her eyes, trying to think. "Where are you now Buddy?"

"Uh, I'm down near the water, on Broad Street somewhere, in a coffee shop called Josie's."

"Yes, I know where it is. I can meet you for a short time. I'd like to get out for a while anyway."

It was a cold, raw day, and looked like it might snow, but Josie's wasn't far and she'd be back before dark. She pulled on her black jeans, took her leather jacket from the closet, and grabbed her helmet.

She saw him waiting outside in the cold. When she rode up on her motorcycle, in her mirror glasses and helmet, he gave no sign of recognition.

She stepped off the cycle and took off the helmet. Her straight blonde hair fell around her ears.

Buddy, his eyes wide, stared at her. "Veronica?"

"Buddy? I guess we both look different in our real clothes." Veronica smiled at him.

"I didn't know that you . . . I mean you do look different, Veronica, very different. I didn't recognize you–that bike and all, your clothes. I didn't know that you rode a motorcycle. Frank never said that you. . . ." He looked puzzled and confused.

"Say, Buddy, you look very different, too. Why don't we go inside? It's a little cold out here." She tucked her helmet under her arm and went into the coffeeshop. Buddy stared at the bike, then at Veronica and followed her inside.

"You seem a little upset, Buddy." She smiled at him as they settled at a table. "Did you expect me to wander down here in the same evening gown?"

"No, of course not. But you're so different from that night."

"Too different?"

"You look different. You seem like a different person, Veronica."

"No, Buddy, I'm the same. I'm just me, that's all. Just the same Veronica."

He kept staring at her, and she sensed him trying to keep a pleasant, non-judgmental smile on his face. "Still, it must be a shock for you, no dress, no heels, no makeup, no teased hair."

"I just never expected . . ."

"What?" She wanted to say it for him.

He turned his head away from her and began to chuckle. "Does your mother know you wear clothes like this?"

"Does your mother know everything about you, Buddy?"

He looked directly into her eyes. "Yes, Veronica, yes, she does . . . the important things about me."

"Are clothes so important?" She wanted to taunt him into blurting out what he suspected.

He smiled uncomfortably. "You know it's not only the clothes, Veronica. It's the way you are now, the way you walk, the way you talk . . . that's so different." He looked away and there was a long pause before he turned to her again. "Why did you agree to meet me?"

"Why did you want to see me?"

Buddy asked the waitress to bring two coffees and was silent. He twisted the napkin on the table until the coffee arrived.

"You know why I wanted to see you again, Veronica. I told you that at the wedding."

"Buddy, did you like that girl at the wedding? Tell me. Why?" She genuinely wanted him to answer.

"Okay." He leaned back into the booth and put his head back, shielding his eyes with his hand. "Whew. What a shock, Veronica."

She kept pushing him. "So tell me, you did like that girl? Why?"

"Look, I'm just a guy from Newark. You don't have to sit here with me. You can go home. My friends will be here soon, and I'll be going back to New Jersey."

"I guess you want me to leave before they get here, so you won't have to introduce me or explain me. You're embarrassed you made such a mistake. I didn't trick you, Buddy. No, I just went along with all of your assumptions. You made it easy. But don't worry. There are loads of nice Italian girls just waiting for you, Buddy."

"Yeah and for you, too, I guess," he remarked with some sarcasm.

"Definitely for me." She laughed, showing a broad grin and running her hand through her hair.

"Then it's true. It's not only the clothes, the bike."

"Whatever you're thinking now Buddy, it's the truth." She was feeling empathy for him as if they were old friends sharing intimate secrets. "I'm sorry I came on so strong just now. I apologize for that." She looked away from him out the window. "You did call at a bad time. Someone who was important to me left a while ago, and I'm still pretty upset. But it's got nothing to do with you. So I apologize if I was taking it out on you." Her eyes were filling with tears. "Well, so much for the tough Dyke image. Guess I'll have to switch roles now." She rubbed her hands over her eyes.

"I'm sorry you're unhappy, Veronica."

"Again, I apologize. You always see me crying." He reached for her across the table, and she backed away. "No . . . oh no. Don't get any ideas . . . I may be unhappy, but you're not the answer for me."

He softened. "But why that night? How come then?"

She clasped her hands and sighed. "It's very complicated, Buddy, hard to explain. I think it has to do with becoming someone everyone else wants you to become. You do things to make others happy. You forget who you are or who you want to be because you know that wouldn't make them happy." She threw up her hands. "Oh, who knows about these things?"

"I do understand, more than you think. My parents wanted me to go to college. I didn't want to go, but I knew it would make them happy, so I went. I was a terrible student. I just don't have the head for college. I don't know if I really even tried. Maybe I just went through the motions, made it look good. I failed, and I left. Then I did what I always wanted to do. So in some ways I understand what you're saying, but . . ."

"Buddy, you're a really nice guy. What you see in front of you is a big part of me, not all of me, but it's the image I want to have of myself. That girl at the wedding–I didn't ever want to be that girl. I'm sorry . . . I don't mean because of you. It has nothing to do with you. It's only me."

Buddy nodded, looking down into his coffee cup.

"I don't want to hurt you or make you uncomfortable, Buddy."

"That's easy for you to say."

"No, no, it's not. Not at all." She wanted to reach out and touch his hand, but was afraid that he would misinterpret the gesture.

"Don't you ever feel that it's wrong? That you should try to change? You don't seem very happy. Maybe if you . . ."

She held up her hand.

"Please, Buddy, no simple answers, no pop psychology. You wanted to see me again, and you have. Don't get into water that's too deep for you."

"Does that mean I'll never stand a chance?" His look was so earnest that Veronica was disarmed.

"Buddy, Buddy, you want me to say it out loud? I'm a Dyke. I like women. I want women lovers. I don't want to have sex with men."

"I can't believe it."

"Believe it, Buddy. It's the truth. This is Veronica. I'm not an illusion, a fantasy, or a bridesmaid. And I'm one bridesmaid who never wants to be the bride. I know it's hard for you to believe." She held both his hands in hers and pressed them together. "Believe it."

"I will if you tell me to, but . . ." His laugh was a little uncontrolled.

"I guess I'm a living dirty joke in your world, right?"

He nodded in agreement but would not look her in the eyes.

"So now you have to make up your own mind about me. Try to ignore the scrawl on the bathroom walls, the Sunday church sermons."

He wanted to get away from her and pulled his hands out of her grip.

She looked down and shook her head, got up from the booth and held out her hand.

"This must be my year for ending things, or not even letting them get started. Good-bye, Buddy."

She held his hand until he looked directly at her. When he did, she smiled broadly.

"Good-bye, Veronica," he said. "Keep well. Good luck." She heard the sadness and defeat in his voice.

She mounted the cycle, fastened on her helmet and started up the engine. She knew that he was watching her, and without looking back, she lifted her arm gave him the thumbs-up sign, and pulled away from the curb.

JOURNEY TO THE WEST

To see a greater distance, one must move to a higher ground.

–Wang Zhihuan, Tang Dynasty

Like the Way I Love You

Elizabeth walked into the small cottage and almost tripped as she attempted to stop the screen door from banging shut behind her. She put the groceries down on the counter and called out, "Carol? Carol?"

The house was quiet. Only Matilda and Penelope, the two tiger cats, came when she called. Carol had left a note, taped to the refrigerator, saying she would be back soon, but she hadn't said what time she left or what time she would return.

Elizabeth tensed. She rationalized that this was not the first time Carol had left unexpectedly. Carol taught several studio classes, and there were department meetings and other lectures. Occasionally she drove to Portland, Seattle, or San Francisco to meet with gallery owners.

It wasn't that she had gone. That was very like Carol, who hated schedules and worked best when she was free of constraints. What that freedom meant and how far it extended, Elizabeth could only guess. During the first few weeks of her move to California, they had talked about living together again as an experiment.

"You know how much I love you, Carol. I'm here. I don't have to say anymore."

Carol put her hand up. "Right. Don't say any more. I don't want to feel pressured to be something superhuman for you, and I don't want to feel guilty for everything that you gave up to be with me. Surely you see what a burden that puts on me . . . on us?"

Elizabeth, frustrated, quickly crossed the room. "I don't want you to feel that way at all, and that's not what I meant. It was a big step. I can't deny it. You're important to me, and you always knew that." She threw up her hands. "Let's not talk about it anymore. I'm here . . . with you."

She moved close to Carol and held her close and kissed her.
She felt calmed and secure.

Today, Elizabeth wondered whether wishful thinking had deluded
her into coming to California. In New York her feelings for Carol
had been so clear and strong that she coerced the invitation from
Carol. Veronica would probably call her reaction to Carol another
illusion.

She felt like a foreigner. People spoke English, but that was
where it ended. She had no reference points for life here. She
poured herself a glass of white wine, and noticed that it was a
California vintage. Why am I questioning everything here, even the
wine? She berated herself. California wines were world class now,
but sipping the wine, she didn't think it had the mellow taste of a
French Bordeaux. Snob, she told herself, stick in the mud, eastern
snob, Euro-centered, old wave, traditional conservative.

She thought it best not to mention to Carol some of her
negative impressions of California, when she realized that Californi-
ans were very sensitive to the disparaging remarks of East Coast
visitors. She couldn't help it, but she felt everything in California to
be so transitory; in fashion one minute and discarded the next. You
needed a certain state of mind to live here. Shortly after her
arrival, she was invited to dinner with two of Carol's new friends.
Diane and Karen kept on all evening trying to get her to
acknowledge the superiority of the California wines. Diane told her
that when the French vineyards were at their best, French wines
tasted just like the variety of the California wines today. Now the
California wines were at their peak and French wine was *passé*
and the only reason people still preferred French wine to domestic
was snob appeal. She didn't know how to respond to this assault.

Diane was a painter. Karen taught English literature at the local
college. They were both very friendly. They were lovers who led
their own lives, although they saw each other most weekends.
They liked having no permanent attachment. They were uncom-
mitted. She felt that there was no connection to a past tradition
here or any long-term plan for a future. People just keep

reinventing themselves, moving on from one fad to the next. It was the beauty of the scenery and being with Carol that allowed her to believe that she could fit in here. She would try not to be so critical. She wanted to see herself as one of the early California settlers, leaving the constraints of the East to begin a new life.

Elizabeth walked into Carol's studio. Her latest landscape painting, a large canvas of the redwoods in snow, was propped against a wall. Elizabeth noted the boldness of color in Carol's new paintings. The earlier paintings of the Southwestern desert blended the muted colors of green, rose, pink, mauve, and tan. Elizabeth tried to link the change in Carol's painting with the changes she saw in Carol and she realized that she spent a lot of her time comparing her present situation with her past. In searching for clues she might be able to stop the apprehension, the uncertainty she had felt from the minute she arrived. Recalling the past was a way to understand the present.

They met at a gallery in New York that was exhibiting Carol's desert landscapes. A large canvas of desert plants, sagebrush, cactus and bluebonnets fascinated Elizabeth.

"You've been looking at this painting for a long time."

Elizabeth glanced at the blonde woman who moved next to her. "Yes, I think it's so mysterious and beautiful, another world, almost another planet."

"You like it?" Carol asked.

"Yes, very much. I wonder if the desert really looks like that? The painting seems so stylized and fixed, but the colors seem so true . . . too true." She turned to face the woman who was standing too close to her, and Carol looked boldly into her eyes.

"Have you ever been to the Southwest?"

"No. I've lived all my life in the East and I'm just down for the day with a friend of mine."

"Down from where?" Carol smiled.

"I'm from Connecticut." She laughed and pointed at the canvas. "This scene is more foreign to me than anything

European. I'm embarrassed at my ignorance of the rest of the country."

"Can you imagine that the desert actually has those colors?"

"They seem to be realistic. The painting makes me want to see the desert in person. I like it very much."

"Yes, I am very fond of this particular one. The setting is not too far from my house, and as a girl, I always thought of the desert as another country."

Elizabeth stared at her. "I'm glad you identified yourself before I really started my critique, otherwise it might have been quite awkward for us both." They laughed.

Carol asked, "Can I get you some wine?" and spent the remainder of the evening talking with Elizabeth, asking questions about gardening and plants. Elizabeth was fascinated by Carol's paintings and intrigued with her stories about growing up in Texas. Remembering that night, Elizabeth was reassured and charged with the possibilities for both of them.

*   *   *

At five o'clock, Carol called. "Hi, Liz, I'll be home soon. I'm just finishing up some work here."

"Where's 'here'?" Elizabeth asked jokingly.

"In my studio, at the university. Where else?" She could hear the annoyance in Carol's voice.

"Carol, I'm sorry. Don't get upset."

There was a pause and a sigh. "No, Liz, I'm not. Sorry for jumping all over you. Being alone for the past few years, I'm not used to accounting for my whereabouts to anyone. I've forgotten how to be civilized and social. Forgive me for snapping at you."

"It's okay Carol. Really, I didn't mean anything. See you when you get here."

"Right."

Elizabeth knew that it was just a matter of time before she would have her own work here and be involved in other things besides Carol, the cats and the house. Carol took her on trips through the redwoods. The beauty and majestic scale of the country impressed her. How appropriate that redwoods should grow in California, home of the colossal everything. Elizabeth again thought of Carol's new paintings and how well they reflected the majestic proportions of the landscape. Elizabeth would be patient and give herself time to adjust.

The Way I Want It to Be

After she hung up the telephone, Carol returned to her office, sat down and put both feet up on the desk in front of her. She looked out the window at the dark evergreens and the bright blue sky. She had been trying all day to focus on her painting and not on her problems with Elizabeth. She got up and kicked the wastebasket as she circled the room. How could I have done this? Again! All she could do was shake her head. This is how I get into trouble all the time. I just never learn. I have no control. The telephone rang. She turned and stood over the desk while she picked up the phone. "Oh Sally, hi. Thanks for returning my call. Do you think we could meet somewhere? I told Elizabeth I'd be home soon, but I really have to talk to you. Okay, I'll meet you there in ten minutes."

* * *

When Carol got to the coffee shop, she saw Sally's car parked near the door. The diner was almost empty, and Sally was sitting in a booth reading the music selections offered in the little juke box over the Formica table. She looked up and smiled as Carol came toward her. When Carol sat down, Sally took her hand and held it for a long time. Carol looked at her, saw the teasing look in her eyes, and pulled her hand away.

"Sally, come on."

"It's been so long since I've seen you. I miss you."

"Sally, I told you once Elizabeth came out here, I would try to make it work again and that we had to stop seeing each other as lovers. You agreed. It wasn't just for Elizabeth. It was for you, too."

Sally clasped her hands in front of her and looked down at them. "Right. So what is there to talk about? We will remain friends, and anything more is a memory."

"I'll ignore your sarcasm. I want to talk about Elizabeth, get your professional opinion on some things." She paused. "I'm worried. She's unhappy here. She's in culture shock and really depressed. Worse, I feel that she's unhappy with me. She calls me at work, and if I'm not there, and call her back later, I hear that suspicious tone in her voice. It's driving me crazy." She looked at Sally who was nodding her head.

"Carol, you never told her everything about your life out here, did you? You never said that you wanted things to be any different from the way they were back East. Something in you wanted it to be the same, even though you knew your life had changed."

"That's true, but Sally, I couldn't work there anymore. The life was stifling, but I stayed on because I really loved her. What could I do? There were no challenges, and I was isolated from new experiences that could excite and stimulate me."

"By experiences, you mean women, right?"

Carol smiled, "Not entirely that–although that was a part of it."

"And I'm just one of those you picked up along the way, right after Jane, as I recall. Isn't that right?"

"Batting one thousand," Carol responded.

"So now that we understand each other . . . what?" Sally held up both hands questioningly.

Carol rested her head on her arm and fiddled with the knobs on the music selection box. She avoided Sally and looked out the window. "Well I thought maybe, you'd be able to offer some advice. You're a psychologist. What do you think I should do about my problem . . . with Elizabeth?"

Sally leaned her head back against the leatherette bench. "Okay, I'm not going to pull any punches with you. First of all, our relationship is not a professional one, so I can't begin to give you advice. This is not a weekly column for the lovelorn, either, and there is no prescription I could write for you or for her. I wouldn't know where to begin if I could. It's not as if you had a sprained ankle and I could give on-the-spot medical advice about it." Sally looked at Carol who was listening intently, a worried expression in her eyes.

"Carol, I don't think you understand. As you've jokingly told me many times, you can spend years 'shrinking' out your life. But I will tell you something as an intimate friend." Sally held up her hand as she saw that Carol was about to object to her use of the word 'intimate'.

Sally shook her head. "You want it all, and when you're finished, or bored and you're not interested anymore, you don't know how to get rid of whatever it is. Let me restate your 'problem', as you put it. You dragged this woman all the way out here. You seduced her without thinking of the results, and now you want out. Isn't that it?" Sally paused when she saw the hurt look on Carol's face. "There's nothing I can say, Carol. This is a serious situation you've gotten yourself into, not for one night, or even a few months' romp. You're talking about a woman who loves you deeply. She left everything to be with you." She read Carol's expression. "Oh, don't look at me like that. Of course I sympathize with Elizabeth. I'm presenting her case to you. I guess it's just a question of how much guilt you have versus your own needs at the moment and your expectations of a future. But, I am curious to know how it came to this. You always told me that you never wanted to be involved with anyone again . . . or was that just for me?"

Carol didn't respond.

"It would help you to try to answer some of these questions. You have to think about these things."

"I'm thinking. I'm trying. It's not easy. I guess it was being back in New York and seeing her again . . . remembering the way we used to feel about each other. She was with another woman, who was much younger, and I was jealous and thought I could still get her back if I wanted to. I'm still more attractive to her than Veronica." Carol wrapped her hands around her elbows as she leaned over the table. "Sally, I'm embarrassed to say all this to you, but it's the truth. Then it all got out of hand, and I tried to believe that it would work out. I wanted it to be exciting."

"And if Carol Travis wants it . . . it's got to be." Sally shook her head. "God, what an ego. Elizabeth probably wanted to believe that it would work as much as you, and is probably aware of the truth now, like you. She must know that it was a mistake. What a mess."

"I suppose you'll tell me next to see some shrink or something?"

"Couldn't hurt."

"I need something now." Carol looked at her watch. "I have to go home, and I want to know what to say to Liz. I want her to feel better, and I want to feel better, too."

Sally was exasperated. "Maybe you really want to be back together with her? You're so ambivalent about her being in your life and being here with you. She senses that."

"Don't be ridiculous. Why would she think such a thing?"

"It always amazes me to see how dense people can be about some things in their lives and really have great insight into other aspects of the world. You really are such a brilliant painter. Maybe you're feeling depressed, too? Maybe you're feeling caught up in something you have no control over?"

"I think I should go away for a while. I've been planning a trip back to Texas soon. There's a gallery in Las Cruces that's been asking me down, and I could see my family at the same time. I can hardly concentrate on my work, and I have deadlines and gallery shows. I can't continue like this. I have to leave. Let's pay for the coffee and get out of here. I'm late already, and I hate having to be in a place because I'm expected."

"You know, Carol, I never realized how really spoiled you are."

"I'm just honest and open about my feelings."

"That's what you think. You know you can't be honest and open unless you have some understanding of what you're about. Why do you do things? What are the consequences of your choices?" She shrugged. "No, I don't just mean you and me. I mean everything you do. Not that life has to be calculated, but you have to explain your actions to yourself, at least. And in order to do that you have to know what you feel, at least some of the time. Do you know what I mean?"

Sally took her arm, and Carol pulled away from her.

"Oh, don't get so sensitive. It doesn't matter to me. It's my training. It's the way I look at everyone, lovers included. You have an instinctive sense about people that comes from getting what you want. You plan well and you usually get what you want, but underneath I don't think you understand why you want anything. You have no idea why any of this is happening to you, and you're beginning to think of yourself as the victim-poor you, putting up with Elizabeth."

"You've never said anything like this to me before, Sally. I had no idea that this is how you see me, cold, calculating, ignorant, and insensitive. What was it that attracted you to me if you saw these unattractive aspects?"

"Carol, I'm reminded here of a quotation from a poem by W. B. Yeats, '. . . only God my dear could love you for yourself alone and not your golden hair.' You're a very beautiful woman and very talented. That's a winning combination for me. How could I resist? Why would I want to? I had nothing to lose. In fact, I still want you. It's hard to find someone who attracts me as much as you do. But I keep looking." Sally grinned up at her and pushed her hands down on the table.

Carol relaxed and sat back. She enjoyed the compliments. This was familiar territory all of her life. "Well, don't look too hard or too far. I might just be back."

"Oh yes, you'll be back with me, with the next one and the next."

Carol grew tense but Sally reached out and took her hand. "It's all right. Really, I'm not making a moral judgment here, just stating the obvious."

"Obvious to you, you mean."

Sally laughed. "Yes, if you like, clear to me. But, I'm not a fortune teller either."

"Well, we'll see. Sally, thanks for meeting me. I promise I will think about what you said. Your hour has not been wasted, and you can send me the bill anytime."

Sally looked at her and ran her hand along Carol's cheek. "I just know that I will be paid for services rendered. Take care and let me know what happens." She got up and left the diner, leaving Carol sipping her coffee.

Dear Veronica

"I don't know if I want to write to you anymore or if this is an excuse for writing in a non-existent journal. I keep hoping for some word from you, as unrealistic as that might be. It's sometimes difficult to see the light if you choose to wear blinders half of the time. I think the light enters my world filtered through a very romantic imagination. You keep reminding me of what's real. You are so tough and, I think, too rough for me. What you called up inside me was scary because it was unknown. I pretended that it was you who made me react the way I did when we made love. I didn't know myself, and I played games with you. I lied to you, and I lied to myself.

"Veronica, I'm going to tell you the truth. I don't know what I want. Sometimes, I hate being here. Carol is changed, and almost a stranger to me. I don't fit in. I'm sitting here alone in this house and I'm not a part of it. I'm so confused now. Why is this happening? Why can't I connect here? I feel as if I am being ripped open but exposed only to myself. Carol and I go out and visit her friends or go to parties. We take walks through the woods. Yes, we even make love and eat and sleep together, but I'm just going through the motions. There's so much to say to Carol, and yet I say nothing–and the times I do try to talk it sounds wrong, even to me. Thoughts go round in my head, but what comes out of my mouth is something so controlled and different from what I am really thinking and feeling.

"I don't sleep. I lie in bed pretending sleep. Some days, I take the car, drive to the redwood forest and spend the afternoon there. The trees are gigantic and it's quiet. Sometimes Carol is home when I get back. When I first came here she would always be there. She would hold me and stroke my hair and *whisper that she loved me. Now it's not like that. Maybe it's too painful for her to see me. Maybe she lied to herself about us and . . ."* Elizabeth heard a car door close and stopped writing.

The screen door slammed shut. "Liz, why are you sitting here in the dark?"

"Well, I didn't notice."

Elizabeth heard Carol sigh as she sat down on the sofa. There was a pause and Carol sounded upbeat. "Liz, honey, why don't we go into town for dinner and a movie tonight?"

"Sure, if you'd like to." She heard her own flat, passive voice respond.

Carol in a controlled exasperation said, "Liz, Liz, what do *you* want? You make it so hard for me. It's only a dinner, an evening. Do you want to go or not? What would you like to do?"

Elizabeth jerked her head up, "Carol, why do I get the feeling that you really are sorry that I came out here? Something is wrong." She breathed deeply to gain control. "I think it's you who should tell me what you want, and I'm not talking about tonight's dinner. Tell me. I can take it." Elizabeth walked towards the sofa, and Carol quickly got up and left the room.

"No! Carol, don't do this to me again. I can't live through your leaving me again." She ran out the front door and headed towards the car. As she opened the car door, Carol caught up with her. She grabbed Elizabeth's arm and turned her so that she was pinned against the car.

"Liz . . . don't." Carol sounded frightened.

Elizabeth struggled to get away, but Carol pressed her body against Elizabeth and held her. A few minutes later, Carol led her back into the house and settled Elizabeth on the sofa. "Liz, you look so drawn and exhausted. You scare me."

Quietly, Liz asked, "Why did you stop me like that? What did you think I was going to do? "

Carol stroked Elizabeth's hair back from her flushed face. "I didn't know what you were going to do. You seemed so upset by what I said, and then, I heard what you said. I'll never be able to make that moment go away will I? I'm sorry, Liz."

"What exactly are you sorry about, Carol?" She didn't want to drop it now. She had always expected too much from Carol, always depended on her for . . . for what? She looked at Carol who was now nervously walking around the room.

"Liz, I'm afraid to say anything to you. Afraid that it will sound so wrong and that I'll be misunderstood."

Elizabeth bit her lower lip and closed her eyes tight. "The question is, what are we going to do now?"

"Liz, maybe I should leave for a while. I told my father I would come home for a visit and there's a gallery in Las Cruces that wants to see some of my work. It seems like the right time for me to go."

"I don't know, Carol." Suddenly Elizabeth understood why she had never been able to tell Veronica the truth about how she felt. Elizabeth told herself that she didn't want to upset or hurt Veronica. That was a lie. She knew now that she didn't want to commit herself to Veronica in any further intimate way. Carol was doing that now, to her. She couldn't let Carol get away from her. She had given up so much for this.

"Why are you running away from me?"

"I want to think by myself. I don't want other factors to enter into this. I have to be alone and away from you. Just for a short while."

"You're not asking my permission, are you?"

"No, just telling you why I want to leave."

"You told me that once before, remember?"

"Yes, I remember. Why do we always have to be reminded of the past? Can't we just move along in the present and slide effortlessly into a future?"

"Doesn't seem likely." Elizabeth shook her head. "At least not for you and me."

The Yellow Rose of Texas

Her father was waiting for her when she stepped off the plane in El Paso. He wore his summer Stetson, boots, western pants and a western shirt. His rugged, lined face and his graying hair made him more handsome than Carol remembered. His pale blue eyes twitched as he saw Carol emerge from the passenger gate. He called to her.

"Carol, honey, glad you came." He bent down, hugged her, and kissed her on the cheek. Then he held her away from him and studied her carefully, cocking his head to one side.

"So, Dad, do I meet with your approval? Everything in place?" She laughed, looking up at him.

"Yes sir, my baby sure meets with my approval all right." He grabbed her flight bag, tucked her under his arm and together they walked out of the airport.

"Made a reservation tonight at Victor's. I knew you'd want some real food right away. Then I asked Owen to get us a little *cabrito* to celebrate for the weekend." He was staring straight ahead out of the car window, a broad smile on his face. "Hope you can change whatever plans you made so we can see something of you. Myrna and I are just so excited to see you. It's been too long baby." He shook his head. "We really miss you. Thought we might even have a few days to go up in the mountains. I have to go check the water levels in the San Juans and thought we could make a trip out of it like we used to do. Remember?"

"Uh huh." She was flooded with memories, and they all seemed to be someone else's past, not her own. It was another Carol who had ridden her horse across those arroyos and through the desert. She remembered the trips to the San Juan Mountains with her father. She was so proud of him. Henry Travis was an important man. He was Rio Grande Compact Commissioner for the state of

Texas, and he would travel to the mountains frequently to calculate the amount of water that would come down the Rio Grande into Texas from the high mountains in Colorado. Inspection trips of the mountain reservoirs turned into hunting trips as she got older, and she still shuddered thinking of the animals she had shot to please her father. She knew that he, too, had been proud of his 'little darlin' as he called her. She was his foreman on the ranch, doing all of the outdoor work when he was gone, fencing pasture, fixing water pumps, and setting postholes. He came to all of the rodeo events she was in, and cheered loudly as she galloped her horse around the arena carrying high the Texas flag. Her father had long ago sold the ranch and the cotton farm and had moved into El Paso.

"Well, Dad, I don't know, I had only planned to be here a few days, and I have to go to Las Cruces for a day to meet a gallery owner who wants to show my paintings. Can we leave it open? But I will take you up on Victor's tonight and on the *cabrito*."

"Great. That's great, honey. How's your painting coming along? Everyone's asking about you all the time. You've become famous here in your own home town."

Inside the cool house, Carol looked at the familiar Western style paintings that had had such a profound effect on her early ideas of theme, color and perspective. Her father's gun collection was still prominently displayed, and above the gun cabinet was the stuffed head of her first buck. The library was filled from floor to ceiling with books on Texas history, novels relating to Texas, Texas law and politics.

In spite of what her father said about her career as an artist, Carol lived with his keen disappointment. She hadn't followed in the footsteps of so many in her famous family, practicing law and eventually running for the Texas legislature. How could she have told him when he asked why she wasn't going to go to law school that choosing to live as a lesbian meant giving up any notion of participating in Texas politics. Life in El Paso or in Austin would definitely put a damper on her personal activities. She had disappointed her mother as well, when she was expelled from her mother's sorority for bringing her favorite roping goat to college with her. She laughed out loud remembering the shock on those prissy little faces when they saw the goat nestled on her bed. Carol told her angry mother that she would never marry, and she would never join the Junior League.

Myrna came running out of the kitchen, calling her name and Carol quickly turned her back to the Texas memorabilia that was her inheritance.

Myrna and Carol's father had been together for almost 15 years. Myrna's first husband had been Henry's best friend, and when he died, Henry and Myrna got together.

"Carol, you look great. Couldn't wait for you to get here. Your Dad has been fussing ever since you called."

"Myrna, come on now, you'll scare her off, thinking we have too many plans for her."

"Henry, you know you're just tickled to have your baby here again. Why don't you admit it?"

Carol looked at her father and smiled. "I'm happy to be here, Dad, and I missed you, too."

Dinner at Victor's was excellent. Carol savored each morsel along with the atmosphere. Quickly she told herself that these were the good parts of life in El Paso. Just passing through, she reminded herself. That's the best way. Was that also the best way to live her life? She'd have to think some more about that. Friends came over to the table to say hello. People who had known her since she was a little girl and welcomed her back like the prodigal daughter.

Her father asked about Elizabeth and how she liked living in California. It was a formal question. She knew he didn't want too many details, just showing his daughter that he kept track of her life and was interested. She lied and told him everything was fine.

"I just can't see Elizabeth out of the East is all. I always liked that woman because she had a sense of where she belonged. She had a real love for New England. What a spread you two had there! That house and those gardens in Connecticut seem as much her home as El Paso is mine."

"Dad, are you saying that you're disappointed I didn't settle in El Paso?" Henry Travis leaned back in his chair and blinked a few times, as he looked his daughter square in the face.

"Carol, honey, we all have to do what we have to do. I left your mother when you went to college, but I stayed with her all those years because of you. It was what I had to do. I just accept things as they come. You should know that about me by now. I'm not disappointed in any one thing about you, not one little bit." Henry Travis leaned across the table and patted his daughter on the cheek.

"Why, Carol, your Dad just pops his buttons every time he talks to someone about you. He's so proud."

Why push it, Carol thought. She cut a piece of the best Chile *Rellenos* in the world, stuffed her mouth, and kept quiet. How upset she had been when she learned that her Mom and Dad were divorcing. She was only finishing her sophomore year, and it shocked her to realize that she had had no idea that anything was wrong. She had grown up believing that she lived in the most perfect, wonderful home in Texas, USA. She made a few trips back to help her mother move into a small apartment in town. It had been very painful to leave the ranch, and when her mother died a few years later, Carol felt that she had cut all of her emotional ties with home.

She realized how good her parents had been at leading superficial lives, putting up fronts, and lying to their friends. Although her father was a big reader, and an educated man who could talk on a variety of subjects, he never spoke of his feelings on any aspect of his personal life or hers. Whatever she did was fine with him. Carol never considered this supportive of her choices; it was just an easy way for him to avoid discussion and possible controversy. And here she was, a grown woman, saying the same things she had said to herself for all these years. Don't push it. Let it be. Yes, she was her father's daughter. No one could question that.

The next day, Carol borrowed Myrna's car and drove to Las Cruces. The gallery was in the old section of town, in the tourist area. Good location, she thought. As she walked into the gallery, door chimes sounded. White washed walls and plain wide board floors polyurethaned to a glossy shine really set off the art.

"Be right with you," a woman's voice called out from the back of the gallery. "Look around, and I'll be right out."

There was an entire wall of primitive *Retablos* on tin, depicting saints and biblical stories. Sculptures of cowboys and horses reminiscent of works by Remington sat on wooden pedestals. There were paintings by local artists she knew, and some work by Mexican artists. She was admiring one of the small retablos of St. Jerome with his lion when a woman's deep voice, in a musing tone commented, "Some people have extraordinary house pets, don't they?"

Carol laughed out loud and turned to face a dark-haired woman. Her arms were crossed in front of her, and she was studying the painting.

"Actually it's one of my favorites, and I'll be sorry when it sells. It's late-nineteenth century, and the reds and golds have held up pretty well considering the house I got it from was damp, with no heating to speak of except a wood stove."

"Where did you get it? It's wonderful!"

"I found it in an Indian's house near Alamosa. They were Catholics and had placed a little candle in front of it. The wife told me that they liked it because it combined Christian and Indian life; all creatures living together in harmony and caring for each other's welfare. Well, that's not really what she said, but my translation of the conversation." She moved closer to Carol and extended her hand. "Hello, I'm Celia Ortiz. You must be Carol Travis."

"Yes, hello," said Carol, taking the woman's hand. Celia was an attractive, imposing woman, with a firm handshake. One of her hands could enclose Carol's two. "I like the feeling in your gallery, and I admire your eclectic art collection."

Celia was a big woman; part Indian and part Mexican, Carol thought. Her skin was dark, and her straight, black hair was braided and then turned up on top of her head, somewhat like a bun. Thick crescent shaped eyebrows framed dark, deep-set eyes. Carol noted the tension lines around Celia's mouth, and the high, flat cheekbones. A long Mexican skirt with its soft folds emphasized her broad hips. Her short-sleeved blouse had no collar and sat comfortably on wide shoulders, outlining her full breasts. Elaborate silver earrings touched her face as she moved, and a silver and turquoise necklace was fastened tightly at her throat.

"Well, do you want to add any Carol Travis work to what's here?" The Spanish accent gave a softness to her voice.

"Sure, let's talk about what you want and when. I have several paintings coming back from a tour and I brought some slides to show you. You already have the slides that I sent you a few months ago."

Celia looked at her watch, and Carol noticed a narrow gold wedding band. Too bad . . . what a waste of a big, gorgeous woman, she thought. ". . . over lunch," Celia was saying, "You can show me the slides later, when we come back."

"Okay. I'm going to be here only a short time, and I'm glad I made the trip up here to meet you in person and get a sense of the other pieces in the gallery. I'm very protective of my paintings and like to make sure that they are in the right setting and shown the way I would want them to be."

"Many of the artists here feel the same way. I always try to place the right painting with the right person. Sometimes I feel like an adoption agency or an animal shelter," and she pointed to the retablo of the lion and St. Jerome.

"Right." Carol shook her head and laughed.

Celia led the way to a small restaurant nearby. It was cool and pleasant inside.

"I miss Tex-Mex food. There's not much in redwood country, at least, not much that's good. Sometimes I really yearn for the real thing."

"How did you to move to Northern California, or is that prying a little too much for an art dealer who doesn't really know you from St. Jerome?"

"I've lived in different places. It's good for my work, keeps the creative energy coming. How do you happen to live in Las Cruces?"

Celia put down her cup of coffee. "I was born here, near this town."

Carol laughed quietly. "Oh, so what you really want to know is why I don't live in the valley anymore?"

"Yes, I guess so. I'm curious after seeing your paintings of the Southwest why you choose to live somewhere else. You obviously have a great love for this area."

"The best answer I can give you, Celia, is that while I love the desert, I feel more comfortable living in other parts of the country."

"Okay. I won't pry any further." Celia coughed and changed her tone. "As you see, Las Cruces is being developed because retired Easterners are coming here to live. These newcomers have money and are interested in decorating their homes in southwestern style that includes artwork as well as furniture. Actually, they have helped start a revival here in Mexican, Indian and early western crafts. So their arrival is a mixed blessing."

After lunch they walked back to the gallery and Carol showed the slides of the paintings she wanted to send to Celia. They agreed to start with four medium-sized paintings of the desert that Carol had done a few years ago.

"So you'll send these and we'll go from there, see how they sell and then we can possibly do more. Your new work is really beautiful, very dramatic, almost epic, but here in Las Cruces, my clients want to be reminded of why they moved here from Cleveland or Boston. Do you think you will paint some more desert scenes, or are you finished with that?"

"Oh, so your question about my location just had to do with the subject matter of my paintings, not with the painter."

Celia laughed. "No, no that wasn't entirely true, only partially. After all, I am in business, and I have an interest in following good artists."

Carol knew that she should get back to El Paso. Her father and Myrna were waiting for her, and tonight was the special *cabrito* dinner ordered from Owen's barbecue, but she was interested in talking with Celia. She looked at her intently.

There was an awkward pause in the conversation. Now was not the time to start yet another involvement with questionable results. "I guess I'd better be getting back now. I'm sure you have work to do, and I don't want to hold you up."

"No, not at all. I enjoyed meeting you, Carol." Celia held out her hand. "I know we'll work well together. There is a clientele for your work here, and with your reputation and the quality of your paintings you will definitely sell. I was wondering if you'd allow me to take some pictures and arrange an interview with the local newspaper before you go back to California."

"I don't see why not. Good idea!" Carol turned to leave and felt that she was going out to her horse hitched up outside, instead of Myrna's two-door Buick parked at the curb.

"I like Las Cruces. It reminds me of El Paso when I was a kid."

"Well, many of the artists live in town or nearby, some even live in El Paso. Maybe you'll move back someday."

Carol said nothing. That day will never come, she thought to herself. Leaving here was like being released from prison, but Celia could possibly be enough of an attraction to consider a short stay. She turned back from the threshold, "Celia, maybe I'll just deliver those paintings myself."

*   *   *

Her father had invited some of their friends for the barbecue, and Carol sat on the patio making small talk till she thought her head would just split open from boredom and tension. She had never fit in here and never would. All the talk about the kids and pictures of supposedly happy couples with their families made

Carol want to scream. Having children, and especially grandchildren, was the great accomplishment in life for these women. Carol was glad that she hadn't made that mistake. She had met some lesbians who had their children from early marriages. Carol always avoided getting involved with them, even on the most superficial of levels. She had never wanted children and she thought herself lucky that Elizabeth hadn't wanted them either. That was the period in which she had been most vulnerable to settling down.

She suffered through the evening being polite. Occasionally she thought about Celia and what kind of man her husband might be. Probably she had kids. It was a lockstep, knee-jerk life, no matter who you were. She was intrigued with Celia, and tried to remind herself that she should be thinking about Elizabeth and what she was going to tell her when she went back to California, instead of lusting after some married woman in Las Cruces.

She turned to Royce and Libby Hayes, who were sitting next to her, talking about their daughter who had moved to New York where she was designing commercials for a famous jeans company. Carol remembered Harriet well. They had gone to camp together for several years. Harriet had run the family ranch by herself for a long time. She had been by herself out there in Hayes canyon. Carol had gone to help out, and would trailer her horse up there to break the ice on the water troughs during the coldest parts of the winter. Goodness, that was a hard life and Harriet was one good rancher, too. She always had admired her. But the Hayes ranch was so large it was impossible for one person to keep it going, and they didn't have the money to hire help. They had to sell the ranch, and move into town. It was a sad story, and one Carol had heard many times before. Harriet left home and became someone far different from the cowboy she had been all her life. Just like me, Carol thought. She wondered why she had never called Harriet when she was in New York. Maybe she would next time.

Mr. Hayes grabbed her around the shoulders. "Well, pretty lady, how come no one's lassoed you yet?"

Carol couldn't believe that people still spoke that way. Norman Rockwell is alive and well in El Paso, she thought.

"Well, sir, I guess I've kept indoors with my work, so it's hard to find me." She smiled at Mrs. Hayes, who was sipping her third bourbon and soda.

"Harriet's the same way. She never married, and lives by herself. She's dedicated to her work. I really do admire that, you know, but we were really hoping for some grandchildren."

Why, she wanted to ask, but restrained herself, knowing that they wouldn't be able to answer anyway.

"Carol . . . Carol Travis." A woman about Carol's own age came running towards her. She was tall with brown hair, wore a brightly colored flower-print dress and had rhinestone eyeglass frames. Carol looked at her with a vacant expression.

"Carol, it's me . . . Barbara . . . Barbara Collins–we went to camp together and to Austin high, and Crockett elementary. I'm just so proud of you and all you're doing. Why, it's like knowing a movie star or something." She smiled at Mr. and Mrs. Hayes. "Jimmy and I read about you all the time. When we went to New York once, we even went to an art gallery because they were showing your paintings. Jimmy saw it in the papers in the hotel. We asked the woman for your address, told her we were friends from Texas, but she said that she couldn't get in touch with you. What a shame! I was so disappointed."

Carol remembered her at last. A stupid, silly, flirtatious girl who always wanted to play with her dolls, even taking them to camp each year, propping them on her narrow bunk bed. She never liked to ride, never liked to get herself dirty or sweaty.

Barbara left for a moment but came back with an overweight, balding man, dressed in a western suit. She introduced him to Carol as if she were showing off a prize horse. Maybe she thought Carol would be envious of Barbara's good fortune. "This is my husband Jim. He owns the Cadillac dealership here in town, and we're thinking of opening a Chevy dealership next year."

Carol shook his hand.

"Is your husband here with you, Carol?"

"I'm not married, Barbara." Carol was becoming annoyed with Barbara's fatuous assumptions. It had been too long since she had been in company like this. Barbara looked guilty, as if she had said something rude. Then that pitying look came over her face which Carol had seen so many times in similar groups and which she could write dialogue for: "Carol couldn't get a man. Poor thing! No one to take care of her. She's an old maid." Carol said nothing to clarify her private life after her declaration of not being married.

Carol had to spend the next few, uncomfortable, minutes listening to Jimmy inform her about the pros and cons of selling Chevys versus Cadillacs. Barbara told her everything she never wanted to know about her children and childhood friends who had gone to school or camp with them. They had a group. They all went to the club for dinner every Saturday and once a month they would get together to do something "fun." Sometimes they went out to the rodeo dance or they arranged bridge matches. Barbara and Jim and Shirley and Tom Smiley had traveled to Europe last year. They had seen it all, had eaten all that foreign food, and were glad when it was over and they could come home to Texas.

Carol shivered, thinking about the life she might have had.

"Why don't you give me a call while you're in town here, Carol, and I'll get some of our old friends together and we'll have lunch."

"Oh, sure, sure, Barbara, but it may not be this trip–maybe the next one when I have more time."

"Well, we do need lots of catching up, Carol. I'll be waiting for your call."

Barbara dashed away with Jimmy in tow, moving on to a couple they knew, sharing anecdotes of children and bridge and "the club."

Later, after the guests had gone, Carol helped her father and Myrna clean up. She listened to the two of them extolling the virtues of their friends, complimenting themselves on the success of the party. Carol told them how much she'd enjoyed seeing some of her old friends, and they looked very pleased with themselves.

"Honey, you know your old man goes to bed early and this is way past his bed time. I'm turning in. See you tomorrow. Glad you had a great evening. Owen really did great with the *cabrito,* didn't he?"

Carol smiled, "Yes, Dad, just like old times."

The house was very quiet. Carol sat alone in the living room. She felt that she should call Elizabeth, but didn't know what she ought to say. The physical passion which they had shared for a long time was no longer a primary drive. Could Carol live with that? Could she live without it? Be honest, she told herself. That's the bottom line. Sally had told her to think of Elizabeth. Liz hadn't cut all of her ties with Connecticut. She had only rented the house in Connecticut and had taken a leave of absence from the university. She could still go back. Yes, but in what condition would she return? Carol couldn't speak with her on the phone. Elizabeth would hear the false tone of cheer and the superficiality of Carol's concern. She thought it was unlikely that they would remain friends after this. She felt guilty and depressed. She felt sorry for herself and dreaded confronting Elizabeth.

The Morning's Hard

"Carol." There was a knock on her bedroom door. Myrna was calling her. "Carol, Carol, honey there's a telephone call for you."

She was still asleep and for the moment didn't know where she was. "What? Oh, oh, Myrna? Telephone?" She panicked, thinking that it might be Elizabeth. "Who is it? No, wait. Tell them I'll call them back. Get a number and name. Thanks, Myrna."

She sat up in bed and stared at the wallpaper trying to find the courage and the words she would use to tell Elizabeth that it had been a mistake. She was afraid of Elizabeth, afraid of what she might do. Telling her the truth is best, even if she doesn't understand it. After all, I don't understand it much either.

When she had washed up and put on her bathrobe, she went into the kitchen and found out that the caller had been Celia Ortiz from Las Cruces. "She left this number for you, Carol, and said to please call her this morning about that newspaper interview."

"Oh, yes, the newspaper." Carol was relieved. Postponed execution, she thought.

She called Celia and they set up an appointment for that afternoon at a restaurant in El Paso. Carol had never heard of the restaurant, but Myrna said it was the new 'in' place. Carol smiled, thinking she might run into Barbara Collins and some of the 'fun' folks from the 'club'.

Carol put on her best cowboy boots, a pair of fawn-colored soft pants and a white silk blouse. She searched through her bags and took out a tan suede vest. When she was finished dressing, she looked in the mirror and said to herself *Are you kidding? Who are you dressing up for? As if you didn't know.* She laughed out loud.

The Rio Grande restaurant looked like a Mexican hacienda. Inside there were little alcoves, and terra cotta floor tiles. It was so dark that candles burned on the tables in the middle of the day, yet it was a relief from the glare of the hot El Paso sun. Carol's photo gray glasses needed a few seconds to lighten up, and then she saw Celia stand and wave to her. She nodded in recognition and strode towards her table. As she neared the table, she saw two men, seated on either side of Celia. The man with the short brown hair, wearing the blue suit, white shirt and tie, was quite young. The other man had a dark complexion, wore a western suit and a bolo string tie with an Indian turquoise clasp. He was about Carol's age and looked familiar. Celia took Carol's elbow and Carol felt the strength in Celia's hand as she turned her towards the two men. They both stood up and smiled. "Carol," Celia took the arm of the younger man, "this is Tom McCrory from the newspaper in Las Cruces. He's here to interview you and take a few pictures. We'll supply him with some photos of your paintings later. The newspaper has decided to do a full story on you for the Sunday edition. It will feature the gallery, too, so we're very excited." She introduced Carol to the other man.

"This is my husband, Roberto."

Carol forced a smile. "Yes." She was sorry he was there. "I'm happy to meet you."

"Celia has told me so much about your work. I saw your paintings, and I like them very much. I'm in El Paso for the day on business. I can't stay long. I have an appointment this afternoon, but wanted to see you."

"I'm flattered that you took the time."

He held out his hand. "Carol, do you remember me, Roberto Ortiz?"

Carol's face went pale. Yes, she remembered him clearly, and he knew about her life too. They had gone to school together, been friends for a short time, but Anglos never socialized with Mexicans. She had never brought him home to meet her parents. It was in the second year of high school that Carol had discovered her feelings for women. She had somehow confided this to Roberto. She couldn't remember exactly what she had said to him or how she had told him, but it's probably not the kind of revelation that a young boy forgets. It was soon afterward that they stopped being close friends. He dropped from her life. He had been very smart in high school, good at math. That's why he went to Stephen Austin. It was all coming back to her. What had he told his wife? What would she think of Carol?

"We knew each other for a short time in high school, Carol." He held her hand and Carol saw the kindness in his dark, brown eyes.

"I thought you might like to meet each other again." Celia was smiling.

Carol searched for a way to begin to talk. "I thought you looked familiar when I saw you, Roberto, but it's been such a long time. What are you doing now?"

"Carol, you didn't know it, but you were my inspiration. You had such defiance and courage. Mr. Adams, the school counselor-you remember him, Carol, a very nasty, prejudiced man-wouldn't let me take the test for a national scholarship. But because of your example, I persisted and forced him to allow me to take the test. I passed, and won a scholarship that changed the rest of my life. I became an electrical engineer."

"That's wonderful." Carol grasped the water glass and drank slowly to ease her anxiety. Then she told him about the party at her father's house, last night, and the meeting with Barbara Collins. She thought that they even laughed together about that group being the same after all these years, but it was all a blur because she was so nervous.

Roberto looked at his watch. "Well, I'm sorry but I have to go. I just wanted to say hello to you again, Carol. It's been a long time, and I think of you often, my brave friend. I hope, now that you and Celia are working together, we will see more of you."

"Carol, we both owe you a great deal." Celia took Roberto's hand in hers and beamed at the two of them.

Roberto shook Carol's hand and left.

"Your husband is a very nice man, Celia." Tom turned to Carol. "What did he mean by 'brave'?"

Celia quickly put her hand on Carol's arm. "Tom, it's hard to be different in a small town, and Carol wanted to be an artist. Not many young women had such strong ambitions, and it took a lot of courage to say to the world, 'This is what I want to do with my life,' especially when all of your friends are dating and thinking about marriage and children, and hoping to lead the same kind of life that their parents had. It takes a lot of strength to go against that."

"That's true," said Tom, thoughtfully. "Dad wanted me to carry on the family farm, and I felt bad, because I just couldn't wait to get out of there. I know what you mean. I can use that angle in my article." He took out a little notebook and began to write something down.

Celia knew about her. Her reassuring, strong arm held her. Their eyes met, and Carol knew that she wanted this woman, even if she was Roberto's wife.

Tom looked up from his notebook, smiling. "I suppose El Paso is like any other small town where everyone grows up together and knows everyone forever."

He asked Carol why she didn't live in El Paso anymore, and she gave him some vague answer about seeing the world and widening horizons.

"Celia told me that you studied art in Paris?"

"Yes, for a few years. I learned as much as I could about technique from my European teachers and realized how different the southwestern art I grew up with was from the European models. I tried to blend the skills I learned to recreate the spirit of the western landscape."

"Carol's paintings are unique, Tom, not really a primitive southwestern style, but not traditional either. Although Carol's work is not abstract, her paintings seem to interpret a landscape not just to portray it." Celia took over the interview.

It was difficult to concentrate, but Carol forced herself to present the kind of image that would be important for Celia, and the gallery. What was important to Carol was the intense rhythm of the blood in her head and the tingling in her right forearm where Celia's hand rested.

They ordered lunch, and Celia carried along the conversation, relating much of Carol's history in Texas. Tom was impressed with Carol's story. "From Rodeo Queen to international artist." He described the headline of his piece. "Prodigal Texan artist returns home. A fifth generation Texan," Tom said. "Your family history is really the history of the state." He crunched on his taco.

After lunch, Tom wanted to take a few photos outside. Carol looked over at Celia whose Buddha-like expression told her to be calm and that she would wait for her to return. At least that's the way Carol interpreted it. She and Tom came back in a few minutes.

Tom thanked them both for the interview. "This is going to make a very exciting piece. Thanks for calling me, Celia. It was a pleasure to meet you, Carol. I'll drop by the gallery to get photos of Carol's paintings to go with the story." He shook hands with both of them and left.

There was a tense silence following Tom's departure. Carol stared down into her plate. There was no way for her to proceed. She was uncomfortable, waiting for Celia to choose the direction.

"Carol, I hope that meeting Roberto did not upset you too much. I think perhaps it was a mistake to see him again?"

Carol looked up. "For you or for me?"

Celia looked puzzled. "What do you mean? I was thinking of your embarrassment, the painful memories of your youth here."

Is this how I end it, Carol thought. She sadly shook her head, a wry smile beginning to form on her face. She looked up brightly at Celia.

"You're right. I was upset for a minute, but I'm fine now–really. It was so unexpected seeing Roberto–and with you." She stopped herself. Her fantasies would have to remain just that. Well, it wouldn't be the first time.

"It was thoughtful of you to bring the reporter here and save me the trip back to Las Cruces. I hope he writes a good story and

you get lots of publicity. I think that I have to go now and pack.
I'll be leaving tomorrow to go home." That was a lie, but Carol
thought that it might not be a bad idea. She pushed her chair back
from the table and stood up. Celia did not move right away. It
seemed to Carol as if there was something that Celia wanted to
say to her.

"Look, Celia, why don't I ship down those paintings that we
spoke of instead of waiting till I come back here again? It might be
a long time, really." Carol couldn't tell whether Celia was disappointed or relieved to hear this. And it didn't matter really. The
moment was past and they would go their separate ways. That's
how most things turned out anyway; Carol knew that much.

Walking on the Edge

Elizabeth didn't fall asleep till dawn. When she awoke about noon, it was raining softly and the bedroom was dark. Matilda and Penelope were heavy weights pressing on top of her stomach and between her legs. She remembered that Carol was gone and she lay in bed for a while, trying to sort through the recent events. She was disgusted with herself. She had behaved outrageously, losing self-control. She wanted to trust Carol and trust those feelings of love and optimism that had brought her to California. She got up, opened the bedroom curtains and stared at the small backyard. It was too cold in the winter for many plants to survive, still she thought, Carol could have done something to create a garden if she really wanted one. Then she remembered that it was the gardens in Connecticut that made Carol feel like a caretaker. Carol would only take care of herself. That was all. She went into the kitchen to fix breakfast for the two cats. Afterwards she brewed some coffee and toasted a piece of bread for herself.

Elizabeth sat at the kitchen table, slowly sipping her coffee, trying to put together another day. The telephone rang, and she almost tripped over the chair to reach it before it triggered the answering machine.

"Hello?" She was expecting to hear Carol's voice on the other end, and she was tentative and nervous, not knowing what she could say to her.

"Hi, is this Elizabeth?"

She was disappointed. "Yes."

"Elizabeth, it's Diane. Karen and I were wondering if you and Carol would like to come to a party we're having Saturday?"

"This Saturday?" Elizabeth glanced up at the wall calendar.

"Well, I know it's short notice, but Karen and I are entertaining a friend from Paris and we thought that you and Carol might like to meet her."

"Diane . . . Carol's not here. She went home to El Paso and to a gallery in Las Cruces. I don't know if she'll be back by Saturday."

There was a long pause on the other end of the phone. "That's why I couldn't get her in her office. Is everything okay at home?"

"Yes, yes, her father's fine."

"If you're not busy, we'd love to have you, with Carol or without. Please come. It will give you a chance to meet some more people here. I think you'll have a good time."

"Thanks, Diane. I'm free Saturday, and I guess I'll see you then."

"Great. I'll tell Karen, and we'll count you in."

The invitation from Diane and Karen gave her a lift. She felt energized, took a quick shower and got dressed. Then she sat down with the telephone book and looked up the department numbers at the university. Although she intended to take her sabbatical year, she thought that having a professional involvement now would give a direction to her life and make this move seem more permanent. Taking a leave from the university in Connecticut was playing it safe. She had to cut her ties to the past. As she retrieved the list of names given her by colleagues and friends, she wondered if it was too late. She spoke with the Director of the Forestry Department at the university. As it turned out, they had several friends in common, and he had heard a paper she had presented at last year's conference in Massachusetts. He was delighted that she had relocated to the area, and eager to meet with her. He had so many projects that needed her expert advice. They arranged an appointment.

*   *   *

Saturday came, and Carol still had not called. Elizabeth had the telephone number in El Paso, and each day was another battle not to call. She wanted it to be Carol's call.

When Saturday evening came, she fed the cats and left a note on the kitchen table just in case Carol returned. She drove the few miles to Diane's house, stopping in town to buy a bottle of wine. She had dressed carefully for the evening, black slacks, white blouse and black blazer. Diane lived in a single-story contemporary house set in deep woods several miles outside of town. The first time Elizabeth had gone there with Carol, she noted how dark and damp it was. Diane had not cleared much of the land around the house, so there was no garden of any kind, and not enough sun to grow anything anyway, she thought. It did seem strange to have this house just suddenly appearing out of the woods. There were several cars parked along the dirt roadway as she drove in. Elizabeth walked up to the porch and rang the doorbell. She heard music and laughter inside the brightly lit house. No one answered her ring, so she let herself in.

She walked into a large living room. Women were sitting and standing, talking in groups or in couples, others were dancing at the far end of the room. She was nodding to some familiar faces when Karen came up to her and took her hand. She pulled her into the room and hugged her. "Elizabeth, we're so glad you came. You look great. Let me introduce you to some people, and then you're on your own. Diane is busy in the kitchen. Come say hello to her. But first, . . ." she put her arm around Elizabeth's shoulder and steered her over to the bar. "What can I offer you?"

"Oh, just some white wine, thanks, Karen. I never knew there were so many lesbians living around here."

"Oh, they're not all lesbians, and not all local people. There's a women's conference at the university this weekend, and we know some of the women here, but not all of them."

Elizabeth felt shy about walking up to someone and introducing herself, so she went into the kitchen where Diane was taking some quiche out of the oven.

"Can I help?"

Diane smiled at her. "Hi, Elizabeth, glad you're here. Yes, please could you could grab a pot holder and take out the other quiche before it burns while I just set this one down?"

After the quiche was left out to stand, and the salad removed from the fridge, Diane kissed Elizabeth on the cheek, thanked her for her help and shooed her out of the kitchen to talk and meet the other guests. She was on her own again, and wandered over to the table with the various dips of vegetables and cheese. A heavy set, gray-haired woman was putting some cheese on a cracker.

"Want one?"

"Thank you, yes."

"Do you live here in Eureka?"

"Yes, but on the other side of town. A few miles from here. And you?"

"I live in Arcata."

"Do you teach?"

"No. I'm not connected with the university. I used to live in San Francisco, but moved up here a few years ago."

"I just moved here myself. It's really beautiful, so quiet and remote. Must be quite a change for you from a large city like San Francisco?"

"Yes, it's a big change, but a good one, I think, not quite so hectic. When did you move here?"

"Oh, just a few months ago. I'm still settling in."

She looked at Elizabeth. "Do you teach at the university?"

"No, I don't."

They took some more pieces of cheese and started to turn away from each other after the polite small talk. Elizabeth wanted to make the effort to meet someone. She called after her. "I'm sorry, I didn't introduce myself. I'm Elizabeth."

The other woman turned around. "I'm Sally."

The doorbell rang, and more women kept arriving.

"I had no idea that this was going to be such a big party," said Elizabeth.

Sally turned and smiled. "I suppose most have come from the university. There's a women's conference this weekend."

"Yes, that's what Karen said." Elizabeth was watching the

dancing. "I always like watching women dance together. It seems so natural."

Sally looked at the dancing area and back at Elizabeth. She thought this woman was attractive, tall with wavy brown hair, broad open face, light brown eyes.

"Would you like to sit down?" She pointed to some chairs near the front windows.

"Sure." Elizabeth picked up her wine glass and cheese cracker and walked in the direction of the front window. "I'm happy to meet someone who's also new to the area. How did you happen to move here, Sally?"

"Well, I used to drive up for vacations from San Francisco and liked the simplicity of the area. I love the redwoods, and it can be very private when you want it to be. In San Francisco I couldn't go anywhere or do anything without everyone knowing. Even though it's a large city, the lesbian community in San Francisco is very much like a small town. Moving here was difficult, and I feel I'm still adjusting, but so far, I don't regret it." Sally laughed, "Sometimes, if I'm feeling lonely or bored, I tell myself I can always go back to San Francisco, anytime I want, and that seems to keep me here."

"You give me a lot of confidence. I've just come here and I love the scenery and the town, but I know how very difficult it is to leave your home. I'm still adjusting, and to tell the truth having a hard time of it, too."

"Where did you come from?" Sally asked.

"I'm an eastern transplant."

"How did you happen to settle on this area?"

She was reluctant to reveal too many details about her personal life. "I came to California to live with someone."

"Oh, then you're not too lonely. That's great. What kind of work do you do, Elizabeth?"

"My field is horticulture and gardening. I taught in Connecticut and also worked with several arboretums in New England, but I'm still getting my bearings here in California and thought I'd take some time off till I get adjusted."

Sally was silent. This was Elizabeth Sanderson. Sally was engrossed in her own thoughts and in her assessment of Elizabeth.

"Are you all right?" Elizabeth asked.

Sally stammered, "Yes . . . I'm fine." She smiled at Elizabeth.

"What do you do, Sally?"

"I'm a psychologist."

"Oh, really." Elizabeth was pleased. "This really is a coincidence and very interesting."

It was Sally who saw Carol first, as Elizabeth's back was turned to the door.

"Carol!" Elizabeth jumped up from her chair when she turned and saw who was behind her. Carol's expression softened as she looked at Elizabeth. She took her arm as if pulling her away from Sally.

"When did you get in? I'm so glad I left the note. I remembered you said you might come back over the weekend." Elizabeth was relieved to see her.

"Yes, I decided to come home early." She looked at Sally, "And I'm glad I did. I saw you both through the window from the porch."

Sally was amused by the implications in Carol's voice. She decided to say nothing.

"Carol, this is Sally . . . I'm sorry. I never did ask your last name."

Sally stopped Elizabeth before it became too much of a farce. She tried to sound casual and friendly. "Actually, we know each other already. Hello Carol."

Elizabeth looked from one to the other. "Of course, I should have guessed. Everyone knows Carol." She stepped back.

"So, what have the two of you been talking about?" Carol asked.

Elizabeth sat down. "Sally was telling me why she came here and how much she likes northern California."

"I'll bet she likes it a lot better now," Carol responded sarcastic-ally.

"Carol," Sally jumped in, "Elizabeth and I just met. I was about to tell her that I knew you when you appeared."

"What's the matter Carol?" Elizabeth asked.

"Nothing. Nothing. I'm just tired that's all. I wanted to see you, so I drove straight here after I dropped my bags." She placed her hand possessively on Elizabeth's shoulder.

Sally looked at her and smirked. "Well, I'm touched by such a display of affection, Carol. Really, I don't think I've ever seen you quite like this."

Elizabeth was humiliated. She understood instantly that Carol and Sally were more than acquaintances.

"Carol, Carol Travis." A dark-haired woman came over to them. She took Carol by the shoulders and kissed her on each cheek. "Carol, you look wonderful. I went to see your paintings after our dinner in San Francisco and they are, as usual, brilliant and exciting, just like you, my dear. I took Diane up on her invitation to visit before my return to Paris, hoping I would see you again. Where have you been the past few months? Come, we must talk."

Ignoring both Sally and Elizabeth, she started to pull Carol away.

"Nicole. Let me introduce you. This is a friend of mine, Sally Lerner and . . . and this is my lover, Elizabeth Sanderson."

"Oh, oh, I see. I didn't know that you were with anyone. You didn't say . . ."

"Yes, Liz came here from Connecticut a few months ago," Carol interrupted.

Elizabeth had never seen Carol blush from embarrassment, only anger, so there were no visible signs to indicate whether or not Carol was troubled by Nicole's brash behavior.

Nicole held out her hand. "I'm so happy to meet Carol's girlfriend. You must be a very special person."

Elizabeth understood that to these people, she had an identity only in relation to Carol. She was Carol's girlfriend. She shook Nicole's extended hand, but wanted to leave as quickly as possible without making a scene. She couldn't respond to Nicole. She was too hurt and too angry. Carol turned away from the three of them. Probably trying to avoid any more disasters, Elizabeth thought. How could she face these people ever again? She had to extricate herself. She took Carol's arm. "Why don't we go home so you can get some rest after your long trip?"

Sally stood with her wineglass in hand and started to cough.

"Sally, I hope you're not coming down with something." Elizabeth sounded concerned.

Diane and Karen came over to the little group. "Oh Carol, when did you get here?" Diane leaned forward to kiss her on the cheek. "We were so happy that Elizabeth could come tonight and get to know some more people in the area."

Diane put her arm around Nicole. "Carol, what great luck that you should have the chance to see Nicole again before she goes back to Paris. It must be a while since you've seen each other."

"Actually not that long, Diane. Nicole said that they met just a little while ago. Isn't that right, Carol?" Elizabeth kept her voice calm.

Diane looked quickly at Carol. "You never told me that you . . ." Elizabeth looked at her. It was obvious that neither Diane nor Karen had known anything.

Elizabeth said, "I think Carol and I should go home. She's really tired. Could I leave my car here so that we can drive back in one car? I'll pick it up tomorrow." She assumed her most formal and cold manner.

"Sure, sure, Elizabeth, there's no problem." Diane turned to Carol. "Yes, you must be tired. It's a strain . . ." Her voice dropped off.

"No. I'm not tired, actually. I was up for a party after a visit home with the folks." She took Elizabeth's arm. "I wanted to make a big party like this when you first came out." Carol looked around the room. "Elizabeth, would you like to dance?" She gently caressed Elizabeth's hair.

Elizabeth had nothing left. She placed her arm on Carol's

shoulder and closed her eyes. She followed Carol's lead. It was so easy to do. "Yes, if you like. We can dance." With Veronica she had allowed her emotions to choose instead of her head. On the motorcycle, she had pressed herself close to Veronica, her cheek resting against Veronica's cold leather jacket. In Veronica's room, she had been able to give herself up to the excitement of the moment, but then she had had help from Veronica. Now she would have to rely on her own instincts.

They danced one slow dance before Carol led her out the front door. She didn't look at Elizabeth when she guided her to the parked car and opened the back door. She lay down, pulling Elizabeth on top of her, removed her jacket, began to undo her blouse, reaching up to unhook the bra. She placed her hand between Elizabeth's legs.

"No, no. Damn you." She pushed Carol away. "What are you trying to prove?"

"You're so wet. I could feel it." Carol stroked Elizabeth's leg. "You still want me."

"And you?"

"Yes, I still want you, too. I didn't realize that until I saw you tonight." Carol sounded pleased.

Elizabeth covered her face. "No, Carol. Is this how you get excited, humiliating me in front of your friends, and now in the back seat of a car?"

Carol ignored the question. "Liz, I know what I feel, and I also know you. You wouldn't have taken that first step onto the dance floor if you didn't want to and want me."

Elizabeth lifted her face. "You're wrong. It was a way out of there. That's all."

"Don't fall back on that Miss Proper New England, will you? You did what you wanted. You got what you wanted."

"Yes, and I think that's the problem. I have to talk with you."

"Yes, I want to have that talk, too."

"You've discussed me with your friends, haven't you, Carol?"

Elizabeth didn't wait for an answer. "I don't know whether to be upset or flattered."

"Liz, Liz, you're such a private person. Everything is so personal. Approval is hard to come by in your world, where everything is judged, categorized. Your code is too much for me. I told you about me before you came out here. It's just like this moment. You enjoyed it, but now you're upset. There's nothing logical or reasonable about what happened, but you want to discuss it, try to understand it."

"Carol, let's be honest with each other. I didn't turn you on. Seeing those two women got you excited. You've slept with Sally and Nicole, haven't you?"

"Wait a minute, now, just wait. That was before you came here, before we got together again."

"Sally, maybe, but that's not the impression I got from the Parisian pin-up." Elizabeth shook her head. "I sound just like the accusing wife."

"It's true, I did meet her in San Francisco when I went to the gallery, but we only went for coffee."

"Carol, I don't believe you. I just don't . . . the way she came over to you and presumed so much about your friendship."

Carol studied her. "Look Liz, I'm telling you the truth. Why would I lie to you now?"

"I know very well why you'd lie; first, you hate scenes; second, you don't want to upset me; third, you don't want me to leave you like this. You can pick any of the above reasons or all of them."

Carol said nothing, but turned away from Elizabeth and leaned over the front car seat, looking out the windshield into the dark woods. Elizabeth slumped back and closed her eyes. Finally Elizabeth gently placed her hand on Carol's back. "It's cold here. I think we should go home. Can you drive? I'm very tired."

They drove in silence.

Carol was desperate for something to say that would ameliorate the tense situation. She looked in the rear-view mirror. Elizabeth had her eyes closed, her head rested against the back of the seat.

Carol felt guilty. This was not what she had planned. This was just what she had wanted to avoid. She was being pushed into what she regarded as a final confrontation, and she didn't really know how to deal with this. Did she really want to give up Elizabeth? Did she want to accept her situation even though she felt trapped by it? She had left her once. She might as well face whatever it was and get it over with. That was her father talking, trying to simplify complicated situations. In his philosophy, you never consider emotions or anyone else's feelings or even your own, so it's fairly easy to do things with impunity, and move through life avoiding obstacles to pleasure.

Her emotions shifted erratically from feeling sorry for herself, to feeling sorry for Liz, to anger at the whole situation. When they arrived back at her house, Carol was so paralyzed she didn't know what she should do or say. Elizabeth got out and quickly walked towards the house, pulling her jacket tightly around her. Carol watched her go and then got out, prepared to face whatever was to happen. Outside the door, she hesitated, shuffled her feet and kicked at the loose pebbles in the driveway.

The telephone rang as she hung up her coat, and although Carol did not want to answer it, she thought it might be her father and Myrna checking to see if she had arrived home safely. She picked up the telephone on the fourth ring.

"Hello."

"Hello, Carol?"

"Yes."

"It's Diane. I'm so sorry if I said anything that I shouldn't have. I had no idea that you and Nicole . . . I feel so badly. I didn't mean to say anything to upset Elizabeth or you, and when you two didn't come back into the house . . ."

"Diane, it's okay, really, you didn't do anything. It's got nothing to do with you or Nicole or anyone else. It's something that Elizabeth and I have to talk about. Look, this is not a very good time now. I'll speak to you soon." She hung up the phone and covered her eyes with her hand.

Elizabeth was leaning against the far wall of the living room glaring at her.

"You just lied to Diane."

"What do you mean?"

"You told Diane that you and I were going to talk, but that was a lie."

Carol took a step towards her. "We will, and we have to, but I think we should wait until morning when we've calmed down a bit and can make sense out of things."

"By 'things', I guess you mean our so-called life together?"

Carol started down the hall to the bedroom. "Liz, I don't think this is the right moment, that's all."

Elizabeth followed her with her eyes. She knew that she should make a break, now. She should sleep in the guest room, lie down on the couch in the living room, but it would only be an empty gesture. She still wanted Carol to love her and she was angry Carol didn't. She wanted to sleep next to Carol, feel the steady beat of her heart underneath her hand. She wanted to put her hand between Carol's legs and feel the heat even in her sleep. She wanted to own her, possess her, if only in her sleep, if only in their own bedroom, if only in the hours that she was with her. She knew what she wanted. She wasn't confused. She couldn't trust her feelings. She never could, and she didn't trust Carol either. She went into the bedroom behind her. This is not a contest of wills. The question still remained, what does Carol want? But that question didn't seem so important anymore. At least it wasn't the fulcrum around which everything else turned. Her thoughts turned to the first night with Veronica. She went into the bathroom where Carol was brushing her teeth and stood behind her. Carol lifted her head and looked into the mirror over the sink, and their eyes met. She turned Carol around to face her and read the look of panic in Carol's eyes.

"Maybe the truth is that you don't know what or who you want? Isn't that it?" Elizabeth wasn't afraid anymore. It was like an epiphany, a flash of insight. She was her own self, independent of

Carol. It gave her a great sense of freedom to realize this all at once. She felt so light. It was the car, the dancing. In spite of everything that had happened, Carol turned her on. It had felt good, so spontaneous and out of character. Carol had been right, it had been what she wanted. She smiled.

"I do love you Liz. It's just I don't know what to say to make it right." Carol was wary.

"Just trust your feelings, honey. Isn't that what you told me a short time ago?"

Carol held her at a distance and scrutinized her face for some clue to this sudden change. She was relieved not to have to deal with a sullen, disappointed and angry lover, but she was distrustful of this person who was now nuzzling her neck and kissing her hair.

"Now, I don't want to talk about anything, at least not yet. It's not that I don't have anything to say. I wouldn't know how to put it."

Carol softened. She kissed Elizabeth's cheek, moving her mouth closer to Elizabeth's lips and then she lingered for a long time on a mouth that willingly opened to her and took her inside. It was so yielding and empty of everything except sensation that Carol thought she could go on kissing her. There was nothing she couldn't do, nothing Liz could ask of her that would be too much, nothing that they wouldn't find pleasurable. Elizabeth played with her, teased her, moving over her body with her hands and tongue, pushing inside of her, opening her wide. There was nothing complacent or perfunctory in the way Elizabeth held her down on the bed or thrust herself inside her, and she followed her body's responses, allow herself to submit to the sensational pleasures her lover was creating inside her. When she had come and come again on Elizabeth's hand and mouth, she opened her eyes and looked at the stranger who had made love to her. She lay on her back, knowing that there was no way she could reciprocate the intensity of Elizabeth's emotions and passion. Her heart beat with a fear that she could not name. Elizabeth's fingers were still inside her and Carol knew she could not push them out, even if she wanted to.

*   *   *

The next morning Elizabeth sat up in bed, watching the leaves blow past the window. She burrowed deeper under the warmth of the covers and wished that she could listen to the Connecticut weather to see what today was like on the shoreline. It was time to cut back all the perennials, but leave the tall grasses till the spring, plant some more bulbs around the new clump birch. She turned her head to observe the sleeping Carol, and brushed her hand affectionately over Carol's hair. Quietly, she got up and went into the kitchen. She fed Penelope and Matilda, knowing that they wouldn't let her do anything else until they had their breakfast. She brewed the coffee to take back into the bedroom. Weekends had been very special when they had been together in Connecticut. After a long work week of Elizabeth teaching, designing gardens, and working in her own gardens, and Carol locked in her studio, they looked forward to the weekends together. They would lounge in bed Saturday and Sunday mornings, and one of them would bring coffee. They would sit, hold hands, make love and talk about weekend plans. On Sunday morning, Carol's father would make the weekly phone call to catch up on their lives. Carol would spend some time talking with him and Myrna, but that was usually the only interruption to their privacy. She had wanted to recreate that time again.

Elizabeth looked out the kitchen window as the sun melted the thin layer of frost covering the lawn. There was nothing as beautiful as riding through the New England woods in the fall when the leaves were all turning. Every bend in the trail brought another spectacular vision. Deer and first-year fawns seemed to be every-where. She would come across them feeding or drinking or she'd just catch sight of their white tails running into the deep brush. Her horse would skitter out from under her, hearing rustling in the brush, scaring up pheasant, partridge and wild turkey from their cover. Fall was her favorite season; everything beginning to shut down for the long, dark winter. It must be just as wonderful to ride through the redwoods in California, and she would like to have a dog again, some company for the rides. She took the two cups of coffee to the bedroom and placed Carol's on the night table next to her side of the bed. She drew the covers over her and looked at Carol sleeping on her stomach, a strand of her blonde hair falling over her cheek. She placed her hand on Carol's head. She felt different now. She loved Carol, but it was not with the same desperation and neediness that she had felt before. She turned Carol over and took her in her arms. Carol was warm and soft, still asleep. She pulled Carol up so that her head rested on Elizabeth's breast. Images that she had so frequently dismissed from her consciousness, believing that they would impede her integration into Carol's world, flooded all of her senses; the color of her gardens in the full bloom of summer; the smell of her horse after an early morning ride; the solid feel of the tumbler turning in the lock to the front door of her house. She had a home that was hers, something she had created herself, out of her imagination and her will. Carol would no longer be a part of that world. Was the answer as simple as going home? Admitting to herself that, next to Carol, it was what she most wanted. If she stayed, was she willing to continue to sacrifice everything for Carol's happiness? If she stayed here, every part of her would be cut away, like some pollarding operation. The natural growth, the directions she would have taken on her own, would have to be trimmed and altered to allow her to remain with Carol. She would always be a transplant, and her life would be artificial. She shook her head as she held Carol a little closer. That's not what she would want or what she would be happy with either.

Carol opened her eyes and smiled, and for a moment Elizabeth thought that any sacrifice would be worth staying with Carol. But just as quickly another part of her remembered the day-to-day reality so far, the life without an identity. What would that do to her after a time? Carol reached up to put an arm around her, but Elizabeth had already begun to extricate herself from Carol's embrace. She let Carol fall back onto her own pillow, turned and picked up the cup of coffee on the bed table next to her. Carol again moved closer to her, pushing her head into Elizabeth's waist and placing an arm across Elizabeth's stomach. Elizabeth smiled. Who could resist her? Not too many people, judging from the party last night. Carol's charm always was impetuosity, urgency, and passion. She was so volatile, so unlike Elizabeth in that. Yes, Carol was exciting to be around. But now . . . now she wanted something quiet. She needed time for repose and consideration. Carol propped herself up on the bed.

"I'll be right back." She couldn't look Carol in the eye. Feeling like a boat come loose from its mooring, she wandered around the living room. She sat down on the edge of the sofa. She was scared. She couldn't face Carol. She could never duplicate last night. This wasn't her. She knew it. It was only time before Carol again was disappointed in her. It was over. Without her passion for Carol she had to invent a world again. What would that mean? Carol called to her from the bedroom, and she didn't answer.

Carol stood in the doorway to the living room, stretching and yawning. "Why didn't you answer when I called?"

"I don't know. I don't know what to say."

Carol crossed the room and took her in her arms. She whispered, "Liz, you don't have to say anything. I loved how you made me feel last night." Something about the stiffness in Elizabeth's body made her look up into her face, and she dropped her arms and walked away to look out the window.

"You seem so different this morning, Liz. I should have realized that . . . last night. The way you look at me . . . you really hate me because of what I do to you, don't you?"

"No, no, that's not true at all." She quickly went to Carol and held her shoulders. "No, don't think that! Never think that! I don't hate you. That's not it." She paused and moved away again. "I have to sort out my thoughts."

"No, tell me now. Tell me what you're thinking now. I don't want to wait for a rehearsed speech."

Elizabeth took a deep breath. "I don't know what I want to say to you. I don't know what I should say to myself."

"Well give it a try. Come on, Elizabeth." She was pleading now.

Elizabeth looked out the window and said calmly. "I want to go home. I think I have to go home . . . now."

"Why? I thought after this morning . . . you and I . . ." her voice trailed off. "You sound so final. I would never have guessed after last night." *It had been a mistake to try it again. Elizabeth would leave, leave her alone, and wasn't that what she wanted? Wasn't that what she had told Sally?* Carol looked down at the wooden floor.

Elizabeth stared at her, trying to guess what Carol was thinking. She felt the tension between them. She could go to Carol, tell her that she would try again, but the truth was she didn't know what she would try, and the "again" part seemed a physical and emotional impossibility. Something inside her had shifted, broken, snapped. The morning sun filled the small living room, its rectangular pattern like a blanket covering and warming Elizabeth. The sun shone on Carol, too, framing the outline of her slim, angular body and casting her light hair and fair skin in shadow. She's a shade, Elizabeth thought, and she began to shiver. She sat down in the rocking chair and closed her eyes. The picture of Carol as a spirit, as someone dead, would not dissolve or fade out. Carol's vulnerability was enticing and seductive, and she struggled against the desire to take Carol in her arms, forgive her, repress her own anger. Exhausted, she couldn't open her eyes.

It was early afternoon before Elizabeth woke. When she got up from the chair, her muscles ached and her back was tight and stiff. She looked out the window and discovered that Carol's car was gone. She wondered if Carol had gone to her studio or to visit Diane or Karen. She thought for a while and then looked for Sally's telephone number. She was tempted to hang up when the answering machine took her call, but she forced herself to leave a message. About half an hour later the phone rang. She let her answering machine screen the call and when she heard the speaker on the other end, she picked up the receiver.

"Hello, this is Elizabeth. Thanks for calling back so soon. I need to talk with someone, Sally. It's about Carol and me. Yes, I know that you and Carol are friends, but you're the only one who would understand." She was convincing enough for Sally to agree to see her.

Show and Tell

It was late afternoon, and the sun was low on the western horizon, making driving difficult. Strips of light filtered through the redwoods and driving through the towering, ancient forest, Elizabeth thought her personal problems insignificant. The cluster of homes on the edge of the forest was an alien settlement disfiguring the majestic, natural landscape. She needed the wilderness, but not the wildness. She needed to believe in the order of things, not in the chaos. While it was true that change was the only real constant and could not be controlled, she trusted that there was an underlying pattern to everything, even if it was obscure to her.

She pulled her car into the gravel driveway, turned off the engine and sat for a few seconds, trying to compose what she would say. She stepped outside the car and inhaled the smoke from a wood fire. Sally's house was set behind a large spruce with the usual nondescript foundation plantings too close to the house, and a broad patch of lawn ending at the front door. A cement path led from the parking area directly to the house. Elizabeth automatically redesigned the approach, replacing the unimaginative walkway with gravel or stone, removing the spruce, taking up the lawn and adding plants and smaller shrubs. As she walked towards the door, the little tract house had already transformed itself into a charming cottage–inviting, cozy and unique. She pressed the buzzer and waited, glancing around, distracting herself with plans for renovating the site.

Sally smiled as she opened the door, but her concern was visible to Elizabeth.

"Sally," she paused. "I feel very uncomfortable. What sounded like a great idea a little while ago, now seems ridiculous. You can chalk this one up to my erratic emotional state."

"I know what you mean. I'm feeling awkward myself. Let's sit down where we can talk. Can I get you some coffee or tea?"

"Is that part of the herbal cure?" Elizabeth attempted to break the tension.

Sally smiled and shook her head. "No, I don't think I have a quick California cure-all." She walked ahead of Elizabeth. "Why don't we sit in my study."

There was a sofa covered in a chintz floral pattern facing a small fireplace, flanked by two armchairs in a blue and white stripe. "What a wonderful room. It's so warm and cozy. It reminds me so much of my own living room in Connecticut."

"Sit anywhere you like, Elizabeth."

Elizabeth sat down in one of the armchairs, and Sally sat directly across from her on the sofa.

"I'm sure that you were surprised by my phone call."

"Yes. I've been thinking about you and Carol since you called, actually since that night at Diane's house. I know how difficult it must have been, and I'm sure that you wouldn't have called me if you'd had any other alternative." Sally shifted uneasily in her seat and looked directly at Elizabeth. "You and I know that this meeting is very unorthodox. I have never seen anyone professionally who is, in any way, connected to my personal life. That was somewhat easy to do in a large city like San Francisco, but up here, it's been very difficult, and I've had to rethink many of my ethical . . . nevers. This is such a small lesbian community and so closed off from anywhere else. The only other therapists are a straight woman and a Freudian male psychiatrist. Not much choice for any lesbians who feel they can only communicate with another lesbian. So, I'll consider this a visit, not a therapy session." She paused. "I can see that you're quite upset. I don't mean to sound cold and detached."

Elizabeth focused on the books on the library shelves. She shook her head.

"It's going to be harder than I thought. The truth is, I don't know what I was thinking about when I called, except that I would talk to you . . . you would listen . . . sort it all out for me . . . and somehow it would be clearer. I mean . . . for me . . . and with Carol . . . I'm sorry . . . I'm really confused . . . and can't quite find the words to say what I want." She brightened and looked up. "And you would listen and then give me terrific advice, something like a horoscope."

Sally managed a tight laugh. "This may all be a little bit of hocus pocus, but I'm no fortune teller and certainly never had a talent for reading palms."

"I'm sure you could have foretold the outcome of Carol and me a long time ago. Right?"

"No you're wrong." Sally shook her head. "Even though I know Carol, people behave differently in different situations. Maybe I could have predicted what the problems would be between Carol and whatever woman she got involved with, but I could never say what the outcome would be. Are we there already?"

"I don't know. That's why I wanted to see you." Elizabeth gripped the sides of the chair. "No, no, I do know. That's the real problem. I know and . . . I'm afraid. It's not as if she were a stranger, not someone I didn't care about, not even someone I didn't love." She looked up at Sally. "I don't think I can live with her anymore. When we came back from the party I wanted to make up. I wanted to feel the pull I've always felt to go to her. We made love and afterwards, I knew that it would be the last time. I was numb, deadened. It's so hard to explain."

"You're doing pretty well. You must be very angry with Carol?"

"Maybe, . . . angry because of what happened in Connecticut. Carol must have told you why she left." Sally prodded her for information.

"Yes, she did explain." Elizabeth related the final scene.

"But even so you chose to come out here with her. Why did you do that?"

"It took me a long time to recover after Carol left, I had been seeing someone when Carol reappeared, but I never allowed myself to become deeply involved with Veronica. I felt my life, after Carol, as temporary. I believed Carol would return, and when she did, it was natural that we would get back together."

"You mean Carol would see that she needed you, that you were as important in her life as she was in yours? Was that how you interpreted the two of you getting back together?"

"Yes, maybe, sort of . . . that she had realized that leaving was a mistake and had now come home."

"But she didn't. She didn't want to come back to Connecticut, and she didn't want to change. You were the one who had to do all the changing. You accepted her as she was."

Elizabeth responded, "I moved out here to be with her and I've been unhappy ever since. I feel isolated and betrayed, not just by Carol, but by my own feelings. I have nowhere to turn. I've made so many bad decisions, Sally." Unable to speak above a whisper, she said, "I feel pretty weak and helpless."

Sally got up from her chair and crossed the room. She touched Elizabeth on the shoulder and said softly, "I'll get some coffee and be right back."

Sally poured coffee into two ceramic mugs and realized that what she had told Carol in the diner was true. *Elizabeth has sensed Carol's misgivings about her move out to California all along. But what are her feelings about Carol? How honest can I be with Elizabeth? It's arrogance to think that I can retain my objectivity and do the right thing for both of them. I'll tell Elizabeth that I really can't talk with her, but that sounds so pompous. Who do I think I am anyway? And what real power do I have over these two people? Am I magnifying my involvement? In small towns, doctors, lawyers, accountants, ministers socialize with people they see in a professional capacity. They have to or they would have no friends. Isn't this a similar situation?* She placed the coffee on the tray with some sugar and milk and returned to the library. Elizabeth was looking at the titles of the books on the shelves.

"You have quite a varied library: psychology, poetry, classics, mythology. I'm impressed, but there are no books on gardening or landscape design."

Sally put the tray on a table. "I'm definitely interested, but there's so little time." She motioned for Elizabeth to take some milk and sugar with her coffee. Elizabeth picked up one of the mugs and returned to the chair she had been sitting in. "Sally, I . . . I really want to thank you for meeting with me."

Sally replied, "I know how upset you are. I feel awkward too, if that helps. I know Carol too well. I may be doing you a great injustice, perhaps even hurting you in some way." She tried to sound firm and decisive. "I don't think we should continue this discussion."

Elizabeth shook her head. "No, no, Sally, . . . you can't. There's no one I can turn to! Surely, this is an exception. You said that yourself earlier."

"Yes, I remember what I said, but I was feeling grandiose, ignoring my own role in this situation. You have to trust my professional . . . and personal judgment on this. I can't be objective."

"Sally, I knew that before I called you. You don't know me at all, and I'm asking you to help me. Carol is just the catalyst. This is not about Carol. It's about me. I realized that when I called you." She paused, but Sally said nothing. "When Carol and I were together, her work and mine really blossomed. It was an outburst of energy for both of us. We shared years of passion in our creative and personal lives." Elizabeth paused. "I was desperate when I sensed Carol's feelings for me begin to change. I tried just about everything to get her back. My coming to California to be with her is the ultimate extension of that effort." Elizabeth looked down into her lap and was silent for a few moments. "You know what it's like to feel so needy you become nerdy? You become a zip, a zero. Nothing's right, and every time you try to do something, say something, it's inevitably the wrong gesture, the wrong word. My failures make me feel worse and worse. After she left me, I tried to understand what it was I had done."

Sally interrupted. "Maybe it was Carol who had changed?"

"Yes," Elizabeth whispered, "that's what she said when she left. She said that it wasn't anything I had done. She needed something different. It was over for her."

"Yes, but not for you."

Elizabeth put her face in her hands. "No, no. How could it be? I didn't even know that she was feeling so removed from me, from our life. It never occurred to me that she was so unhappy."

"Surely by the time she left, things between you must have been different?"

Elizabeth grabbed a tissue from the table next to her chair. "I couldn't believe that she would leave me. I thought that it was one of Carol's moods, that, in time, she would snap out of it."

Elizabeth sat for a few seconds. "There was nothing I could have done to have kept her then. We never really discussed it in any great detail, but I suspect that a life with anyone would have had the same outcome, would have led to the same finality. That's the way Carol is."

Elizabeth looked directly at Sally. "Is that what you think, too?"

Sally was flustered. "I think we have to let Carol answer that for herself. You can ask her when you see her again."

"I don't have to ask her. It's what she said as she walked out the door. I could never forget those words. She said the life was killing her and she needed more chaos, wildness, disorder."

"And what do you need? Is what you needed then any different from what you need now? Have you changed? What do you want now? You know the answers. The difficulty is acting on the answers, making the changes that will give you back your sense of self."

Sally went on. "Elizabeth, I'm going to tell you what I think, not as a therapist, just as a friend to you and to Carol. You're as respected in your field as Carol is in hers. Think about how you have put these illusions of Carol together, sewn them into a comforting quilt to keep you from everyone and everything. It's much better, in the long run to face the truth, no matter how awful or painful it might be."

They sat silently for a few moments. Sally leaned back in her chair. Elizabeth got up and walked over to the bookcases. "I knew all of this before I came here today. The truth is, I've known this for a long time. Living with the romance of Carol and me has affected my life in many ways. I have Carol safely in the back of my head as a retreat should anything go wrong. Moving here was only an attempt to retrieve the past. But I wouldn't see it. I can't live in Carol's shadow. There's no need for me to do that, and now . . . there is no desire to do that." She ran her long fingers down the spine of one of the books and kept walking slowly around the room. Sally followed her with her eyes. Elizabeth walked back to the chair. She leaned over the back of it and looked at Sally.

"There's so much more to say. More for me to explore, uncover and discover, about myself and about Carol. You've been very kind and very helpful and . . . very blunt and honest. I know we can't continue; you've been generous, and very helpful. This has been an important afternoon. I want to thank you, but it seems such an inadequate thing to say."

Sally stood up from her chair, went to Elizabeth and put her hand on her shoulder. "I'm sorry. We've all been there, so we know the pain too well."

"You're very understanding, Sally, and I don't think it's simply because you know Carol. Carol has a good friend in you." She reached out to shake Sally's hand, but Sally took her by the shoulders and gave her a warm hug.

"Elizabeth, I think you're a very brave woman to have risked so much. I know you'll be fine."

"Yes, my confidence comes and goes, but I think I'll be all right."

When Elizabeth got back to her car, she felt drained. So many thoughts and images were exploding inside her head, she couldn't keep up with them. They were kaleidoscopic snatches of scenes of her horse, her house, her dog Jewel; fragments of conversations; a fast rewind of her life with Carol, and images of Veronica. Everything jumbled all together. She shivered, frightened that she would never be able to block them out and yet not wanting to give up the memories. She would always have to guard against this romanticizing of the past, but it was Carol who was the true romantic, painting huge, dramatic landscapes, not really replicating the scene, but creating an epic, greater than anything that was real on this earth. Even if you stood in the same spot, had the same vantage point that Carol had when painting, her vision supplanted the reality of the scene. The portrait of me in Connecticut is bigger than life, grander than my life. Carol must have seen it that way, because that's the way she wanted it to be. The real was ordinary, not exciting enough, she would say. Expansive, unrestrained, passionate, that was Carol.

*   *   *

She took the long way back to the house because she was nervous about facing Carol and needed to strengthen her resolve. She drove into the Redwoods State Park. There would be a few hours of daylight, so she could take a short walk in the magnificence of these first-growth giant redwoods. Her thoughts shifted from appreciation of the woods, to the realizations about what she had done to her life. As she walked deeper into the woods, the path became less clear. The light slanted through the trees and seemed to give the effect of a spotlight, highlighting a particular aspect of a tree, a section of the forest floor, a leaf. The random beams emphasized the variety and magnificence of the woods. She heard rustling noises all around her and was aware of the animal life. After about half an hour, she began to feel chilly, and the light was becoming fainter. Two red squirrels running through the leaves stopped when they saw her, and ran up one of the huge trees. She heard birds in the foliage, but couldn't see them. The giant trees now completely blocked the remaining light from coming through the canopy of the redwood grove. Elizabeth had some difficulty finding her way back to her car and considered what it would be like to spend the night in these woods.

It was dark when she arrived home. There was no light inside the house, and Carol's car was not in the driveway. Perhaps Carol had gone to her office at the college, or was visiting with Diane. She hoped Carol had left a note.

Penelope and Matilda blinked and meowed as Elizabeth turned on the light in the kitchen. Their food bowls were empty, and even the water dish was half-empty. This was not like Carol, who was very responsible about her animals. After putting out some fresh water and food, Elizabeth looked on the kitchen table for a note. She turned on the answering machine, thinking that Carol might have called and left a message, but there was nothing. She walked into the bedroom and saw the envelope on the pillow.

"Dear Liz, I don't want you to worry. I'm fine. I wanted to get away and so have decided to drive down to San Francisco. I will call you soon."

Elizabeth wondered if Carol had spoken with anyone in San Francisco before she left. She sat down on the edge of the bed. The two cats wandered into the bedroom, lifted their heads and looked up at her. She smiled down at them, and they hopped up on the bed. Penelope stretched out alongside her and Matilda nestled in her lap. She stroked their heads and they purred. Elizabeth relaxed and leaned back on the pillow.

The insistent ring of the telephone broke the silence.

"Hello. Carol . . . ? Who is this? Who's calling?"

There was a long pause and Elizabeth sat up abruptly, dislodging the two cats that had imprisoned her between them.

". . . I . . . I live with her. Yes. She said that she was going to San Francisco. What happened?"

Elizabeth brushed the hair out of her eyes and held her forehead. She tried to keep her voice calm. "Where did you say you were calling from? Could you repeat that?"

She went on asking questions and repeating the answers out loud, then asking them again. She waited for the moment when the voice at the other end of the phone would tell her what happened. Then it would be too late for her to change anything, too late to explain anything to Carol.

"Immediate family? You mean like husband, mother, father? No

I'm not any of those. No, I told you, we live together . . . have been together for many years. It's not what you would call immediate family.

"This can't be true. Is Carol . . . she's not . . . yes, I heard what you said, . . . seriously injured, what do you mean? How badly is she hurt?"

The police officer gave her the name of the hospital where Carol had been taken by ambulance when her car had run off the road near Ukiah. He told Elizabeth to say that she was Carol's sister, so she could claim she was a family member and have no trouble at the hospital.

Elizabeth quickly called the hospital and was connected with the floor nurse. Informing her that she was Carol Travis's sister, she was given the information that Carol was in intensive care with internal hemorrhaging. Both legs were broken and she had a collapsed lung. Elizabeth listened in horror. Carol was listed as critical. She had lost a lot of blood, would need transfusions, but the doctors were optimistic about controlling the internal bleeding.

When she hung up the phone, Elizabeth went into the bathroom and washed her face under cold water. She pressed a cold washcloth to her forehead. She had told the nurse that she would be at the hospital in a few hours. The picture of Carol bleeding made her nauseous. She was frightened, and her hands shook. She put together a schedule for the next few days. There were the cats. She would have to find someone to take care of them. At least someone should come in and feed them till she knew more clearly what she would be doing.

She decided not to call Carol's father until she could give him some more definitive information. She spoke with Diane and Karen. They would take care of the cats. If she were going to be gone for a long time, then they would take them into one of their homes. She should call Sally and tell her what happened. She looked at her watch. It was already 11:00 at night. Not late, but maybe too late to call Sally. But this was an emergency. It would

be okay. Her call was answered by Sally's answering machine. She
started to leave a message that was interrupted half way through.

"Elizabeth, it's Sally. I had the machine turned on . . . what's
wrong?"

"A police officer called just a short while ago to tell me that
Carol was in an automobile accident on 101 near Ukiah. They
took her to the hospital, and her condition is very serious. I don't
know anything very much about the accident. She's in intensive
care. I told the nurse that I would be there tonight. I'm just getting
ready to go."

"Elizabeth, calm down. Listen to me. I don't think you should
drive down there tonight. You're too distraught, besides they
probably won't let you see her until tomorrow anyway. You need
to sleep and be alert tomorrow. I really think you should wait until
morning."

"Yes, yes, maybe you're right. They probably wouldn't allow me
to see her anyway. I'm really in no shape to drive anywhere now.
I'll stay here tonight and leave early in the morning." She paused.
"Sally . . . I feel so guilty and responsible. I was so cold to her
this morning. I just want to help her, and be there if she needs
me. I'll call you as soon as I know what her condition is." She
hung up the phone. There was nothing she could do for Carol
tonight. Still, if anything happened . . . if she wasn't there with
her and . . .

The phone rang. She picked it up before the second ring. It was
Karen who wanted to drive down with her. She told Karen she
would go alone, but would wait for daylight, and promised to call
them as soon as she got there. She knew that she wouldn't sleep,
but got into bed anyway. The telephone rang again. Her voice was
a tentative question.

"Hello?"

"Hello, Carol? It's Celia. I'm sorry to call so late at night, but
someone came into the gallery today to look at your paintings and
wants to buy several. I'm very excited and I wanted to tell you

about it. I hope I haven't woken you up. Carol? Is this Carol Travis?''

"No, this isn't Carol, but . . . yes, it's the right telephone number. I'm Carol's friend, Elizabeth.''

There was a long pause at the other end of the line. "Oh, oh, I'm sorry. I was looking for Carol Travis. I'm Celia Ortiz from Las Cruces. I wanted to speak with her about some of her paintings that I'm showing in my gallery. Is Carol there?''

Carol had never mentioned the gallery owner in Las Cruces. A flash of anger ripped through her. Another of Carol's ever-widening circle of girlfriends, no doubt.

Her voice was cold. "No, Carol isn't here now. I don't know when she will come back. I'll take a message and tell her that you called. She does have your telephone number, I'm sure.''

Elizabeth practically banged the receiver down on the hook. Then she felt terrible for being so rude. Maybe this was someone Carol really cared about. If she wasn't still in love with Carol, why did she care who called Carol and for what purpose? And why did Elizabeth assume that every female caller just had to be one of Carol's lovers? And what the hell did it all matter anyway, when Carol was in such serious shape in a hospital? That was the only important issue now. The rest would sort itself out later . . . much later. She didn't know the name of the gallery. She couldn't look through Carol's papers or records. She decided to let it go until she saw what Carol's medical condition was. Then she would tell her about the call and let Carol decide what she wanted to do. Elizabeth was sorry that she had allowed her feelings to interfere with Carol's life. Even more confused about Carol and herself, she turned off the bedroom lights, got into bed and lay there in the dark, waiting for daylight.

Beyond Recognition, Beyond Repair

The medical center did not have that odor of antiseptic that made her gag every time she walked into a hospital. Elizabeth went up to the information desk and asked for Carol's room number. She was told that a staff doctor would be down to see her in a few minutes.

"Why? Where is Ms. Travis? Is anything wrong? I know that she was badly hurt." She was nearing panic and wished that she hadn't been so insistent turning down Karen's offer to come with her. She was thinking about calling Karen when someone tapped her on the shoulder.

"Excuse me, are you the person asking about Carol Travis?"

She looked up to see a middle-aged man with a serious expression behind his dark-rimmed glasses. The nametag on his white lab coat read Dr. William something.

He held out his hand. "I'm Dr. Clifford, in charge of Miss Travis's case. You must be her sister, Elizabeth Sanderson. The floor nurse said that she had spoken with you last night."

"I drove down first thing this morning. Can I see her? How is she?"

He spoke in a reassuring voice, anticipating her fear. "Miss Travis is still critical, but better than last night."

"Why wouldn't they let me see her? What about her injuries? The nurse said that she had broken her legs and that her lung had been punctured. What happened?"

"Your sister's car went off the road. There were skid marks. She said that she swerved to avoid a deer that ran in front of her car, but we couldn't get the full story. The police may want to ask you some questions. In terms of her medical condition, we set the fractures. Her face was cut on the windshield, and required stitches, but we expect her to heal without too much scarring. We're still working on the collapsed lung. We stopped the internal bleeding, but she's weak from loss of blood. We're reluctant to give her any transfusions, even though the blood is carefully screened these days. It does take a longer period for recovery, but it's safer. When the nurse told me of your call yesterday, we were hoping that since she's your sister, you would have a similar blood type and we could give her some of yours."

"Well, I don't really know what blood type I have . . . and I'm not really. . . ."

He went on. "Actually few people do know, but we can find out fairly quickly and it would help your sister enormously. As I said, she is very weak."

He led her into a room, told her to sit down on a chair with an armrest and to roll up her sleeve. After he had taken some blood, he rolled her sleeve back down and said he would take her to see Carol.

"Don't be too upset when you see her. She probably will look very pale to you, and her face is pretty swollen. We're giving her something for the pain."

Elizabeth followed Dr. Clifford through the labyrinth of turns and passages. Finally he stopped at a door and turned toward Elizabeth. "You can go in for a little while. Don't let all of the tubes bother you too much." He took her shoulder as he ushered her into the semi-darkened room.

Carol was lying in the bed with her head slightly raised. There was a tube coming out of her nose, a needle in the back of her hand. A bottle of glucose with saline hung from a metal pole, and other tubes led to collecting bottles by her bedside.

"You can come closer." Dr. Clifford carried a chair from the corner of the room and placed it next to the bed. He motioned for Elizabeth to come towards the bed. For a moment she was paralyzed, keeping her distance from this strange apparition, trying to tell herself that it really was Carol.

Dr. Clifford said, reassuringly. "Don't be afraid, Ms. Sanderson. It's okay. You can hold her hand. You can talk to her. It really would help if she knew that a family member was here. She's probably pretty frightened herself." He stood for a few seconds looking down at Carol, then looking at the bottles, adjusting the drip. When Elizabeth still hadn't moved, he walked to the door and led her to a chair close to the bed.

"Just sit here for a while until you get used to her. I know it must be a shock."

Elizabeth was panicked. Seeing the legs exposed and in casts, she remembered the pain. The smell of the hospital came back to her. She wanted to run. She stared at Carol, recognizable now even with both eyes swollen. There was a bandage over her forehead stained by recently coagulated blood. In other places on her face, the wounds were still fresh. It appeared as if there was not a single plane or surface that had not been cut and bruised. Strands of damp blonde hair lay over her forehead, and Elizabeth brushed it back.

"I'll leave you two alone, and I'll be back in a little while." Dr. Clifford paused at the door and left.

Elizabeth, even more frightened now that Dr. Clifford had gone, noted that Carol's breathing was very shallow and there were long pauses between each gasp for air. Elizabeth began to worry that her breathing would stop altogether. Carol looked so vulnerable, so fragile. But how had it happened? The doctor said that she had tried to avoid a deer. Carol turned her head and moaned softly.

Elizabeth put her hand on Carol's forehead and in a soothing voice whispered that she was there and that she would look after her for as long as Carol needed. She took Carol's hand and held it gently. Carol opened her eyes at the sound of Elizabeth's voice, and Elizabeth thought she saw a faint smile. Then it was gone, and Carol's face was again expressionless. She continued to stroke her hair. "Carol, you'll be okay. I love you, Carol. Please know that. Don't worry, Carol. You'll be all right. You'll be fine. I'm sorry. I didn't mean to upset you so much. I mean I didn't know you were so. . . . Carol, I . . . I'm sorry."

There was a knock at the door and a uniformed California policeman came into the room.

"Are you Elizabeth Sanderson?"

"Yes," she answered.

"Good morning, ma'am. I'm Officer Malone. I called you last night about Miss Travis."

"Oh yes. Thank you so much, and let me thank you again for your practical advice regarding immediate family."

"Well, unfortunately, that's the way the world is, especially the world here in some parts of California, so I thought it would be best and less trouble for everyone if you claimed to be a blood relation. I don't approve of lying, but I'd hate to think that you couldn't get to see her because of some stupid, bigoted laws."

He was a young man, probably in his early twenties. She wondered if he were speaking from personal experience, but she thought that it would be presumptuous to ask. It was enough to know that he was sympathetic.

"I appreciate your sensitivity. I know that Carol would, too. I guess you want to tell me something about the accident." She sat down in the chair.

Officer Malone seemed somewhat uncomfortable. He studied Carol. "Believe it or not, she sure looks a hell of a lot better today than she did yesterday when we pulled her out of that wreck. I didn't know if she would make it then." Elizabeth's hands began to shake involuntarily. She clasped them together and put them in her lap.

"I think we should go outside and talk. Would you like some coffee? There's a cafeteria downstairs. I don't want to talk in front of Miss Travis."

Elizabeth looked down at Carol. "No, no, I guess that's not a good idea. Sure, coffee sounds fine." She leaned down and whispered in Carol's ear, "I'll be right back," and kissed her hair.

Seated in the hospital dining room, the police officer took out his notepad, read a few notes and then closed it. He looked at Elizabeth and shook his head.

"Look, I still have a lot of questions about this accident. Your friend is certainly in no condition to answer them now. Maybe a deer did run in front of her car. We did find deer prints all along the road, but they could have been made any time that night." He paused, glanced around, sighed and started up again. "What I'm saying is that the deer is her story. It was very foggy last night. It was hard to see. I just don't know. Maybe there was a deer, maybe she fell asleep, or maybe," he cleared his throat, "maybe she drove her car off the road."

When he saw the look of shock on Elizabeth's face, he tried to soften his blunt pronouncements. "The truth is that there was no evidence of drinking or of drugs. There were tire marks showing that she had swerved her car sharply. That's all true! I put down what she said . . . I mean about the deer. That's what I put down in the report. If I even mention anything else, she'll have to be evaluated and transferred to the psychiatric unit. The doctors are suspicious. Usually when a deer runs out in front of your car, it's too late to avoid hitting it." He moved restlessly in his seat. "I wanted to speak with you, to get your opinion. When I looked in her wallet, I saw you both have the same address. I'm assuming you live together. Is that right? Do you think it's possible that she would try to . . . I mean do you think she would drive her car . . . ? Did she ever do anything like this before?"

Elizabeth considered how much she should tell him. She was worried for Carol. She had to protect her. Would her position at the university be jeopardized if she were labeled an attempted suicide? Was it even possible that Carol could have done this? She shook her head. "No, no. You have to believe what she told you. I'm certain it's true. Carol would never do such a thing. She wouldn't. I can vouch for that!"

Officer Malone did not seem totally convinced. "Have you known her long?"

"We've been . . . together for quite a long time, more twelve years. Yes, I know Carol well. I can tell you that running off the road is just not Carol's way of handling a situation. Definitely not!" Elizabeth was upset that anyone would think that Carol would attempt to run away from her problems. But wasn't Carol driving to San Francisco to avoid her, and didn't she go to El Paso to avoid talking? How certain could she be that it was the deer that made Carol go off the road?

"Carol can be very stubborn at times, and she has her own ways of doing things, but this is certainly not one of her ways of dealing with life's problems."

"Well, you see," he leaned closer to her, "that's just it. If I believe her story, and if I believe your story about her, and if it's not true, I'll be responsible if she tries it again. I have to put something in my report that will satisfy the doctors and my chief. I have to tell it the way I saw it . . . with all of the possibilities."

He reached into his shirt pocket and handed her his card. "This is my name and telephone number down at the station. You can call and leave a message. They'll know where to reach me. Call at any time." He got up and rested his hands on the table.

"I see what a shock this has been to you, Miss Sanderson. I'm sorry that my news has complicated the situation."

Elizabeth looked up at him. "Please Officer . . ." she looked down at the card, "Malone, you had to tell me the truth. It's important information. I'm grateful." She shook his hand.

His jaw was set tight, and he responded in a resigned way. "Yes, ma'am."

He walked out of the dining room slowly, leaving Elizabeth staring into her half-empty coffee cup. She knew that she should call Sally. Of course, she would have to tell her everything that the police officer had said. Should Sally come now? She was uncomfortable asking Sally for advice again. But Sally was Carol's friend. She had promised Karen and Diane that she would call them as soon as she got to the hospital. She had to call them, too. And Carol's father? Should she call him now? Should she tell him what the police officer thought? She would only tell him that there had been an auto accident. She looked around the room and found the public telephone. She dialed Diane and Karen first. The phone was picked up at the first ring.

"Hello, Diane? Oh, Karen. Well I'm here at the hospital and she's in serious condition. Her lung is still collapsed and there are all kinds of tubes going in and out of her. Her face was cut badly, but they think it will heal without leaving many scars. Yes, that's good for Carol." Reminding herself how handsome Carol was and how she had used her attractiveness, Elizabeth knew that her physical beauty was something Carol took for granted.

"Her legs are in casts. The police who arrived on the scene after the . . . accident think that she must have swerved to avoid a deer. They said that it was a foggy night and visibility was bad." Elizabeth answered their questions honestly, but omitted the part about the possible attempted suicide. She didn't believe it to be true at all. "Yes, we'll have to wait for Carol to tell us what happened. I don't think that you have to come right now. She's not really in any condition to see people. Yes, I'll definitely call if I need anything. Thanks."

She hung up the phone and waited a few minutes before making her next call that would be more difficult. She reached Sally's answering machine. "Hello, Sally, it's Elizabeth. I'm calling from the hospital. Carol is going to be all right. It will take a long time, but . . . there's something I learned that I should talk with you about." She paused for several seconds. "I don't want to leave a message on the machine, so I'll call you back in about an hour." She hung up the phone and went back upstairs to Carol's room. Carol lay still and immobile. Elizabeth sat in the chair next to Carol's bed and looked at her. She fought against the impulse to shut down all of her conflicting emotions. Carol needed her now and that's what she would focus on. She would concentrate on herself when Carol was out of danger. Leaving now was out of the question, and Elizabeth wondered if it had ever been a real possibility anyway. Could Carol have done this? Knowing how Carol refused to acknowledge any weakness, she wondered if she would ever really learn the truth about what had happened. She realized that what she had told Carol a short time earlier was true. She would always love her. Did that also mean that she would always be with her? What if Carol wanted her now as much as she had wanted Carol back in New York? It all seemed so long ago. Could she ever just walk away from Carol, walk out of her life, as she had walked away from Veronica that morning?

She was startled out of her speculations by a light tap on the door. One of the floor nurses poked her head in to tell her that there was a telephone call at the nurse's station.

As she followed the nurse down the hallway, she inquired about having a telephone put into Carol's room.

"Sure, that's no trouble. As soon as we know where she'll be, you can call down to Services and have it done."

"I appreciate your calling me," Elizabeth said. "I won't be long." She picked up the phone.

"Hello, Elizabeth?" Sally's voice sounded tense. "I couldn't wait till you called back. I might have been with someone, and I didn't want to chance that. Tell me about Carol. What happened?"

"Sally, can I call you back on a pay phone? I'm at the nurse's station, and I don't want to talk too long and take up their line."

"Yes, yes call me right back. Call collect if you want, if it's easier. I'm free now for a few minutes."

Elizabeth went back to the pay phone, called Sally and told her what the police officer had said. She waited for Sally's response. "Sally, are you still there?"

"Yes, Elizabeth, yes, I'm here. I was just looking at my schedule for the rest of the week. Is Carol awake? Can she talk?"

"No, not really. She's been sedated and I don't know how long she'll sleep."

"Could you call me when you think she can see me? That way I can reschedule my appointments. I'll be there as soon as I can."

"Thanks, Sally. I . . . I know you feel very close to Carol and I know that Carol considers you one of her best friends, so . . ."

"Elizabeth . . . call me. I have to go now. But tell me where you'll be staying later. She paused. "How are you doing Elizabeth? I can imagine what you must be thinking. I hope you're not feeling responsible for this? I mean for Carol going off like that."

"Well, it had crossed my mind that we had a fight and she drove off."

"Elizabeth, you forget what we spent the afternoon talking about. Carol is always running off somewhere, or running away from something or someone. I want you to remember that and not believe that you precipitated this."

"Sally, I know you're trying to be supportive, but she looks . . . so beat up, so helpless."

"I know. I know, Elizabeth, but you are not the cause of her condition. Just remember."

"I'll try."

"Elizabeth . . . you try to get some rest yourself. I'll speak with you later."

Elizabeth had been given permission to stay in the room with Carol. At night, her sleep was light as she listened for any change in Carol's breathing. When she heard Carol moan in her sleep, she got out of bed, sat down next to her, smoothed her cheek with her hand and pressed her face close to Carol's. After the third night, Carol's breathing was better, her blood count was higher, and the doctors and nurses were optimistic about her recovery. Carol was still in a great deal of pain, and the drugs she was given kept her in a semi-conscious state. Elizabeth was exhausted.

By the fourth day Carol was awake enough to speak. Elizabeth wanted to hold her as close as possible, and to protect her from . . . she didn't know what. Carol kept drifting off into sleep, and was awake only for short periods. Even so, Elizabeth was buoyed up by the progress that Carol was making.

Elizabeth made a reservation for Sally at a motel near the hospital. When she arrived, they had an early dinner and Elizabeth spoke about Carol's physical state. When she revealed the suspicions of the police, they agreed that Sally needed some time alone with Carol to assess the situation. She would visit her in the morning when Carol was most alert.

Even with Carol lying there flat on her back, her face marked with scars and bandages, Sally still thought that Carol Travis was a beautiful woman.

"Sally, it's good to see you." Carol attempted a smile.

"Well, Travis, at least we know that your ego is still intact." She looked over the helpless body stretched out in the bed. "Can't say the same about the rest of you, though." She reached down and rubbed Carol's arm.

"No, no," Carol mustered. "Guess I'm pretty busted up."

"You're going to be fine, Carol." She noted the clean dressings on Carol's face that concealed the stitches underneath. "In fact, those facial scars will only make you more attractive and mysterious, my dear." She patted Carol's hand and sat down.

Carol turned her head away. "I guess I'm not as invincible as I thought."

"Well," said Sally ironically, "I would say that you're a hell of a lot stronger than you think. After all, you're still here. Must be that old Texas stock. What's the expression, tougher than a boot?" Sally laughed.

They sat in silence for a while until Sally spoke, "Carol, do you know what they said on the police report?"

Carol glared at her. "I know. Elizabeth told me. She looks at me as if I'm ready for a rest cure in some psych ward. It's ridiculous."

Sally was all business. "Well then, we're going to have to put this police rumor to rest . . . for good. Why don't you tell me what happened."

"Sally, I've already told the doctors, Elizabeth, Diane and Karen, my father, the administration at the university, and of course–the police. I'll tell you exactly what I told them, but I'm tired and exasperated at having to repeat it."

Sally expressed concern. "I know, don't get so upset. They have officially filed an accident report and that will be the end of it."

"It was an accident. The night was foggy, the road was wet. A deer ran out in front of the car, and I swerved to avoid hitting it. It was instinctive. Anyone would have done the same. Imagine a dog or a cat, even a squirrel, wouldn't you have done the same? I don't know why everyone is making such a big fuss about this?"

"Well, it's because usually. . . ."

Carol interrupted. "Yes, it's true. Usually a deer freezes and you hit it straight on. Well, I was lucky. I managed to slow down enough and brake enough and turn my wheel fast enough to let it go by me. A miracle . . . but look at the winner." She tried to lift her arms off the bed but was held back by the tubes. "Ow." She groaned.

Sally winced. "Carol, calm down. I didn't come down here to upset you. I'm your friend, remember me?"

"Sally, do you remember those stories I told you about my dad and I on those hunting trips in the mountains? I hated shooting those animals. Stupid, macho crap. I would have done anything not to hit that deer."

"You almost killed yourself to avoid killing the deer."

"It was a split second. I wasn't even thinking. I saved myself *and* the deer."

"Did the deer matter that much?"

"It matters to me a great deal. I did the right thing. I'm alive, the deer is alive. Sally, it was an accident. Believe it! If you want to help me, tell the police that my story, as they call it, is true. I can't take the stares of the nurses anymore. Jesus, Sally, what is this, some kind of inquisition?"

"Well, now I know you're getting better. Back to your old oppositional self."

Carol spoke in a controlled voice. "Sally, you and I have been pretty honest with each other concerning our feelings. I have never lied to you, not when we were lovers, not now as friends. I remember our last conversation very well. Surely you can't deny that I was open and honest with you then. Can you?"

"I'm listening. Go on."

"There's nothing to go on with. I left the house. Liz and I had reached an impasse. I was upset. I couldn't face her anymore. She was leaving me. I didn't know if what I was feeling was loss because she was leaving or guilt for what I had done. It hit me for the first time. I always liked being alone, but at that moment, I felt desolate, deserted. I couldn't stand it. I decided to drive somewhere. Then I thought I would go down to San Francisco for a few days and think things over. It wasn't even planned."

Sally rubbed her hands over her face. "Yes, yes, Carol's famous exits."

"More inquisition?" Carol's voice was weak with fatigue. "Sally, my dear friend," she said dryly, "I don't know how much more I can stand of your 'concern' for my mental health."

Sally was determined. "I'm concerned for you. I want to make sure that it really was an accident."

Carol said bitterly, "Well, no one gives guarantees about anything in life, do they? You should know that, Sally. It's your business, after all."

"Yes, but at least some people know why there are no guarantees. Do you?"

"I give up. I'm tired." She turned her head away and closed her eyes.

"Yes, I can see that. I'm going to go and think about what we've both said. I'm sorry if I doubted you."

Carol opened her eyes, "What about Liz? What will she do now?"

"Now?" Sally sounded surprised. "Why should what happened now make any difference to what she had planned?"

Carol's eyes narrowed. "What do you mean? You sound as if you know what she planned. Has she been speaking with you . . . about me . . . about us?" She paused. "I guess she has every right to speak to you. Why not? You're good at what you do."

"What is it you think I do . . . boil magic potions in a pot?"

Carol spoke defensively. "Just you remember, Sally, Liz loves me, always has and always will. That's definitive."

"Always is a word I thought I would never hear from you,

Carol. Is it important that Liz love you, or important that you can count on it? You need her now, but after this? What?" Sally sighed. "In any case, the real question is what Liz is feeling and what she wants to do."

"Elizabeth and I have had some important talks, and . . . maybe . . . did she say when she would be here this morning?"

Sally looked at her watch. "Soon." There was an uncomfortable silence. "I'll see you later, Carol." She slowly left the room. In the hospital corridor, she leaned back against a wall. It was awkward to sympathize both with Elizabeth and with Carol. Perhaps that's why she never could get completely involved with anyone. She always saw both sides of the issues. She walked towards the elevators, preoccupied with the ambivalences of these two women.

"Sally." Elizabeth came towards her. She took her arm and led her to the visitor's alcove.

"How was she this morning?" Elizabeth looked at her intently.

"Let's sit down here for a minute." Sally took a deep breath. "She said that it all happened in a split second. It just seems so unlike Carol to hurt herself. I agree with you that it was an accident."

Elizabeth sighed. "Oh God, you have no idea how relieved I am to hear that." She spoke softly. "I don't know what I should do now."

"I don't know what to say to you. Carol is a person of extremes. You know that. She has strong feelings, and sometimes she can't control them. The question is how much do her passions rule her life."

Elizabeth said ironically, "They *are* her life."

"Yes, yes, of course. You're right, Elizabeth. You're absolutely right."

"Since the accident, I haven't been able to think of anything but helping Carol. I have to stay to see her through this, go home with her to make sure that she's all right." She took a deep breath. "After that, I have to leave as I had planned to do . . . but I don't know. Carol and I never talked about my going home."

She put both hands up to her head. "What a nightmare this has been." She looked away from Sally. "Carol will do what she wants to do. Nothing . . . and no one has ever stopped her. My bet is that no one will . . . ever."

"That's very definite, Elizabeth. You sound so detached."

Elizabeth's voice had an edge. "No Sally, just realistic. It's taken a long, long time to get some resolution about Carol and me. I'm relieved she wasn't killed. I would have found that hard to live with, much harder than being left alone in Connecticut." She rubbed her hands together. "Still I'm nervous every time I see her and it's difficult keeping all of my emotions in check."

"I don't know what to say, but I'm sure Carol's just as ambivalent as you. She's pretty upset now, but I'm sure that she thinks you're going. I don't believe it will be as great a shock as you think."

"You don't think I'm doing the wrong thing, do you Sally?"

Sally spoke with conviction. "No, no. I think you should plan to leave, if that's what you still want to do. Tell her. Carol will be okay."

"Yes, I know you're right. I don't know if Carol would understand me anyway."

"She might not want to face certain facts, that's why she left the other day, but I think that she knows what's up between the two of you." Sally's tone was defensive.

"I'm sorry if I sound so patronizing."

"Carol is waiting for you. I'll be down in the cafeteria for a while if you need to find me."

"Thanks again, Sally." She walked down the corridor towards Carol's room. Her attempt to remain aloof faltered as soon as she saw Carol helpless in the hospital bed. She gently caressed Carol's cheek, careful not to put any pressure on the bandaged areas. "Hi, you look better today. Did you sleep well?"

Carol reached for her. "Yes, fine." She chuckled. "But, every day you come in here, I feel like little Hansel who has to stick out his arm to see if he's fattened up enough. I know you're leaving,

Elizabeth. I knew that the night this all happened. I've been thinking that as I get better, your leaving me gets closer. I want to shut my eyes when I ask you when you're going, as if I'm about to be executed, waiting for the bullets to rip through me."

Elizabeth shook her head. "So that's what I've become to you, an executioner, your assassin." She paused, her voice slower. "I'm sorry. I'm so edgy and nervous when I see you. I don't want to say or do the wrong thing."

"Still the good little girl, right?" She pressed Elizabeth's arm. "Don't get angry, Liz. I don't know what to say to you either. I know you're only staying to make sure I'm going to be okay. I guess I'm going to live, so I assume that you'll leave. That's all."

"That's all?" She couldn't trust her own resolve, especially with Carol's rare moments of vulnerability that she found so seductive.

"Carol, I don't think of this as a real breakup. Not like the last time, I mean. Too much has gone on between us. I know you'll always be a part of my life, and I want you in my life, but being with you these last months has made me realize that we want very different kinds of lives. I'm . . . I was too dependent on you. I don't know what I thought when I came out here. One of the few impulsive acts in my life." She laughed quietly. "Probably seems very tame to you. I knew from the beginning that you were ambivalent about my being here. Maybe you were acting on impulse back in New York, too. I'm not saying this to change my decision."

"I know that, Liz. It's too late to go back, but I don't want you out of my life either. I need the security of knowing you love me. I always thought of you as strong because you knew what you wanted. You're always so sure."

"Me?"

"Don't look so surprised. Your love of gardening, your sense of a home astonished me. Your trust in the constancy of nature and by extension, to my mind, of people was one of the qualities that I found so attractive in you, but our feelings for nature are very different. I don't want to control nature and redesign it, I want to observe, let the feelings wash over me so I can recreate it in my paintings."

Carol continued. "Remember when we planted that row of sweet gum trees? I'll never forget the name . . . liquid amber. The saplings were as tall as the top of my head and so fragile. I thought one good northeast winter wind would do them in. I'll never forget the look on your face while we were planting. It was a dedication . . . a consecration of us . . . our life. . . . I was overwhelmed."

"I thought that you loved the house and the gardens . . . our life."

"Liz, I did, but-there was nothing that wasn't planned in some way. You thrived while I was being choked off, smothered, like some western weed that had to conform or be destroyed. It took me a long time to realize all of this." She shook her head. "I should have gone to a much more remote area than this after I left, but you already had half tamed me and," she smiled, "there is always the need for women and a place to work. I have to support myself and sustain my ego."

Carol reached for her glass of water. She looked up at Elizabeth as she raised the straw to her lips.

"Liz. I've had time to think in the hospital . . . captive audience with myself. I'll be okay, I'm sure. I know my legs will get stronger. I'll be up in no time. I don't want you to worry about me."

Elizabeth was concentrating on Carol's analysis of their life in Connecticut. Her throat felt dry. "You know, Carol, the only thing I can think to say is about the sweet gum trees. They're fast growing for a deciduous tree and fairly strong."

Carol laughed. "See, you prove my point."

"Yes." There were so many times Carol had caught her off guard. "I don't have to be back for the spring term, but I would like to be in the house by April for the gardens."

"Right. Of course. It's the gardens after all-the call of the wild iris and potentilla, coreopsis, and all of those other glorious Connecticut flowers I loved to paint. I still picture that palette of unbelievable, vivid colors. Liz, I'm not being sarcastic. I'm glad that you have the gardens and the house to go back to. It gives a focus to your life."

"And what will you do, Carol? I called your house this morning, and there were several messages. One of them was from Dean Reynolds who called to say that he would try to get down to visit you this weekend."

"Lucky me," groaned Carol.

"He also said not to worry about your classes. He has a graduate student taking them till you get back."

"Great. The way my luck has been going, they'll probably discover she's a better teacher and takes less money than a visiting artist from Texas."

"Never! There's only one Carol Travis. How can you even think that a graduate student could teach them what you could?" She paused and then blurted out, "I am worried about you."

Carol waved her hand to dismiss any further discussion of the accident.

"Liz . . . the deer really was there . . . in the road . . . in front of the car."

Elizabeth picked up her cue and decided not to press for more intimacy when she was trying so hard for distance. She changed the subject. "Diane and Karen will be here to see you soon, and a woman called from Las Cruces, a gallery owner who wanted to speak with you. This is the second time she's called. I couldn't make out her name, but I assume that you know who it is."

Carol had always hated that tone in Elizabeth's voice. That smug condemnation of every woman Carol knew. The implication that she might be Carol's lover. There was no point in defending herself or Celia now.

"Yes, Celia Ortiz. She's showing some of my earlier western landscapes and probably wants me to send her more paintings."

"Your paintings are special. You're a great painter."

Carol smiled teasingly. "Is that why you put up with me for so long?"

"No. No, I loved you."

"Past tense?"

"In that way-yes." Elizabeth felt awkward. There was no place to go with this conversation, but it was hard to leave it like this. Everything seemed so unresolved. But that was just what she had to accept about her love for Carol. It would not ever really be resolved.

"Carol. I'd like to stay to help you with the house and the physical therapy you'll need afterwards. I'm going to be here until you feel that you can manage by yourself."

Carol's gaze bored into her. "Thanks, Liz. I'm sure that Karen, Diane, and even Sally would help, but I accept your offer. I am glad that you'll be here with me for that. In some ways, I am very dependent on you, at least on your constancy."

"Yes, you know you can always count on that." Elizabeth knew they had found a safe ground.

Inside the Calm

Elizabeth was grateful for the November snow in northern California, which she saw as a sign of her transition to New England. As she drove the roads of the coastal towns, seeing the pines and firs covered in white, she was more certain about returning to her home. Carol was out of the hospital, and Elizabeth was involved with her recovery, driving Carol to physical therapy sessions and assisting her at home with the painful and tiring exercises that Carol was required to do to regain her mobility and strength. The progress was measured in quarter inches: extended range of motion, decreased tension of ligaments and strengthened muscles, and increased ability for weight bearing on atrophied legs.

Friends and students from the university came by to help. She and Carol again had a life that was ordered by external schedules, planned doctors' appointments and therapy schedules, but it was a temporary life. Its only function was to provide a smooth transition for both of them. During this interim, there was contentment with the everyday. Knowing that this would never be enough for Carol prevented Elizabeth from getting lulled into the deceptive pattern of these easy, uncomplicated, unemotional days.

She admired Carol's perseverance and relentless determination. If the therapist told her to repeat an exercise ten times, Carol would do it twenty times. Then she would repeat the same exercise later in the day five more times. She never sat still. She discovered a friend at the university who knew about health foods and began a regimen of mega doses of vitamins and minerals. Each day had to show some improvement over the previous day. If there was no discernible improvement, Carol would become angry with herself and push even harder the following day. The therapist was concerned that Carol was asking too much from her body too soon. Carol just looked up at her and laughed.

"As they say, honey, you ain't seen nothing yet."

Elizabeth shrugged her shoulders and looked at the therapist. "I'm not going to be the one to stop her. Are you?"

The therapist smiled. "Well, you seem so much stronger, so I guess you know what's best for you. There is the possibility of straining a muscle and that would set you back some."

"I'll stop when it hurts too much." Carol smiled at her reassuringly.

"And when would that be?" asked Elizabeth.

"You'll hear the screams. Don't worry." Carol patted her hand.

By Christmas, Carol was walking with crutches. They had dinner with some friends at Karen's house, and exchanged gifts in an unusually sentimental mood. Elizabeth fought down her instinct to read into the moment something more than what it was. It was odd how much closer to Carol she felt, now that the tension of their relationship was eased. When it became more and more difficult to accept this interim life, she knew that it was time to go. Her house would be vacant in January, so there was nothing to stop her. She had worried, initially, about Carol being alone, but Carol had many people in her life now. In this small community, friends would drop by for coffee, or in the evening, come by to visit and talk. Carol had spoken to her art dealer in Las Cruces, and she had agreed to come to see Carol's California paintings sometime late in January. Elizabeth knew that she should leave before Celia arrived. She could only speculate why this woman was coming here in the middle of winter. She felt no jealousy. Instead there was relief that Carol would have someone here to help.

Elizabeth began gathering her possessions together. She hadn't actually brought that much. Why was that? Had she sensed that it was not going to be a permanent move? Maybe it meant that she wanted to discard everything from her past and start fresh, a romantic commitment to a life with Carol? Had she really been willing to sacrifice everything for Carol? She heard one of the cats padding its way down the hall. Penelope looked in the doorway, then sidled up to Elizabeth, who sat on the floor and held out her hand. Penelope rubbed her head against the out-stretched hand, eyes closed, ears flattened, then stepped daintily into Elizabeth's lap. The cat stretched and purred as Elizabeth stroked its silky fur, remembering her dog, Jewel. She missed him and knew that her decision not to get another animal had been made out of fear. It had seemed a safe decision not to get too involved with anyone or anything.

* * *

After the New Year, Sally and Carol drove Elizabeth to the Arcata-Eureka airport in McKinleyville for the connecting flight to San Francisco. As they drove away from the house, Elizabeth turned around.

Carol said, "It's not as if you can never return, you know."

Elizabeth smiled wistfully. "Yes, but it will be different the next time."

Sally interjected, "Yes, and won't we all be, too."

They laughed to break the tension.

Carol took her hand. "Liz, it's not like the last time–you know that–don't you?"

She smiled. "Yes, I know. It's so hard to leave you."

"But you'll be back. You owe me some time in California. And you do like it here? So I expect you for yearly vacations. That is, if you can extricate yourself from the gardens for a while."

"Oh, Carol, I'll miss you so much." She reached out and held her close.

"I feel the same, Liz. I'm trying hard not to cry."

"Don't get femme on me now, Carol. It's too late for that."

They laughed.

When Elizabeth's flight was announced, they walked her to the gate. She remembered how frightened and excited she had been when she came to live with Carol. Now she was only frightened about starting her life in Connecticut.

WINTER DREAMS

The Garden

A tomb of life, not death,
Life inward, true,
Where the world vanishes,
And you are you.

–Vita Sackville-West
Winter

Similar Features

The short winter days were cold, and clear. Five inches of new snow covered the ground so that it was impossible to see the condition of the gardens. Elizabeth was first disappointed and then relieved, because it meant she had the luxury of time to adjust to being home. She was content to be alone and surprised that she could admit to the tension she had felt with Carol. Always wondering if she had said the wrong thing, done the wrong thing. What would Carol think of this? Would Carol be upset over that? Everything hidden was lifted to the surface of her consciousness. She had no control over the memories and the intuitive understanding of the memories. Other women whom she had known in college and women she had barely been with flickered in and out of her daily thoughts. They were fragmented, flashing glimpses into her private life. Experiences that seemed so disconnected from each other were recollected as if there were some kind of order and plan to each and all of them. In her ruminations, she thought that if she could find the link between all of these memories she would come to some important understanding of her life, save herself. From what? Future pain? She didn't really know, but the images persisted, running into each other, like a badly cut film, moving from scene to scene without any real story line. The most frequent reflections had to do with Veronica. Elizabeth supposed that was because Veronica was nearby. She thought of these memories as a video autobiography. At times she was depressed by them, and sometimes disturbed. At other times it seemed that she was detached from her deepest feelings, removed from feeling altogether. This worried her because she understood that it had always been a part of her self-protection. Don't give too much, so you won't get hurt too much.

She carried in some logs from the woodpile and started a fire in the fireplace. When it began to crackle, she lay down on the couch in the living room with a lap robe over her and stared at the painting over the fireplace. She could almost hear her dog bark, and she drew in her breath and inhaled the strong, musky odor of the sweated horse. The aroma still lingered in the closet where she kept her riding boots and jodhpurs. Agitated now, she threw off the lap robe and went to the long French doors looking out over the gardens and the lawn in the back of the house. The snow lay in drifts over the shrubs and plants and accumulated like white birds' nests in the notches of the tree trunks and branches. The lawn sloped down to the river, and in the swift current Elizabeth could make out tree limbs and branches being carried downstream. There was an eerie light; the sky was flat gray and cloudless. She knew it would snow again soon and the temperature would not warm up above what it had been this morning.

She pulled on another heavy sweater and her insulated boots, zipped up her down jacket and walked out into the cold afternoon. She wondered what the weather was like at Carol's house in northern California. She drove into town to the big supermarket and parked in one of the plowed parking spaces. Some people had their headlights on already. Couples were bringing their canvas bags and sacks ready to store up for the terrible weather they knew was on she way.

Elizabeth took a cart and started making her way up and down the food aisles. She reminded herself to stop by the pet shop and pick up some more birdseed, just in case she couldn't get out tomorrow. As she entered one aisle, she saw a familiar face.

"Excuse me, aren't you Kelly? We met a few years ago."

Kelly looked at her with a blank expression, then smiled. "Yes, of course. We met at a hospital party." She held out her hand. "Kelly Hodges. You're Elizabeth Sanderson." She paused, "I thought you'd gone out to California. I'd heard that you and Carol . . . is Carol here?" She looked around. "I heard you both were in California."

"No, I'm back here for good now. How's your friend Lilly?"

Kelly shuffled. "Lilly and I aren't seeing each other anymore. In fact, we haven't spoken for over a year. Lots of bad feelings between us. That's the way it goes sometimes."

"Oh, I'm sorry. Anyway it was good to see you . . . a familiar face." She smiled.

"I'd better get going before the snow," Kelly said.

"Sure." Elizabeth looked out of the large glass windows at the front of the store. "Yes, looks like it's going to be a big one."

"Take care." Kelly walked away.

"You too," Elizabeth called after her.

She stood in the aisle for some few seconds after Kelly left, not expecting that she would be so nervous telling people about Carol. She didn't want to bump into Kelly again. Kelly had been Carol's friend. Maybe they had been lovers. *I'm sure she felt uncomfortable seeing me. Well, there are so many people to call. Friends whom I just about deserted when I left. And . . . Veronica.* She hadn't realized how many of Veronica's physical movements she had unconsciously stored in her memory, the way her hands moved, the silhouette of her body in the dark, the way her hair swung away from her face as she turned her head. She stopped short as soon as she realized how she was now romanticizing Veronica. She was furious with herself for always needing someone to fantasize about, someone to take up her thoughts. She wouldn't call her. It was too embarrassing. She had to let her go. And if she were Veronica, she certainly wouldn't want to see Elizabeth anyway. She finished her shopping, avoiding Kelly, and drove back home just as the first snowflakes started to fall.

There was still a small fire going, and Elizabeth threw on some more wood that blazed up instantly. She put the groceries away and thought about what she would do for the rest of the afternoon. She didn't want to call any of her old friends just yet. She sat down to read the local paper. It was Friday, and she thought about going out someplace. There was always the danger of running into Veronica or someone who knew her and she wasn't ready for that meeting.

Turning the pages of the paper she saw an article that caught her eye. There was a dog show scheduled for Saturday in Hartford. That appealed to her. She would go to bed early and get up early, go to the dog show and find a dog to replace Jewel, to make this place alive and like her home again. She was tired of living in the past, looking at the ghosts in the portrait above the fireplace. She hoped it would stop snowing so she wouldn't have any trouble with the roads.

The next morning there was a slick crust covering the hardened snow in the driveway, but Elizabeth was determined. She was excited and hadn't felt this way for a long time. If only she could find another dog like Jewel. She slowly maneuvered the slippery driveway, listening to the frozen top layer of snow break under the weight of the car. The highway had one lane open, and she drove carefully, following the signs to Hartford.

A front loader blocked the entrance to the large parking lot. They were still clearing away the snow. She waited impatiently in the line of cars, assured by a large sign fastened to the metal link fence of the parking area that the lot would be open in just a few minutes. Elizabeth noticed vans unloading dogs and searched for the German Shepherds. Inside the lot, against the fence, one woman had already opened her van door and was beginning to take out the dogs. Elizabeth wondered what the breed would be. A large dog bounded out of the side of the van. Seeing the snow, it immediately began to roll in it. It shook itself a few times, lifted up its pointed head and began to howl. For a minute, Elizabeth thought that it must be a wolf. The woman was having trouble controlling the excited animal. Elizabeth was so involved with this scene that she didn't notice the cars in front of her moving into the lot, nor did she hear the honking of the cars behind her. She drove ahead and parked in one of the marked spaces. She was intrigued with the dog she had just seen. There was something so wild looking about it. It could have been a wolf. It certainly did not seem like a household pet. It looked like it was born to be outside. She quickly locked her car and walked to the van she had been watching. The woman was still there. She had unloaded three dogs. They stood in the cold, their noses pushed into the snow that was piled up against the metal fence. When Elizabeth approached, they looked at her in an unconcerned way, wagged their tails and howled. She couldn't read the howl. Was it threatening? Was it a greeting? She remembered that Jewel would bark whenever someone came too close to her. She smiled, remembering that Jewel had protectively walked next to her in the house, suspicious when Carol first arrived, and constantly positioning herself between the two of them, her body tense, ready to spring at this strange woman who had invaded their world. What did these dogs mean by their howls? The owner of the dogs was having a hard time getting all of her equipment together, watching to make sure that the dogs were securely tied and trying to shush them. Elizabeth walked up to her.

"Hello, you look like you might need some help. I'm going to the show, but I'd be happy to help if you need me to do anything."

The woman looked up startled. "What? Oh, yes. These dogs . . . they're just so crazy about the snow. I hope I'll be able to get them inside. I should have taken one at a time, but when the first one came out and started howling, the others started up, so I thought I'd better let them all out at once."

The woman was older than Elizabeth was and much shorter. Her gray hair, cut in a bowl shape around her head, complimented her gray-blue eyes. She wore corduroy pants tucked into barn boots that came up to her knees, and a dark green, heavy wool turtleneck under her short, bulky, quilted jacket.

"My sister was supposed to come with me today–we're from Springfield, Massachusetts. But she got the flu last night and could hardly walk this morning. I thought about not coming, but I paid so much for the entry fees, I decided to try it alone."

Her voice was deep and gruff. Elizabeth thought she must have smoked too many cigarettes for too many years. The dogs howled again and strained against the leashes. The woman glanced down.

"Quiet, you guys. Can't you see you're scaring the hell out of people?"

Elizabeth looked around as people were judiciously avoiding that area of the parking lot and crossing into the building at another entry. She thought that the dogs did seem ominous.

The woman looked Elizabeth over and finally smiled a half-twisted smile that forced one side of her face to turn up, and crinkled one eye. "Don't worry. They're harmless. Sometimes I wish they could deliver half of what they threaten. Then I'd at least feel safe in my own house. Anyone could walk in there, kill me, steal everything from the place and they'd all still be howling, wagging their tails and probably pointing out the hidden places for silver and jewelry, if they could." She laughed. "They're not stupid, just critters from another world. Take another few thousand years for *this* breed to be voted house pet of the year."

She walked over towards the nearest one, scratched its head and tweaked a large furry ear. "Now you just be quiet." The dog looked up at her, wagged its tail more vigorously, and howled in a higher pitch with more enthusiasm.

Elizabeth realized that the sound was not an aggressive one. She was drawn to these animals that were like wild creatures. The size of the animal and its howling reminded her of something primordial and ancient. They had thick black, white and gray coats. Black patches surrounded their eyes. She reached out to touch one. The long outer hairs were coarse, but the coat underneath lay close to the skin and was soft and thick, like goose down. She put her hand deep into the coat and felt the powerful muscles underneath. When she patted the dog, it turned its large head and faced her. It stopped howling and sat down, its tail still wagging back and forth smoothing the snow. It did not attempt to lick her hand, or rub against her, but seemed to like her touch. She liked the feel of the dog as well.

The dog's owner watched her. "Malamutes are a very independent breed. They never show how they feel, but the bonds can run deep, in a strange way. They're rugged and very strong, as you can see. If you're used to dogs that curl up on your lap or sit next to you in the living room, you'll never get that from this breed. They are a presence, but not always what people expect from a dog." She had trouble holding the largest one back.

"No, I like that about them. I see they have their own ways. They might not even adapt to my ways. It's refreshing. Like living with a creature that has its own world and doesn't want to become part of yours, only share some parts with you. It's companionable, not slavish."

The woman looked at her. "Looks like you've got the hang of the breed right away. My name's Parry. Parry James." She held out her free hand, and Elizabeth shook it.

"I'm Elizabeth Sanderson. I drove up here from New London, hoping to find a dog. My German Shepherd died a few years ago, and it's taken me this long to decide to get another dog." She paused and looked into the amber eyes of the Malamute whose head was larger than hers. "I thought I wanted another German Shepherd to replace my last dog . . . now . . . I don't know if that would be such a good idea." She looked up at Parry. "Some losses are irreplaceable. Watching you and the dogs from my car, I suddenly realized that. I don't want to recreate the past."

"I know what you mean."

"But I'm holding you up, aren't I? Let me help you into the building. I'll be happy to carry anything or to take one of the dogs, if you like."

"Thanks, I would be grateful." She looked at her watch. "We're not due in the ring until this afternoon, but I would like to get them settled and brushed out some before then. I have some carriers and some kennels. If you could help me wheel them in, that would be great."

They managed to get the three excited dogs into the building and locate the area reserved for Malamutes and Huskies. Elizabeth helped Parry set up, holding onto the dogs while Parry assembled the metal crates and set up the grooming bench.

"Are you going to lift them up there? They must weigh a lot."

"About 90 to 110 pounds," she said. "Got to keep up your strength."

"Do you do this *every* weekend?" Elizabeth asked.

"About once or twice a month is all I can do. I have to work, and between that and this I'm pretty busy. Showing is what you have to do if you want to be in the dog breeding business. And that's what I want to do."

"Do you have a kennel in Springfield?"

"Well, I don't know what kind of picture you have in your head, but I guess some runs and an out-building would classify as a kennel. Most of the time I just let them stay in the house with me. They keep me company, and especially when the puppies come, I like to keep them warm, at least for a while. Can't say as *they* much like it though. As soon as I open the door, there's a mad dash for the exit. So much for being a stay-at-home." She reached down and scratched the head of the largest dog that looked at her, its head cocked to one side as if listening to the story. "Isn't that right, Kotz? Just can't wait to get out."

The dog instantly started to howl. "Whoops, said the magic word, didn't I? Sorry fella, I forgot."

"What's his name?" asked Elizabeth.

"Name's Kotzebue's Arctic Dream. We call him Kotz for short. He's the champion. Best in breed for the last two years in New England. I don't have the money to take him all over the country. Some of these breeders have handlers and people to show the dogs. I have to do it all myself." She looked over at the large dog, who was listening to her. "Yup, just you and me boy, right?" The dog got up, howled and wagged its bushy, raccoon-like tail. She looked at Elizabeth. "Thanks for all your help . . . and for the company."

Elizabeth thought she was keeping Parry from her work. "Oh I was glad to help. I'll just walk around and look. Maybe I'll *see* you later." It was more of a question than a statement, and Parry did not respond.

Elizabeth walked around the benches and dog crates, talking with the dog owners and handlers at the show. She walked into the arena where three judgings were going on at once. One ring had Irish Setters, another Golden Retrievers and a third English Cocker Spaniels. These were all popular dogs, and she knew that it would take quite a while to choose best in breed. She wandered back towards Parry's section, stopping for a while to look at the Siberian Huskies. Too small and wiry, she thought. Still, they, too, had that exotic look of a wild animal, somehow unrelated to any domestic dog. Parry had Kotz on the table and was brushing and combing his coat. Elizabeth stood back and watched. Parry's skilled hands smoothed and then ruffled the coat to give it depth and bulk. The outer bristles shone. Kotz stood calmly, seeming to enjoy the attention. Elizabeth decided not to bother Parry any more. She looked for the German Shepherds. When she came upon their area, her heart beat a little faster. They were so beautiful . . . their coats blue black and orange brown. That's the problem. I'll always be thinking of Jewel, comparing this one to Jewel. I can't afford that now. She tore herself away from the Shepherds feeling that she would begin to cry right there. She went to the dining area and sat down with a cup of coffee, trying to get this feeling to pass. It was paralyzing. Her first instinct was to go home. This was all a mistake. She didn't want another dog. She wanted her old dog back. She wanted her old life back. That was it. God, she thought, how it creeps up on you when you are least aware.

"Mind if I join you?"

It was Parry, carrying a tray. "I'm famished. Haven't really eaten anything at all today."

Elizabeth looked at the donut and coffee on the tray. "That's hardly going to keep you."

"Well, I'll just come back later for the greasy burger and Coke."

"What time do you go in for the judging?" asked Elizabeth.

Parry looked at her watch. "Oh, about another two hours if they manage to stay close to schedule. You know, I never gave you my card. Just in case you ever get up to Springfield, or if you decide you want a Malamute instead of a German Shepherd."

Elizabeth took the card. "I've just been sitting here thinking about whether I really want any dog at all." Tears came into her eyes, and she looked down into her coffee cup.

Parry paused between bites of her donut. Elizabeth had a moment of anxiety when she thought that Parry would lean across the table and pat her hand, but Parry did not move.

"I'm sorry. You must think I'm some kind of case, but I . . ." She decided not to embarrass herself by confessing her whole life story to this total stranger.

Parry concentrated on her coffee. "My offer for the dog still stands." Her voice was low and soft. They sat silently, Parry finishing her meal. She wiped her lips, pushed herself up from the table and leaned down, forcing Elizabeth to look directly at her. "I've had those feelings at times. Sometimes we think we want to relive the past, but it's best not to repeat it."

Elizabeth started to say something in response. Parry stood up and smiled warmly at her. "There's nothing you have to say. We'll be in touch." She walked away towards the benched dogs.

Elizabeth sat there for a while longer, listening to the barking dogs, and the snatches of conversation from people who passed her table. *I'm not ready to move on yet. I've just moved back. I have to have time. Time for what? Time is all I have anyway.* She felt confused and upset. Even a simple afternoon had become an emotional event. Was nothing casual for her anymore? How could she continue like this when she felt so raw?

Elizabeth concentrated on the handlers, the dogs, and the judging in the various rings. When the Malamutes appeared, she applauded for Parry and for Kotz, who looked in her direction; Parry smiled, and Kotz howled, his tail wagging. There were not many entries in the Malamute breed, and Parry's dogs were far superior to the others, whose coats were not as thick and bone structures not as heavy or sturdy. Even she, a novice with the breed, could see that Parry was going to win again. After the judging she went to congratulate the best Malamute breeder in New England. She found Parry sitting on a stool, holding forth to some other breeders. All of them gathered around Kotz. When Elizabeth approached, Parry waved her hand and motioned for Elizabeth to join them.

"He wants to buy Kotz and use him in a breeding program in Missouri." She pointed her chin in the direction of a man in a western suit talking to another woman who glanced now and then at the dog sitting in front of Parry.

"Sell Kotz? No, no, Parry. He's the best you have. He's very valuable. You can't. You shouldn't." She realized that she was getting too involved with a woman she didn't know over a dog that wasn't hers. Still it wasn't right either for the dog or for Parry. His life and Parry's too, she suspected, would be changed forever and not for the good, either.

"But, he's offered me a lot of money for Kotz, and I need it if I'm going to continue. It's what it's all about, anyway, buying and selling dogs and breeding them."

Elizabeth could hear her voice harden. She had already made up her mind.

"You . . . you don't have to tell him now do you? Not right this very minute?"

Parry laughed a sad, cynical laugh. "Yes, yes, I do. Right now. He's leaving and wants to take Kotz with him."

Elizabeth looked over at the man. He had glanced up at her and half smiled, not knowing who she was or what her relationship to Parry was.

"Come on. Let's get some coffee." She took Parry by the elbow. "First let's put Kotz back in his crate." They walked over to the food area. Parry looked glum.

"You need some food. Your head isn't too clear. I'll get you a hamburger and some fries. We'll sit and have a coffee together and discuss this after you've eaten something."

When Elizabeth returned with the food, Parry was staring blankly down into the Formica table, her head resting on both hands. Elizabeth put the food down and sat opposite her.

"I know you mean well, Elizabeth. You're a dog lover, and so am I, but you don't understand. I have to do this."

"No you don't. You just think you have to. What will your own breeding program be worth if you sell your best dog?"

"He offered me pick of the litter as well as the money."

"Parry, you can get that from anyone. Can't you see? Your dog has been a champion for a few years. Things are starting to happen for you. Don't sell it for the short run and sell your future opportunities."

"But I need the money. The money would allow me to travel and show the other dogs. They're not as good as Kotz, but I could build up the breeding program again."

"No, no you couldn't, you wouldn't. I know. Once you sell your favorite, your best dog, you'll regret it. You'll never have the heart to start again."

Parry looked up at this woman who spoke with such conviction and passion about her dog.

"I bet you're the one on the block who feeds all the strays."

Elizabeth laughed and grabbed her hand. "Parry, don't do it. You'll be sorry if you do. You'd be making a terrible mistake. He's not the only one who wants Kotz. Other breeders will want a puppy of his. You'll see. Have faith and wait."

Parry pushed her hand away. "Okay. Okay. My sister would never talk to me again if I came home without that dog, anyway. But you surely are some talker." She laughed.

"I'll help you out. I love your dogs. I know things are starting to break for you now." Elizabeth had not realized that she was going to say that, but as soon as it was out of her mouth, she knew that it was true. She wanted one of Kotz's puppies. She wouldn't go back on her offer now.

Parry looked at her. Her eyes glinted as she appraised Elizabeth's offer.

"What do you mean?"

"I mean I'll help. I'll help you show more often so that Kotz can become a champion, the way he deserves to be, and you can become the breeder you want to be."

"And what do you want from this?"

She contemplated for a while. "I don't know yet. I only want to stop you from making a terrible mistake." She looked over at Kotz. "I want that dog, myself." Parry looked startled. "No . . . not really him. He belongs with you. But I would like to have one of his puppies. The one that is most like him. And I'll pay you top dollar, and you can show and breed him, too."

Parry looked at Elizabeth and then over to Kotz. "Well that's an easy, honest request. I can absolutely guarantee you a wonderful puppy."

"Look, Parry, I don't want to be your partner or go into the dog breeding business, but I can offer some advice, as a disinterested stranger."

"No, I know that you're right. I was tempted, but I won't sell him." She paused, still looking over at the dog. Her voice wavered when she turned to Elizabeth. "Thank you."

"Whew." Elizabeth smiled. "I'm glad that's settled." She looked at her watch. "I can help you load up the dogs if you'd like. It's getting late."

Parry pushed herself away from the table. She paused and squinted her eyes to look up at Elizabeth. "I think you got more than you bargained for today, didn't you? I know I did." She held out her hand.

Elizabeth took Parry's hand in both of hers and squeezed it. "Thank you, Parry."

In the parking lot they exchanged numbers, and Elizabeth said that she would call her and see how everything was going. Parry was going to send her a schedule of all of the upcoming shows in the New England area.

She drove home in the early darkness, thinking that she hadn't thought of Carol or Veronica all day. Somewhat confused, but excited about her meeting with Parry and the dogs, she felt good about involving herself in Parry's life.

The house was dark and cold when she walked in. She made a mental note to always leave some lights on or to get a timer to turn on the lights automatically. Still, she did not feel her usual depression, but was energized and hopeful. She looked forward to speaking with Parry and waiting for her new dog. Having a puppy to train would be exciting. Walking into her study, she saw the blinking light on her answering machine. She rewound the tape and listened to the anxious voice of Al De Simone, the Dean for Academic Affairs. After the prologue of welcoming her home, the Dean told her the real reason for the late call. Tom Hogley, one of Elizabeth's colleagues, had just been taken to hospital with a stroke. He obviously would not be able to meet his classes in the spring semester. Al had heard that Elizabeth was back in Connecticut. Would she please, he begged her, step in and teach Tom's classes? He went on apologizing for the short notice, but it was an emergency. The classes were filled, and there was no one to take over and no way to cancel the classes, either. Elizabeth sat back in her chair. Al had left his home number, asking Elizabeth to get back to him. She sat and thought about this. First, she was not prepared. Second, she didn't want to do this. She really didn't know if she could walk in and teach a class again. She needed the spring and summer to pull herself together. But what excuse could she give for not doing it? The university had been very good to allow her the extra leave to go to California. She looked at her watch. She didn't have to call him immediately. She would think about it overnight, and try to find a good excuse to gracefully decline the request.

Monday morning, Elizabeth knew that she had to call the Dean.

"Good morning. Is this Dean De Simone's office?"

"Yes, the Dean is in a meeting. Can I take a message?"

"Ummm, yes. This is Elizabeth Sanderson. He called me last week about some classes that Tom Hogley was scheduled to teach, and I wanted to . . ."

"Oh, yes. Isn't it just awful, someone so young? There was nothing any of the doctors could do. He went so fast. He left a wife and two small children. It's just terrible. I'll tell the Dean you called. Let me get down the name and number."

Elizabeth realized that this must be a new secretary because she didn't know who Elizabeth was.

"He'll know my number. Just tell him that Elizabeth Sanderson called. That's like Anderson but with an 'S'. Thanks."

She hung up the phone. She had known Tom just slightly. He had come on the staff last year. How could she refuse to teach now? And maybe it was what she was meant to do anyway. She would get all of the details of the classes and begin preparation. Tom had probably ordered some books, maybe set up some guest lectures and site visits. She should try to get his class syllabus. A call to the college bookstore confirmed that the books Professor Hogley ordered had arrived and were on the shelves. The manager said that Elizabeth could get them when she came in. The roads had all been plowed, so getting to the campus would not be a problem. No, she thought, the only problem will be what to do when I get there. She would have to find her old notes on landscape design and theory. She was certain that Tom had probably set up some practical site development projects for the spring besides the conceptual class drawings. The second course on conifer maintenance and pruning would be a practical one on corrective shaping with lots of hands-on work.

Walking on the campus again seemed foreign to Elizabeth. It was still beautiful, especially in the winter with the bare outlines of the old trees setting off the stone buildings. The wide walkways had all been cleared and sanded, and the entire scene looked like a typical New England winter painting. The day was sunny but cold. It would not get above the 20 degrees that had been predicted by the weather report but, at least, it would not snow again. Elizabeth wanted to go to her office first, to look for her old notes on the classes that she had taught several years ago. Then she had an appointment with Dean De Simone to discuss her programs for the spring semester. Opening her office door felt like she was entering the life of another person, the person she had left here, before

California. Truly BC. Now, she was AC. She turned up the fan in the radiator behind her desk. The room warmed up instantly and seemed cheerier than she remembered. Mail covered the top of her desk, and she was overwhelmed with the thought of going through all the requests for letters of recommendation, thank you notes, journals of one kind or another, examination copies of books, announcements of lectures and conferences. She looked at her watch and realized that she had no time for sorting things out now. In her file cabinet she discovered the lecture series on landscape history and design she had given several years ago. She looked over her notes and thought that they would do as a beginning for this class. She would write the syllabus for the course on conifers after she picked up the book reserved in the bookstore. She went to the window again and leaned against it, looking out on the compact campus. It was so removed from the life of New London, or any city for that matter. She picked up her briefcase and left her office to keep her appointment. Hunched up, her long tweed coat lined with thinsulate seemed to do little to prevent the bone-chilling cold from stiffening all of her muscles. She had wrapped a long scarf around her neck and pulled it up to cover as much of her head as possible. She walked faster than her usual pace, the wind running up her flannel trousers and penetrating through her coat and thick sweater into her very backbone.

*   *   *

Looking out of the second story library window, Veronica was stunned to recognize the familiar walk and body movements. She looked away from the window and then returned her gaze. Maybe it was an illusion caused by the bright light, the blowing snow. But no, it was she. There could be no mistake. She watched Elizabeth braving the cold, head down, walking quickly towards the administration offices.

When Elizabeth entered the building and could be seen no more, Veronica went back to her chair and her notes. She sat still, her head resting against the large green leather club chair, her arms tense in her lap. She closed her eyes. It had been almost a year since she had received the first letter. She had not responded, but she had kept the letter, had kept them all, as a matter of fact. Sometimes she took them out to look at them again. She hadn't expected Elizabeth to return. *Why has she come back? Is it for a short time, to collect her things and give up her appointment permanently?* Veronica's head dropped to her chest so that no one sitting at any of the tables close by could see the tears forming. She covered her eyes with her hand and took several deep breaths. *How long has Elizabeth been back? She hasn't called. Obviously, she doesn't want to see me.* That realization hurt more than she wanted to admit. Even after that last morning in New York, Veronica wanted to believe that she had been someone special in Elizabeth's life. *I should call her, go to her home, and tell Elizabeth that I've missed her terribly. And then what . . . more of the same? Nothing has really changed. Where is Carol? Maybe she returned with Elizabeth. Probably set up their wonderful little household together again.* She slammed her hands down on the chair arms and made such a loud sound that all heads turned towards her. Veronica looked up into the puzzled faces of the other students. She had suffered by allowing herself to be open and vulnerable. She quickly gathered up her books, threw on her leather jacket and walked out of the library as quietly as possible, but she really wanted to break things, throw books all over the room, take a steel bar and shatter every window in the place.

She ran to her motorcycle, her knapsack slung over one shoulder, swinging against her back, as she again fought back the angry tears. She pulled on her helmet, buckled it too tightly under her chin and pinched the skin. She swore and kicked at the snow with her heavy black boots.

"*Stop it. Stop it. You're out of control. Take deep breaths. Don't start the engine until you've calmed down,*" she said to herself in a half whisper. She kicked the starter, turned the throttle and the engine came to life. She turned on the lights, as a precaution, and slowly pulled out of the parking lot.

* * *

Elizabeth extended her hand to Al De Simone, who pulled her close and gave her a warm hug and a friendly kiss on her cheek. He was an attractive man in his forties, with thick gray hair trimmed closely around his round, fleshy face. He was about six foot three, and in his younger days had been involved in professional sports. Basketball, maybe, she tried to remember. He was always carefully dressed, which seemed out of place on this campus whose students and faculty had dirt under their fingernails, wore ankle-height boots, and sometimes came to class in muddied overalls or jeans. With his tall frame, large shoulders and handsome face, he could have been a model, she thought.

"Everyone's missed you. I'm sorry that you had to come back to teach earlier than we had planned, but because of the circumstances . . ." His voice faded off. He put his hand to his forehead and motioned her to the small settee on the side of the room opposite his desk. He pulled a chair alongside for himself, and coughed to clear his throat. "I'm really grateful. Is there anything I can do to help you, Elizabeth?"

She didn't know what he meant. Was he referring to Carol? Her body became tense. She didn't want his sympathy about the failures in her personal life. She didn't want to reveal too much about how she felt or what she thought.

He went on. "You know, Elizabeth, it was such a shock. He was so young. Just last week, we had all been together, both our families for dinner, and . . ." He looked up at her and there were tears in his eyes. Elizabeth was relieved, grateful to him for avoiding any reference to California. He did not ask about Carol, even though he had met her several times at university activities. She met his gaze trying to convey some sympathy for the loss of his friend. She waited for him to regain some control, and finally he spoke again, very professionally academic, almost impersonal, but Elizabeth understood that that was the only way he could continue.

"I spoke with the bookstore. They said that you had called. I got the class rosters for you. You know you don't have to follow Tom's syllabus if you don't want to."

He got up, walked behind his desk and reached underneath some papers to remove a manila folder.

"Tom's syllabus, his notes and the class rosters." He gave the folder to Elizabeth.

"Thank you, Al. This was very thoughtful of you, considering your own loss . . . to think of me even now. I . . . . I appreciate your concern."

"Well," he attempted a small smile, "for what it's worth, and considering the circumstances, welcome back."

She returned his smile.

"I'll see you at the beginning of term," he said.

"Yes, yes, I'll drop by. Let you know how it's going." She stood for a second, trying to find some consoling words.

Walking back to her office, Elizabeth wondered if there were something more she could have done to express her sympathy. She hadn't realized that he and Tom had been such close friends. *I don't think I've ever really known much about the personal lives of people I work with every day. That's not really such a big surprise. Only two people in this world really know me, and then only aspects of me.* When she got back to her office, she sat at her desk and worked on the syllabus for the class on landscape design. She would come back in a few days to select the slides for her lectures.

Elizabeth returned home late that afternoon to a dark house. She hadn't yet bought the timers. She checked the telephone answering machine for messages. The little red light was flashing, and Elizabeth pushed the playback button. It was Carol.

"Hello, Liz. It's me. I was just thinking about you. I heard that there was lots of snow, and I'm just checking to see that you're all right. Call me when you get in. I'd like to talk with you."

And if I weren't all right . . . what would Carol do about it? Would she fly east and hold my hand? Fix the burst water pipe? Would she be here to shovel the snow from the driveway?

She sat down with a glass of red wine and thought about Carol and California.

Sally had said that Carol was in better spirits although she was on crutches, and the orthopedists felt that she would be able to walk well enough with the help of a cane, but she might always have a slight limp. Her art dealer from New Mexico had visited. Elizabeth laughed when Sally told her that. *But it's not my problem anymore. No. Carol's going to be all right and so am I. We just have to stay apart from each other.* Elizabeth felt awkward calling Carol. The conversation, she knew, would be strained. The transition from lovers to friends was not an easy one. She was unsure about how close she would ever feel to Carol. She warned herself about getting involved in Carol's life. She didn't want to speak with her just now, but would feel guilty if she didn't return the call. She didn't want Carol to worry needlessly.

"Hello."

"Hello, Carol, it's Elizabeth. I got your message."

There was a pause. A woman with a slight accent responded. "No, I'm sorry. I'm not Carol. Please wait, and I'll get her."

Elizabeth's pulse began to hammer in her head. Didn't take long, did it? No, it never did. Elizabeth couldn't believe how her first reaction to a stranger with Carol had been anger stemming from her jealousy. Must be some knee jerk reaction. *Maybe it was a nurse. Sure, sure.* She pictured a nurse dressed in a black lace uniform, cap, with a stethoscope hanging around her neck. She smiled. *Well, whatever Carol wants . . .*

"Hello, this is Carol Travis."

"Carol, it's me . . . Liz."

"Oh, Liz, oh, I didn't know who it might be . . . Celia didn't get your name."

"Oh . . . Celia."

"Yes, she decided to stay longer to help."

"Of course. I'm delighted to hear you're back in form. I'm glad for you and hope you're having a good time?"

"What does that mean?" Carol sounded annoyed.

Elizabeth instantly regretted her hostility. "Nothing. I'm sorry, Carol. It's cold here and I'm tired. I have to begin teaching this spring term because of a faculty emergency, when I was hoping to have the time to myself. I'm a little down." She changed her tone. "How is the physical therapy coming along? I'm sure you'll be as good as ever. You're so strong and determined."

There was hesitation. "I'm trying, Liz, but it's very painful, and the doctors say that I probably will never walk the way I did. I mean . . . I'll walk with a limp and may even need a cane."

Elizabeth closed her eyes tight and blocked out everything except Carol's breaking voice. For Carol, who had traded on her looks, teased, flirted, tantalized women with her athlete's body, with her athlete's strength, the physical imperfections of her body were going to be hard to live with. Elizabeth wanted to tell her that she was still beautiful, that she had never in so many years found someone as exciting as Carol. She bit her lip, and gasped from the self-inflicted pain. She stopped herself from becoming more emotionally involved with Carol than she already was. It wasn't fair to either of them, now.

"Carol, Carol . . . you'll be fine. You're doing fine already." She paused. "You're still attractive. Doesn't Celia think so?"

"She knew me before. What will happen with new people . . . people who didn't know me . . . before? What will they think of me? My body, oh god, Liz . . . how could I have done this to myself?"

She wanted to hold her, kiss her, and tell her not to worry. She would love Carol always, and take care of her. Elizabeth wanted to say this, even though she knew it was not what Carol wanted to hear. Carol wanted to be attractive to everyone, especially to other women. It had nothing to do with whether Elizabeth thought her attractive. She regained her control.

"Carol, I think that you should sit down with the physical

therapists and the doctors and ask them exactly what they mean when they say a limp. Will it be permanent? Can you remedy it in some way? Then I think you should spend some time talking with Sally. If not Sally, because you're friends, then someone she recommends. Maybe someone in another town or city." There was no response on the other end of the line. "Carol, can you hear me?"

"Yes, yes, Liz."

She heard Carol blow her nose. Carol had put her hand over the receiver and said something to someone else who was in the room. "Carol? Carol? Are you still there?"

"Liz, I was just telling Celia not to worry. She saw me crying and came into the room. She was upset."

"I'm glad that you have someone there for you, Carol." There was an even longer pause. "Have you started to paint again?"

"Yes, I'm back to painting." Carol was still sniffling and Elizabeth knew that she was trying to control herself as well. "I've started a new painting of the redwoods. I like it very much. Some days I get very tired . . . but I'm trying." Another long pause. "Celia says that my paintings are selling well. She wants to have a show for me next year, but that will depend on how much work I can get done. I did mention that Celia is my dealer from New Mexico, didn't I?"

"I remembered the name."

"Right, of course, you were here when I went down there to meet with her."

Elizabeth didn't mention that Carol had told her that Celia was married to one of Carol's high school friends and thought it best not to press for any further explanations. Everything with Carol was a roller coaster ride that never stopped. But she reminded herself that she had gotten off the ride. She rubbed her hand on the back of her neck. She was getting tense. There was nothing to say. Anything now might lead into dangerous areas.

"Carol. I'll call you next week, and you can catch me up on all of the events in California."

"Yes, thanks, Liz. That's a good idea. I know you're disappointed about not having the time to yourself this winter to get readjusted."

"Actually, the more I think about it, it's probably better that I work anyway. It's a long winter up north," she reminded Carol. What was she trying to do? Did she want to make Carol feel guilty about leaving her alone? There was no Celia in her life to keep her warm during the cold nights. Elizabeth regretted revealing anything about her emotional state to Carol.

"Right, I remember. This little cowgirl nearly froze her butt off there that first winter." Another long pause. If Carol had picked up on Elizabeth's complaint, she didn't let on, and Elizabeth was grateful for that. "Liz, promise me that you'll keep in touch. Please, it means so much to me. I love you."

She closed her eyes. How desperate she had been to hear those words from Carol. Only now she was able to understand what Carol's definition of loving her meant. "I can say the same thing Carol." She couldn't tell Carol that she thought of her almost all day long. What would be the purpose? "Carol, you can depend on me. Call me anytime. Are you all right now?"

"Sure, sure, just a momentary lapse into self-pity. I'm fine now. I'll speak with you soon, Liz. Maybe I'll send you a Polaroid of the redwood painting to get your opinion. Would that be okay?"

"That would be wonderful. I'll look forward to seeing your latest, but you know I'm already a prejudiced critic. I love all of your paintings."

"Thanks, I seem to need a lot of boosting right now."

"Well, you called the right person."

"Thanks, Liz."

"Good-bye, Carol." She waited to hear Carol hang up the telephone and then she disconnected.

The Way I Want It to Be

Despite the cold and the dangerous road conditions, Veronica had taken the long way home to calm herself down. Her first impulses had been murderous. Elizabeth was back. Why was she back? What happened? She practically shouted at herself, *Let it go. It's gone already.* She shut the door to her apartment and leaned against it, out of breath from taking the stairs two at a time.

The steam heat made a hissing sound. Except for that and her hard breathing, it was silent and empty since Kathy had moved back to Hartford a few months ago. Veronica stood looking around the room. This would be her final winter in Connecticut. In just a few months she would be in Colorado at the forest research station and then on a special project in the Canadian Rockies. But most importantly, she would not see Elizabeth. She could hold out, mark off the days on the calendar. Since that last episode in the hotel room in New York, she had convinced herself that her feelings for Elizabeth had not been as intense as they had seemed at the time. She spoke to Kathy about Elizabeth as if it had been a casual affair. She had seen other women, but did not feel close to anyone. She spent more of her time with her family in New Jersey

She walked into her study, which used to be Kathy's bedroom, and sat down at the drafting table. In front of her was the design for a new herb garden planned for the arboretum. She looked at the drawing and began to play with the positioning of the sections. Pictures of Elizabeth's perfectly designed perennial gardens flashed through her mind. She put down her pencil and stared out the window.

I just want to get through these next few months. She rested her chin in her hands. She would call Kathy and see if they could meet for dinner. No! She didn't want to see Kathy and talk to boredom-come about Elizabeth. She wanted to be with someone who knew nothing of her past, who would ask Veronica the easy, standard introductory questions. She grabbed her leather jacket and headed for the door.

It was too cold to go all the way up to Hartford, so Veronica decided to trust the local talent. She probably knew them all anyway. But there was always the small chance that someone new was in town. She started the engine. It was still warm and turned over quickly. She adjusted her helmet and headed for the best known spot in New London.

Veronica's mood changed as she walked into the bar. It was a weeknight, so people would come early and go home early, but there was still some time for fun before classes the next morning. She ordered a beer, pushed up her sleeves and leaned back against the bar. She loved bars that were especially dark, crossing the threshold, adjusting her eyes to the moving shadows. There was a sense of mystery and sexuality that got her excited with possibilities. She would focus on one person, follow her around with her eyes for a while. Then she would allow her fantasy to take over. Sometimes, the way a woman danced became the inspiration for the fantasy. Sometimes her body would trigger a sensation in Veronica. She savored these experiences, allowing herself the indulgence only a few times every few months. Veronica never wanted her encounters to become a routine. This was the bar she had taken Elizabeth to that first night. She had chosen this one in particular because it was so seedy. She knew that Elizabeth would never come here on her own. Remembering that night intensified Veronica's need for a warm body to take home, but it also distracted her so that she did not see the two young women who came in and sat down at the opposite end of the bar from her. They whispered to each other and looked in Veronica's direction. The taller, heavier set of the two got up and went to sit next to Veronica. She ordered a beer.

"Pretty slow tonight, isn't it?"

Veronica turned slowly. The woman looked particularly pale in the unnatural light of the bar. Dark curly hair fell in soft ringlets

around her ears, framing a face which Veronica decided gave her a
look of a kewpie doll with full bow lips, a short upturned nose and
dark round eyes. Her hands were large and thick with blunt long
fingers. Her facial features seemed incongruous with her height,
which Veronica guessed at almost six feet. There was a thickness
to her, and she guessed that this woman worked out and had great
physical strength. A purple wool scarf was tucked into her zippered
black leather jacket. Glancing down, Veronica saw the motorcycle
boots and wondered if she had also come by bike.

"Leave your bike outside?"

"No, we drove up from New Haven."

"We?"

"That's her, over there." She pointed to the woman at the far
end of the bar.

"But, you're over here?" Veronica seemed puzzled.

"Yes, that's right." She motioned for the other woman to come
over, then held out her hand. "Patricia. You can call me Pat."

"Nancy," said Veronica, and took the woman's hand.

"Jo Ann." The other woman had just joined them. Jo Ann was
shorter than Pat but appeared just as muscular. She had the same
dark curly hair with a more angular face, dark eyes, a long nose
and narrow lips. She, too, wore a black motorcycle jacket, and
held a pair of black leather gloves in her hand.

"Is that your bike parked outside?" asked Pat.

"Yes."

"Pretty dangerous for a motorcycle in this weather."

"Well, I don't live that far."

Veronica regretted having given up even that small detail about
her life. She sensed that these two had come here for a thrill, and
it looked like Veronica was it. Now the choice was hers. This was
the excitement of the bars where anything could happen. Sometimes the adventure stayed in her head and sometimes it was real.
No one was forcing her to do anything. They were simply two
women she had just met. Then why was her heart racing, and why
was this bit of fear adding to her excitement? She looked at the

two closely. They all smiled. There was something about women that she trusted.

"Let's have another beer," Pat said.

They ordered another round, and Pat paid.

"Do you live in New Haven?" Veronica asked

"For the time, yes."

"Where are you from?" Veronica looked at Jo Ann and then at Pat.

"Pat's from Pennsylvania."

"Scranton. Couldn't wait to get out of there," Pat interjected.

"And I'm from Troy, in upstate New York," said Jo Ann. She looked at Pat. "That's me, a little farm girl. Couldn't wait to get out of there, either."

"Although it sure is a lot prettier up there than Scranton."

They both laughed at some inside joke. Veronica felt uncomfortable. These two, one on either side of her, made her nervous. They turned their attention back to Veronica.

Pat asked, "Nancy, you come from around here?"

"No, no, I'm originally from New Jersey."

Now that they had exhausted the geography lesson, Veronica thought they would move on to vocation, followed by hobbies and interests. Instead they listened to the music and said nothing. There was an awkward silence. Maybe there was some signal that she was supposed to give them. After all, they weren't going to jump her here in the middle of the bar. Jo Ann's jacket was unzipped and as she turned back towards the bar to get her drink, Veronica noticed her large breasts crushed against the bar top. She leaned towards Jo Ann and allowed her elbow to brush against one of her breasts. Jo Ann stopped abruptly, looked at her, and a broad smile crossed her face. Pat had seen all of this out of the corner of her eye. She put her arm around Jo Ann and held her close. They kissed, and Pat put her hand under Jo Ann's cotton T-shirt. She looked directly at Veronica and squeezed Jo Ann's breast. Jo Ann began to moan and nestled her forehead in the shoulder of Pat's leather jacket. Veronica felt weak. She had gotten wet instantly. She held Pat's gaze and placed her hand under Jo Ann's jacket and rubbed her back. Veronica removed her hand and so did Pat. Jo Ann looked up at Pat who lifted her chin and kissed her again. She leaned across Jo Ann and, with a seductive smile, whispered, "She likes getting fucked . . . and she likes you."

"Mnnnn. That's right, honey," Jo Ann murmured.

The bartender had discreetly turned away from the three of them.

Pat reached down to Jo Ann's crotch and Veronica knew that she was rubbing her hand up and down just for her.

Veronica swallowed hard. "Follow me."

She pushed herself away from the bar and walked towards the bathroom in the back of the building. Pat and Jo Ann, their arms around one another, followed her. When the three were inside, Veronica shut the door and slipped the bolt. Pat moved forward and pushed her against the door with her full body's weight. She reached down and grabbed Veronica's crotch. Veronica felt the strength of Pat's hands on her crotch. Jo Ann was leaning against the back wall of the small room and rubbing herself, her hand down inside her un-zippered jeans.

"Oh, Nancy, you are one hot babe," Pat whistled in Veronica's ear.

"Do her, honey," Jo Ann called in a low voice to Pat. "Let me see you do her."

"Is that what you want, Nancy? Want me to fuck you, too?"

Veronica was willing to give herself over to whatever happened here.

"Whatever you want," she breathed out.

"Well, I don't want it so fast. That's one thing."

"No, no, Pat, do her slow. Real slow and where I can see her. Inside."

"I'm willing to oblige each of you, just one at a time." Pat gave a husky laugh, and Veronica knew that she, too, was beyond caring that they were in a public bathroom.

Pat squeezed Veronica's breast, moved her large hand down and undid her pants.

"Help me pull them down." Pat was needy, and it excited Veronica to hear the urgency in her voice. She pulled her pants down and stepped out of them and her underpants, leaving them lying on the bathroom floor.

"Yes, oh, god yes." Pat slid her finger up along Veronica's wet crotch. She put Veronica's arms over her neck and moved her hands down to unzip her own pants. Her teeth were into Veronica's neck and she was biting down on her so that Veronica could not see what was happening. Pat pushed Veronica's legs open.

"Open wide for me, honey. Here comes the good part."

She released her teeth from Veronica's neck and used her upper body to pin Veronica to the wall, her heavy thighs between Veronica's open legs. She put a finger inside Veronica, then lifted it up to her mouth and sucked.

"Oh, you taste good. I just knew you would."

Veronica wanted to tell her how she loved the touch of Pat's strong, thick finger, and pushed herself onto Pat's hand. She needed a release from the pressure building in her cunt.

"No," Pat said. "Not that way." Veronica felt something hard pushing against her pussy. Pat's fist was wet against her crotch, and she was pushing into her with a dildo.

"You, you . . ."

"Yeah, I always go out packing. Doesn't everyone?" She laughed softly, put both hands under Veronica's thighs and easily lifted Veronica's legs off the floor.

"Wrap your legs around me. I won't let you fall," Pat whispered in a reassuring voice.

Veronica put her legs around Pat's hips and placed her arms around Pat's thick neck. Pat jammed her shoulders against the door and pumped into her with long smooth strokes, going ever deeper and harder with each thrust. The dildo was pushing against her cervix, and with each plunge, Veronica thought that she would take off and fly.

"Come for me, baby. Come for me. I promise, it's just beginning for you." Pat was sweating and groaning with each thrust that brought Veronica closer to orgasm. Finally, with a scream, muffled in part with her mouth against Pat's jacket, she came, and she came. She bucked and threw herself onto the dildo, wanting it to stay inside her forever. She clung to Pat who was saying something to her that she could not decipher. After a while Pat slid her off the dildo, and Veronica felt her naked ass touch the bathroom's tiled floor. She lay like that for a few minutes till she could catch her breath. She looked up to see Pat standing over her, the long, pink dildo wobbling ludicrously over Veronica's head.

Pat took it in her hand and rubbed the shaft up and down. "This cock goes on forever. No limp dicks here." She looked down at Veronica, and grinned in a calculated way.

Veronica leaned her sweat-soaked head against the back of the door. "After that, I don't think I can go on forever."

Pat looked over at Jo Ann. "Lucky there's more than the two of us then."

Veronica glanced at the back wall where Jo Ann, her hands still inside her jeans, had her eyes half closed and was breathing hard.

"Oooh, you two really did it for me."

"Really?" Pat asked slyly. "Well, I didn't even see it. Did you, Nancy?"

She extended her hand to help Veronica off the floor.

Veronica, her heart still pounding, said, "No, I didn't see it, didn't hear it. Maybe it didn't happen. Maybe you'll have to prove it to us again."

She walked over to Jo Ann and roughly began to strip off her jacket and her shirt, throwing them onto the Formica counter top of the sink.

"Least you could do is let us see it," she said as she pulled Jo Ann's pants down around her ankles, held her legs as she lifted the pants.

Pat was washing the dildo in the sink. It was sudsy with soap and water. She dried it with a paper towel, slipped it back in its harness and walked over to Jo Ann and Veronica.

Pat spoke to Veronica without looking at her. "Jo Ann, here, needs a few things to get her off, don't you? No one hole is enough for her, like any normal person. She needs to be all filled up, don't you, baby? Well, looks like you're going to get what you need tonight. Right, Nancy?"

"We aim to please as well as be pleased," Veronica grinned.

Pat reached inside her jacket pocket and took out a webbed harness and a short, thick, black dildo. She reached into her jeans and took out two condoms. She put the harness, dildo and condom on the sink counter. Motioning to Veronica, she said, "Come and get it while she's hot."

Veronica slipped into the harness, stuck in the dildo and smoothed the condom over it.

Pat had already grabbed Jo Ann and had opened one of the bathroom stalls. She put down the toilet seat and had Jo Ann over her lap. She looked up at Veronica, who was standing against a sink watching them.

"Now for what really warms her up." She had put on one of Jo Ann's leather gloves, and after moving her finger a few times up and down the ass crease, she flattened out her hand.

"Tell me this is what you love, Jo Ann. What you beg me for." Pat brought her gloved hand down on the center of Jo Ann's white ass. She raised her arm higher and smacked her left cheek and then her right. Veronica could see that the skin was turning red. Jo Ann squirmed and put her fist in her mouth to stop from screaming out loud.

Pat looked down at her, her expression fierce with lust. "You love it don't you?"

After a few minutes, it looked to Veronica as if Jo Ann's bottom was going to be pretty sore.

Pat stopped the ferocious pace for a moment and looked at Veronica. "Sometimes she comes just like this. But then I get deprived of what I like to do, don't I, Jo?" And she started in again, this time patting her ass and kneading it like a loaf of bread before each stroke. Now rubbing her ass, now running a finger along the ass crease.

Veronica, watching the two of them, could feel her clit twitching.

Suddenly there was a knock at the door.

"You've been in there a long time, and I really have to go."

Pat paused, and everything held still while Veronica answered. "I'm sorry. I . . . I've been sick in here. I don't know when I'll be out. There's a small toilet out back. Try that."

They heard the footsteps walk away.

"Gave you some time to cool off, huh?" Jo Ann had turned her face towards Pat. Veronica read the expression as fear mixed with pure hedonistic pleasure.

"O.K." Pat pushed Jo Ann off her and stood up. She arched and stretched her back. "Takes a lot out of me, too. But you're worth every last lick, aren't you?" She kissed Jo Ann on the mouth and gave her a strong slap on the ass, forcing Jo Ann's body into hers. She led Jo Ann out of the stall and had her face the mirrors in front of the sink. Jo Ann's arms were on the sides of the sink.

"Now bend over, baby, and take it where you love it."

Pat motioned for Veronica to stand next to her. She leaned over Jo Ann and whispered something into her ear that Veronica could not hear. Jo Ann started to take her arms off the sink and turn around, but Pat forcefully put her arms back in position on the sink and pushed Jo Ann's head down.

She motioned for Veronica to stand closer to Jo Ann. She was breathing hard and Veronica was, too. Veronica wanted to fuck Jo Ann in the ass. She couldn't wait to see the expression on Pat's face, hear Jo Ann grunt her pleasure. Pat rubbed some lube on the dildo that Veronica was wearing, then stepped back.

Veronica moved in back of Jo Ann. She pulled Jo Ann's legs out further away from the sink and pushed Jo Ann's head down. Her ass was exposed and sticking out. Without a word, Veronica began to stroke the crease in Jo Ann's ass.

"All ready for a ride. She's all yours." Pat nodded to Veronica.

Veronica guided the dildo and slowly began to push it into Jo Ann's ass. She got a lot of help from Jo Ann, who pushed herself back on to the cock. Veronica was in deep and she began to speed up her strokes following the desperate moans and groans from Jo Ann. She grabbed Jo Ann's hips and was thrusting harder and faster. Jo Ann was moving her head and crying, holding on to the sink for support. Veronica was practically lifting her off her feet with each inward thrust. Pat removed the pink dildo from her own harness and walked over to Jo Ann.

"Now you really get filled up." She stroked Jo Ann's hair back from her sweaty face and slipped her hand underneath Jo Ann. As Veronica pulled out of Jo Ann's ass, Pat pushed the long dildo into Jo Ann's cunt. When Jo Ann felt it inside her, she began to shake her head from side to side. "Too much, nnnnhhhh, no. . . ."

"No, it's never too much, for you. No, no, baby." Pat reassured her, standing close to Jo Ann, stroking her breasts, smoothing her hair, pinching her nipples and shoving the long dildo inside her, keeping it there as Veronica continued the inexorable ass fucking.

"You know it's what you want. It always is," Pat was saying to her. "Fuck her harder, Nancy. Really slam it into her. She loves it."

Pat moved the dildo around inside Jo Ann, pulling it out and slamming it back into her in rhythm with Veronica's ass fucking. Veronica held Jo Ann up with one arm around her waist, to allow Pat access to her cunt. Jo Ann bent her knees and leaned her weight back against Veronica, who wanted to keep the dildo in Jo Ann's ass as long as possible. Pat nodded, and Veronica pushed Jo Ann back down across the sink again and started to pound into her.

Pat lifted Jo Ann's face and read something there. She looked at Veronica. "She's close now. Very close. I can feel it. Don't stop, no matter what."

Nothing would make Veronica stop. She felt that even her own orgasm could not make her stop. It was as if she and Jo Ann were attached by the dildo. There was no way Veronica would allow it to slip out of her. Jo Ann was getting it in both ends. When she pushed back, Veronica would slide into her hard and deep, when she moved forward, Pat's dildo thrust even deeper. There could be no relief from the pleasure and the pain she was experiencing.

Suddenly, Jo Ann stopped moving. Veronica saw the reflection of Jo Ann's face in the mirror over the sink. She seemed disoriented, her eyes wide, yet unseeing, her mouth open, head thrown back. Pat clamped a gloved hand over Jo Ann's mouth, but Jo Ann tried to shake it off. She pushed back once onto Veronica and nearly knocked her off her feet. Then Jo Ann swung her hips forward, and Pat stepped in front of her and caught her as she fell and slumped in Pat's arms. Veronica watched as Jo Ann's knees buckled and she fainted. Veronica was distressed and looked at Pat.

Pat stroked Jo Ann's hair and hoisted her up so that their bodies embraced. She held her and kissed the slick, wet face. They stood this way for a few seconds.

"Is she all right?"

"She'll be fine." Pat smiled at Veronica. "I could tell that she really liked you. Picked you out right away as soon as we walked in, and was she right."

Veronica was self-conscious, standing naked in a public toilet with a dildo swinging from her hips. She rolled the condom off the dildo, slipped off the harness and went over to the sink. The warm water felt good on her face. She lifted her head to grab a paper towel, and in the mirror saw Pat sitting on a toilet seat with Jo Ann on her lap, knees drawn up, cuddled against Pat's chest. Maybe Pat would have to carry her out of here.

She put on her clothes, feeling awkward under Pat's scrutiny. It was always difficult to know what to say afterwards. They were, in spite of what had gone on, strangers. She looked directly into the mirror and into Pat's open, warm smile. For an instant Veronica wanted to sit on her other leg and nestle as close to Pat as Jo Ann. She continued to wipe her hands on the paper towel.

"She'll wake up in a few minutes," Pat answered her unspoken question.

Veronica turned, "Do you need any help?"

Pat seemed quite relaxed and calm. "Nope, we're just fine. I really enjoyed meeting you, Nancy. Hope you had a good time, too."

Veronica ran her fingers through her damp, sweaty hair. "You two are really the dynamic duo." She shook her head and laughed. "You should bottle it, sell it nationally."

Pat laughed, and her whole body shook. "You're pretty special yourself."

"Well, I guess we've been taking up this bathroom too long. Lucky it's been such a quiet night." Veronica wanted to leave.

"Yes, very lucky." Pat grinned. "You can go whenever you want. I'll just close this stall door till she gets up. Could you pick up her pants and hand them to me? Thanks."

Veronica hung all of Jo Ann's clothes on the hook in back of the bathroom door.

"Bet you'll sleep tight tonight," said Pat with a leer. "Bye, bye, now, hon."

She pushed the stall door shut, and Pat leaned forward to lock it. Then Veronica opened the bathroom door and exited the bar. She did not respond when the bartender shouted a good night.

The cold air made her gasp and cough. Her eyes began to tear. She had trouble catching her breath. Finally, she got to her motorcycle and slid into the saddle. She was sore, and leaning forward hurt just a little. She put her hand up to her bruised neck and winced. She cleared her mind of all thoughts and started up, wanting to get away from the bar as soon as possible. She definitely did not want to be there when Pat and Jo Ann came out.

She looked at her watch. It was one o'clock, but she still had work to do. When she shut and locked the door to her apartment, she began to shake. She knew it wasn't from the cold. She first showered and soaped herself, then sat down in the tub and filled it with water covering her shoulders. She felt the muscles in her body relax and she slipped down deeper into the warmth.

It wasn't until the next morning that she realized the money she had kept in her jeans' pocket was missing. She had taken thirty dollars with her in case of an emergency. Had it fallen out while Pat was fucking her, or had Jo Ann taken it out? There was no way to know. Oh well, she thought, tossing the jeans into the hamper, it was worth the price of admission.

Timing

Veronica stood at the window and read the outdoor thermometer wondering if she had made the right decision to go to Colorado, where the winters would be even colder than the Northeast. She decided to have breakfast at the college cafeteria. It took several tries to start up her motorcycle, but finally the engine boomed, sputtered, and idled nicely. She rode through the snow-covered streets carefully, thinking about the bar last night and what she would do for escape in Colorado. She backed the bike into the parking spot at the arboretum and walked to the cafeteria. The day was overcast and she looked up at the dark sky, thinking another storm was on the way.

Someone called out to her, "Veronica."

She turned around. Jack Meyer waved a mittened hand at her. She waved back, a bit annoyed because she had not wanted to see anyone this morning.

"Wait up." He picked up his pace. She stomped her boots in the wind and the cold.

"Where are you heading?"

"Cafeteria. I need some breakfast."

"Me too. Mind if I join you for coffee?

She looked over at him. They had started the program together. Jack was interested in landscape design and he had already contracted a really good job with a New York architectural firm that designed indoor landscapes for large corporations. They met at a gay bar in New Haven a few months after arriving at school.

The cafeteria was quiet. It was early, and her professors would not be in their offices yet. Veronica got a tray and sat down at a table with her eggs, toast and coffee. Jack joined her with a muffin and coffee.

"Only a few more months of this." He gestured outside. "It's not the cold so much as the dead life here. You know what I mean? I can't wait till I get back to New York."

"Uh huh."

"So I heard you took that job with the Forest Service in Colorado. Where is it? Is it near Denver or Colorado Springs? Lots of dykes in the woods there."

"No, it's in Creede, the middle of nowhere, in terms of Lesbianville."

"Why did you go there?"

"That's why. I need a break from lesbians. Better if I have to search them out." She smiled. "Wouldn't want anything that came so easy."

He laughed. "Not me. The only outdoors I want is indoors that looks like outdoors."

"Right, Jack."

"I'll donate my snowshoes." He sipped his coffee. His narrow, pale face and steel-rimmed thick glasses made his dark brown eyes appear intense.

"Did you hear about Tom Hogley?"

"Yes. It's really a shame. He was the up-and-coming expert in conifers around here."

"You know who's going to take his classes this term?"

She was bored. Did all gay guys enjoy gossiping so much? "No, who?"

"Sanderson. They must have told her to come back or else."

She looked up at him.

"You worked in her gardens one summer, didn't you? I went with a class to see them once. Fantastic! Gave me lots of ideas for moving the outdoors, indoors. Those gardens should be donated to the state and made public."

She grinned. "Right. I'll bet she would just love that."

"I don't really know that much about her."

"Nope, neither do I." She shook her head and smiled at him.

He tried again. "Well, what I meant was . . . you worked for her and all."

"And all?"

"So what's the story there?"

"I don't know. As you said, I just worked in the gardens one summer."

She looked at her watch. "I have to go to the library and do some research." She pushed back her chair. "See you, Jack."

The wind had died down, and she could tell that the storm was going to hit soon. She decided to skip the library and go back home. She turned and walked through the quadrangle towards the parking lot. She fumbled in her leather jacket pocket for the keys to her bike.

She stopped short when she looked up and realized that someone was watching her. Elizabeth stared, and after a few seconds walked towards her. There was a smile on her face. She looked as though she were greeting an old friend. Veronica's fists clenched. Her jaw started working.

"I wondered how long it would be before we ran into one another," Elizabeth said, her eyes never leaving Veronica's face, hoping for a warm greeting in return.

"I heard you were back." She returned the stare and tried not to read too much into the lines around Elizabeth's eyes or the way her mouth drooped.

"You never returned my . . ."

"Let's not talk about that anymore." Veronica cut her off. "I have nothing to say. And if you do . . . you should know it's much, much too late."

"I tried to reach you so many times while I was gone . . . Veronica, I wrote, I called . . . but you wouldn't answer." She looked down at the ground. "So I stopped."

"Gone? You mean while you went off with your 'ex' to live in California?" Veronica moved closer to her. "What did you expect me to do? Wait till you sorted out your life? What about me? What did I mean to you? Nothing, Elizabeth. Nothing. Let's just leave it at that." She waved her hands in front of her. "No, no go away. Leave me. Please."

"Let me explain. You have to know the story. It's important that you know."

Veronica's anger hardened her response. "For who, for me? No! I don't have to know what happened between you and Carol. I don't have to know if she's back here or still in California or what. It's you." She shook her finger and poked it into Elizabeth's chest. "It's for you. You want me to know so that I'll understand *you*. Well, fuck it and fuck you." She shook her head. "You haven't changed. Still beating around the bush. Can't come right out and say or do whatever it is. Still never act on your feelings, or say what you really think."

Elizabeth reached out and grabbed her hand. "Veronica . . . don't." Faculty and students were now parking cars in the lot at a steady rate. Elizabeth pulled her hand away.

Veronica laughed. "See?"

"No, don't go. Not without us talking at least."

Veronica looked at the sky. Her voice was expressionless. "It's going to snow soon. I have to get home."

"Come home with me. Come now!" Elizabeth insisted.

Veronica wavered for a minute, and in that time Elizabeth took her arm and led her into her car.

Inside the privacy of the car, Elizabeth leaned back into the seat. She relaxed her hands on the steering wheel and spoke with a calm resignation. "You're right, Veronica. I know how you must feel." She looked straight ahead out the front window. They sat silently, not looking at each other. Finally, Elizabeth sighed. "It's going to snow. I'll take you home if you want."

"No, Elizabeth. I have to take my motorcycle home and put it inside. I don't want to leave it here with this storm coming."

Neither of them moved.

"I feel so awkward with you. I have nothing to say. We are not who and what we were to each other anymore. It's as if I'm sitting here with a stranger, someone I met for the first time, but not really like that because I feel such a tension between us that I can't say anything."

Veronica shook her head. "Yes, I feel the same way."

Elizabeth sighed. "It makes me so sad."

"Yes, me too."

"Well, what should we do now? You're angry, and I'm embarrassed. I just want to apologize, Veronica. I behaved badly, and you didn't deserve it. I'm sorry. Please accept my apology. You're right. I do feel guilty about you." She paused. "I guess that's all that needs to be said."

Veronica looked up at her. She took a deep breath. "I don't want to know what happened with you and Carol," she said again. Then she smiled. "Well, that's not totally true. I'm curious. Yuuchh! What a crummy word. Curious? More than curious . . . but you don't have to tell me. But if you want to . . . tell it fast." She shut her eyes. "Okay, I'm ready. Is she waiting for you at home in front of the fire?"

"Nooo." Elizabeth drew out the final 'o' sound. "But she's waiting for someone in front of a fire. I'm sure of that."

Veronica opened her eyes. "You don't sound angry about it."

"No, most of the time, especially lately, I'm not angry. I'm glad to be back here. Glad to be on my own. I feel free, and . . . I was going to say happy . . . but I'm not. I'm not exactly unhappy either. I have no expectations and no real plans. Except one."

Veronica hesitated, expectantly. "Yes?"

"I've decided to get a dog again."

Veronica shook her head and laughed. "You mean after a whole year this is the news? You decided to get another dog?"

"Yes, and I'm very excited about the dog, too."

"I don't believe you, Elizabeth."

"Well believe it, because it's true. I went to a dog show last week in . . ."

Veronica interrupted her, "No, not the dog . . . you. I can't believe that this is what you're telling me about the year with Carol."

Elizabeth paused. "I'm following your request. I'm not using you to confide in about my life in California, and I'm not going to tell you anything about Carol. It's no longer of concern to you and me. It's part of my past. Only mine. I'm telling you this to make it easier for you. You and I will not be lovers again, Veronica. I know that. I know that you're leaving for Colorado in the spring."

Veronica looked at Elizabeth intensely. "I don't know how to describe my feelings for you. They were the strongest I've had since Leslie."

"Why not be honest?" Elizabeth reached over and covered Veronica's hands with her own. "Call it love, Veronica, and it was not returned equally with equal passion. I have to be truthful about that. Maybe that's also part of why I feel so guilty about you."

"You weren't going to call me at all were you?'

"No, I wasn't. I've decided to start all over again, and to do that I need to give my emotional life a rest."

"There's nothing new there. You were never comfortable with your own feelings," Veronica said coldly.

"Don't be mean, Veronica. Whether you believe it or not, I still feel close to you."

"I believe it," Veronica replied, "but it will have to be at a distance. My bike's parked over there. I have to go. Take care, Elizabeth." She stepped out, carefully closing the car door. Then she turned and placed her palm flat on the window glass.

"Goodbye."

Elizabeth started to lower the window, but Veronica smiled slightly, turned and walked slowly away from the car.

Whatever she had wanted to tell Veronica about California, or Carol or that day in New York, wouldn't have changed anything, now or in the future. Mixed feelings of frustration and loneliness upset her as she watched Veronica mount her motorcycle and pull slowly out of the parking lot.

Portrait

Elizabeth walked towards the house listening to the crunch and squeak of the packed snow under her boots. Thoughts of Veronica had not left her all day while she sat in her office choosing slides for the landscape course. She had to stop herself from picking up the phone to tell Veronica that she had not meant what she had said. But she couldn't do that because it had been the truth. She removed her boots in the entryway, turned on the lights in the hallway and in the living room. She sighed and studied the lighted rooms. Carol was right; she really did belong here. Her comfort was in the security of her home. She walked into her study and saw the blinking light of the answering machine. For one fantasy-filled moment she thought it might be Veronica. She quickly pushed the rewind and play buttons, and was disappointed to hear Parry's voice.

"Sheba had five puppies a few weeks ago. I thought of you immediately, Elizabeth. They're beautiful and healthy, too young to be taken from their mother now, but they're growing very fast. If you really want one, you should have a look before they're all spoken for. By the way, you remember that fella who wanted to buy Kotz. Well, he called to tell me that he would take my choice of pick of the litter, and he would fly east to look them all over if I wanted. So you were right, Kotz is getting quite a name for himself. I have more people than puppies to go around, but I wouldn't forget you. Call me when you get in. We'll set up a day when you can come up and have a look."

Elizabeth searched for Parry's number on one of the pieces of paper by the phone. "Parry, hello. I just got in and heard your message. Congratulations on all counts. That's wonderful news."

"You were so right about Kotz. He already has a reputation."

"I'm glad you kept him. I can't wait to see them all."

"Do you still want a puppy?"

Elizabeth fairly shouted into the phone. "Of course, of course. How could you think that I would change my mind?"

"Well, the last time we spoke you sounded as if you had so much work to do to get ready for the spring term and all . . . I thought that you had changed your mind."

"About Kotz . . . his puppy? Never."

"Oh, I'm so glad. When can you come and see them?"

Elizabeth looked at the calendar on the wall. "If we don't have another snowstorm, I can drive up on Saturday. You'll have to give me directions."

"Come for lunch, and don't worry about the snow. You can always stay over if a big storm develops."

Elizabeth laughed. "Sure, thank you. You just can't imagine how excited I am about this puppy."

"I think I can imagine that, Elizabeth."

She wrote down the directions to Parry's house and spent the next few days considering appropriate names. At times she believed getting the dog was just another distraction from thinking about either Carol or Veronica. She laughingly thought that she should hire an exorcist to rid the house of ghosts.

*   *   *

She sat in front of the painting in the living room. Lately she had begun to view the portrait with a different perspective. She tried to recreate the moment of the painting.

> *I remember the times she and I . . . I remember her . . . I re-member her.*
> *Memory and creation . . . The past lived in the present,*
> *Re-membering time, people, places. Illusions like silk restraints . . .*
> *The delicate fabric bends under the efforts to cut through.*
> *There is nothing solid in that green field.*
> *My questions are the wrong ones . . . still I persist.*

She looked at the Elizabeth in the portrait with the kind of objectivity that only comes with the passing of time and the waning of emotion. What had that rider been focusing on with that long-distance gaze? She appeared unfriendly, almost arrogant. The expression in her eyes was uncompromising and unresponsive. Had Carol sensed that even then? Surely it had not been conscious. No, it was meant to be a flattering painting of Elizabeth. Art critics had described the painting as mesmerizing, mysterious, and sensual. Yet now she recognized her worst qualities of coldness, distance, lack of passion, amplified in Carol's vision of her. She wanted to speak with Carol and ask her what she had been thinking about Elizabeth when she painted that portrait. Then she realized that Carol would not be able to give her any answers. She sat and studied herself for a long time, until the waning light made it impossible to discern the subtlety of expression on the rider's face, the varied colors of the meadow, or the delineating lines of the horse and rider. She was even more confused about her own interpretation of the persona in Carol's painting.

The Hills of Home

Saturday morning, Elizabeth dressed in her warmest sweater, boots and jacket. She made sure that she took her road map and the directions to Parry's house. It was a fairly simple highway route, and the detailed map of Springfield would be useful.

More than two hours later she turned off the highway onto a single-lane country road. She made a right turn onto Burton Road. A narrow, snow-covered dirt road that gently turned and climbed opening up marvelous perspectives of hills and valleys. She drove slowly, absorbing the pictures of white farmhouses and red barns; Holstein cows in snow-covered pastures pulling hay out of ricks; woolly brown cattle meandering over frozen ground; and horses with thick winter coats galloping energetically in open meadows. This must be just as magnificent in the summer, she thought. Then she saw the wooden fencing, and the horse gate, and the sign above the gate, "Eagle Rock Farm."

She had to step out of her warm car to lift the gate latch to the long approach drive. She breathed in the high country air and coughed. It was colder than New London. There was no large body of water nearby to mitigate the temperatures. Living along the shore of Long Island Sound she still had a New England winter, but it was never as cold as the weather inland. She drove her car through the gate and got out again to secure the latch. She looked up the road and saw the house. It was set on a knoll at the end of a long driveway covered with a hardened layer of snow, which probably turned icy at night.

Elizabeth parked near the house, next to a green pick-up truck. As soon as the car door opened, she heard the howling of several dogs. She was eager to see the dogs again, but walked towards the house. She was sure Parry would want to show her the kennel. Always aware of buildings and landscape, she studied Parry's home.

It was obviously a very old structure. Rounded boulders formed the base, and dark, weathered boards completed the exterior covering for the first and second floors. A large porch gave a feeling of spaciousness. Parry's house didn't resemble the other farmhouses along the road. It looked more like a hunting lodge.

She climbed the steps to the porch and knocked on the door.

"Be right there, Elizabeth."

A few seconds later, Parry opened the door. "Welcome, welcome to my winter paradise," she exclaimed. "I'm glad the snow held up for you. How was the trip? Were my directions clear? You didn't get lost, did you?" She held the door as Elizabeth stepped into the house.

"No, no. Everything was fine. It was an easy drive . . . and a beautiful one, too."

"So you did notice?" Parry grinned. "Anyone who knows anything about landscape can appreciate what we have here." She paused. "But you should see it in the summer. It always takes my breath away. It's so beautiful . . . like living inside a painting."

Elizabeth laughed. "Yes, a true New England winter scene." She looked around her at the huge logs that formed the interior walls; she looked up at the cathedral ceiling and down at the wide oak floors. "This is a very special house, Parry. I'm sure it's special to you."

"Yes, it is." Parry smiled in her diffident way. "Oh, we have lots of time to look at this old house. Sit down–I cooked us up a wonderful lunch. You must be famished after the drive."

"Well, a cup of coffee would be great. Maybe we can take the tour with the coffee in hand."

Elizabeth followed Parry into the kitchen. The room was dark with pine cabinets and red Formica countertops.

"Just what I thought." Elizabeth nodded.

"About what?" Parry asked.

"About this kitchen and how it would look. As soon as I saw the house, I knew how the kitchen would be."

"Really? How could you tell?" Parry sounded embarrassed. "I've been wanting to modernize it for a long time, but . . ."

"Modernize? No way! This is the way it should be." She shook her head and bit into her lower lip surveying the room. "Yes, it's perfect," she nodded.

Parry was at the sink pouring water into an electric percolator. "It'll only take a few minutes. I'm so glad you came. Wait until you see the puppies." She grinned.

"I can't wait, Parry. I feel as if it's Christmas and New Year's all together today."

"Yes, you look happy, Elizabeth. I'm glad." She walked over and patted her shoulder.

"I'd like to see the kennel, but first . . . I can't wait any longer . . . where are the puppies? How many did you say?"

Parry held up five fingers.

Coffee mugs in hand, they set off to see the pups. Parry led her through the dining room. A large oak breakfront stood along one wall. Set up on top of the antique piece were two dozen photos in various sized frames. Some were sepia colored, some old black and white prints. Elizabeth stopped to get a better look, but Parry kept going. She led her into the living room and down a long, wood-paneled hallway. There were bedrooms on each side of the hall, and they, too, were paneled in pine from floor to ceiling. Parry noticed Elizabeth looking into each of the rooms.

"Gets a little monotonous, doesn't it, but it sure saves on painting every few years." She stopped in front of a closed door. "They're all in here." She hesitated, her hand on the doorknob, ready to dramatically reveal the occupants. She opened the door slowly, and Elizabeth followed the sweep of the door, her eyes searching for the puppies. She saw the large Malamute in a far corner of the small room, nestled in blankets and pillows. Suddenly a small furry ball ran between Parry's legs and scrambled down the hallway. Parry shut the door quickly. She started after the lone traveler. "Oh no you don't. That's the second time today you fooled me." The puppy stopped and turned towards the sound of her voice. He sat down on his haunches and howled. Elizabeth was surprised at the depth and resonance of the tone in such a young animal. It must have used every ounce of its small lung capacity. Then it got up, looked at Parry, wagged its tail and took off again, looking back all the time to see if he was still being chased. "It's a big game to him." Parry sounded exasperated. "This has been going on for a few days now. He wants to explore. Now I have to dive under the sofa and chairs trying to catch him. He discovers new places to hide. He's learned that from the cats."

They followed him into the living room. Elizabeth kneeled on the floor looking under the furniture. She heard some panting and saw him lodged under a small love seat attacking the rug with his teeth.

"Oh, no!" She could move the love seat to pull him out, or she could try to reach in and grab him by the scruff. He did seem fairly large and agile for a puppy Parry said was still too young to leave his mother. They stared at each other for a few seconds, both deciding what to do next.

"You've found him?" Parry was out of breath.

"Yes, he's here, safe, sound, and chewing."

"Uh huh! Just as I suspected. All those rawhide chewies I bought down at the feed store aren't good enough." She laughed.

"I'm going to try to get him to crawl out from under," Elizabeth said in an even voice, so as not to frighten the dog.

"I know what he likes." Parry put something into Elizabeth's hand. "Squeeze this. He loves it." Elizabeth squeezed the rubber toy and the puppy cocked its head. She squeezed again, and he dropped the rug and crawled towards the sound of the squeaky toy. When his head emerged from under the sofa, Elizabeth grabbed him and cuddled him in her arms. He lay there on his back looking up at her. His mouth open, pink tongue hanging out. With one paw, he brushed her face. He didn't squirm to get out of her grasp.

Parry leaned against the wall and watched as Elizabeth bent down, kissed the top of the dog's head and rubbed the round belly.

"He seems much older than a few weeks," Elizabeth said. "He's so large."

Parry sat down on the sofa. "He's really my big surprise," she said and smiled. "I tricked you, Elizabeth. The puppies are older than I told you on the phone. I was afraid that if I told you to come up and get one, you'd change your mind."

Elizabeth turned and the conflict expressed in her eyes was obvious to Parry. "I'm sorry, Elizabeth. You don't have to take one if you don't want one." She got up to take the dog from her.

Elizabeth handed Parry the puppy, who looked at Elizabeth and raised his paw to touch her arm. He looked straight at her and howled.

"Trying to get your attention." Parry scratched his head affectionately.

Elizabeth held out her arms, and Parry gave the dog back to her. "Parry, I told you, I've been waiting for this puppy. I'm sure it's what I want." She held him up in the air. He howled a few more times, and then she held him tightly to her chest. She looked at Parry. "Thank you for the surprise. He's perfect . . . a little Kotz."

"Don't you want to see the others?" Parry asked.

"No, I don't have to." She sat down. The puppy relaxed and stretched out on her lap. "Looks as if I've been chosen."

"Well, let's put him back with his brothers and sisters for a while, so we can have lunch."

Elizabeth wanted to hold the puppy on her lap all day, but reluctantly agreed that he should be returned to his litter mates.

Parry took him. He was tired and just dozing off. They opened the door to the small bedroom that served as the puppy quarters, and as soon as Kotz junior entered the room he squirmed to be put down. He greeted the other four dogs with yelps, licks and little nips.

Elizabeth saw the rest of the puppies. They were all gray and black and white, big boned, with shiny thick coats. One in particular seemed to follow Kotz junior, snuggling next to him and licking his face.

"They seem to be attached to each other," Elizabeth observed.

"That happens with litter mates. A few become bonded."

"Are they all sold already, Parry?"

"No, I asked you to come up before I told anyone else."

"I know this sounds crazy, but if it's all right with you . . . I would like to take the two of them. I have a big house and acres of woods where we could take long walks." She stopped and bent down to touch the two puppies. "I suddenly saw the three of us mushing through the snow. I could take them with me to class." She thought of coming home, in the dark, to an empty house. "They would be such good company . . . and protection during those long winter nights."

"I've always preferred their company to most of the people I know," Parry agreed. She watched Elizabeth playing with the two dogs.

"Can I really take them with me? I didn't bring a carrier."

"Don't worry, you can borrow one of mine." Parry looked at Elizabeth and then at the two puppies rolling and playing together on the floor. "Those two do belong together. I'm glad they'll be going with you." She pulled on Elizabeth's elbow to get her out of the room. "I hope that you're still hungry."

After lunch, Parry showed her the kennel area, and they went for a walk in the woods with Kotz and some of the other dogs running in front of them. Parry told her the history of the house. It had been in the James family for five generations, first used as an inn and then as a hunting lodge. "My family originally came from England. Most of them were farmers. Most of the land on this road once belonged to relatives, but now it's all changed. When I grew up, this was still a farm, and I helped with the farm chores. Although my parents didn't encourage me, I always wanted to be a dairy farmer. I think I fell in love with the cows." She laughed and broke off a dead twig from a tree. "It was a sad day when I sold my herd. That was almost ten years ago. Then I took a job with the post office delivering the mail. Did that until I got my pension. Now, I just do what I want to most of the time." She whistled, and the three dogs turned and ran back towards her.

"You have them very well trained."

"I like training dogs. They like it, too. Makes for better communication. I'll be happy to share my secrets with you, Elizabeth, when you start training." She bent down and patted one of the large Malamutes. "The property has all been fenced, so there's no danger of the dogs running off and getting lost. Sometimes, if the snow is too deep and fresh, it covers up the scent dogs need to find their way home."

They continued to walk, Parry pointing out special trees, bird nesting sites, and old stone walls that once served as boundary markers. It was clear that Parry's home was a special sanctuary for her, but Elizabeth didn't tell her how well she understood those feelings. Parry's haircut reminded her of an English schoolboy's, very long on top and shorter along the sides. She considered Parry's lean, wiry body, clearly accustomed to physical work. She looked closely at her hands, which were rough and calloused.

"Have you been here alone all this time?"

"No, no, there was my sister. She got married and lives in town. Her boy, William, used to come up and help me, but he decided to go to college and learn about computers. He didn't want to become a farmer." She wiped her hands on her jacket. "So," she smiled and looked at Elizabeth, "I'm the end of a long line."

"I noticed that there was a wedding picture in the dining room. The bride looked like you."

Parry stopped and regarded her uncertainly. "That's me and Archie. We were married for a time." She laughed. "He was a city boy from Boston . . . didn't have any interest in cows. He never liked being tied down to farming, and when he left, there was no one to help me. I keep that photo around to remind me."

Elizabeth was curious. "Remind you . . . ?"

She said. "To remind me that you can feel more lonely and alone with someone than by yourself." She stared hard at Elizabeth. "I know you understand my meaning."

Elizabeth self-consciously looked away. She felt chilled and looked down at her watch to realize that they had been out walking for more than an hour. "Parry, I hadn't realized how late it was." She wondered whether she should accept Parry's invitation to spend the night. "It's too late to drive back home today. You have to give me all the instructions on the puppies' care and I don't feel safe on the icy roads at night. If it's still okay with you, I'll accept your hospitality and stay over."

"Great, Elizabeth. Give us more time to talk."

"Yes. Yes. Thank you. I appreciate your generosity." She hugged Parry spontaneously, and when she felt Parry's body press against her own, she broke away abruptly.

"I feel like a kid the night before Christmas. I know I won't sleep at all just thinking about those two."

After dinner, they took their glasses of wine and sat in front of a fire in the living room. Elizabeth was tired, and she felt unsettled without the dogs as a distraction.

Parry got up to stoke the fire, then she leaned back against the wall and faced Elizabeth. "I've been thinking all day about you taking two of the dogs. Remember what I told you at the dog show. Malamutes are not good watch dogs. They won't be much help in protecting you."

"Yes, I remember what you said." Elizabeth searched for an appropriate response. "I guess I wasn't thinking of that kind of protection."

Parry quickly asked. "Oh? What kind of protection do you expect from them?"

Elizabeth felt cornered. She was being pressed to answer specifically, and the answer would involve some revelation about her life. She would have to tell Parry about her loneliness, maybe tell her about Carol. She didn't know how she would begin, or even if she wanted to divulge her personal life to this woman she hardly knew. "I'm sorry. I've probably used the wrong word."

"No, I believe that's the right word. You want these dogs to be guardians from what or from who . . . I don't know."

"Parry, it's not what you might think. It's not anything sinister. I respect your responsible attitude and concern for the animals. I meant that they'd be good companions for me, just like Jewel, the German Shepherd I mentioned to you."

Parry spoke gently. "Oh, I'm not worried about the dogs, Elizabeth. I was thinking about you."

"Me?" She sipped her wine and stared at the fire.

"I recognize the signs. It's what animals do when they're hurt. They go some place alone, to recover or to die."

"No. I'm not dying, and I'm not hurting . . . maybe still afraid of pain, though." She shook her head. "I left someone who once meant everything to me. I don't think it was like you and Archie, but she didn't want what I wanted, and we could never reconcile our differences. When I came back home, there was another woman. She had strong passions. Both women have exceptional courage, though they are very different; it was that quality that attracted me to both of them. I've only recently come to realize that I've never tested my own spirit." Elizabeth paused and shook her head. "Parry, I don't know why I'm going on like this. It's not like me to reveal much about my personal life." She stretched her arms over her head and took a different tone. "I don't know what more I can say. I guess I could blame it on the wine. I've been accused of being too private. I don't usually develop friendships easily."

"I understand. Maybe the dogs will give us the opportunity to see each other more often. I could come down and inspect their living conditions." Parry laughed.

"Of course, you'll come down. We don't need the dogs for an excuse."

"I didn't mean to upset you, Elizabeth. I'm too nosy and should mind my own business." There was no response, and Elizabeth did not look at her. Parry waited a few moments. "Maybe we should get some sleep."

"Probably a good idea." Elizabeth heard the detached tone in Parry's voice. She wondered if Parry also hid her feelings out of fear of being hurt. She hoped that she hadn't caused any pain to Parry, whom she genuinely liked and respected.

Parry showed her to a bedroom and gave her a pair of flannel pajamas. "I turned up the heat in this room earlier, so it should be comfortable." Parry smiled and held her gaze a few seconds. "I hope you sleep well."

Elizabeth couldn't sleep. She worried that she had offended Parry, and was angry that she had spoken about her personal life. She had abruptly moved their friendship to a different level and she felt vulnerable and unsure. She focused on the dogs she would take back home with her tomorrow. She thought about going to the little bedroom to check on the dogs, but was afraid that the noise would waken Parry.

As the first light appeared in the sky, she slipped out of bed and walked down the hall towards the little room where her dogs slept. She stood with her hand on the door knob for a few seconds and then took her hand away. She turned and walked to another room at the end of the hall and opened the door. In the dim early morning light that came in from two long windows, Elizabeth saw a double bed against the far wall. She shivered, but moved closer. She stood next to the bed for a few seconds, looking down at the sleeping figure. Then, quietly, "Parry?"

The form under the covers turned towards her.

"Yes . . . yes." It was not a question.

About the Author

Judith P. Stelboum is Editor-in-Chief of *Harrington Lesbian Fiction Quarterly (HLFQ)*, and she is co-editor of *The Lesbian Polyamory Reader: Open Relationships, Non-Monogamy, and Casual Sex*. Her essays, fiction, and poetry have appeared in a variety of anthologies and journals: *Common Lives/Lesbian Lives; Sinister Wisdom; Sister and Brother; Dyke Life; Resist: Essays Against a Homophobic Culture; Not the Only One; Heat Wave; Tangled Sheets; Hot Ticket; Electric: Best Lesbian Erotic Fiction; The Oxford Companion to Twentieth Century Literature in English;* and *The History of Homosexuality: Vol. 1: Lesbian Histories and Cultures*. She is a reviewer/essayist for *The Lesbian Review of Books* and *Lambda Book Report*.